A TOTALLY AWKWARD LOVE STORY

A TOTALLY AWKWARD
LOVE STORY

Tom Ellen and Lucy Ivison

Delacorte Press

Text copyright © 2014 by Tom Ellen and Lucy Ivison
Jacket photos copyright © 2016 by Blackburne/MergeLeft Reps

All rights reserved. Published in the United States by Delacorte Press,
an imprint of Random House Children's Books,
a division of Penguin Random House LLC, New York.
Originally published in paperback as *Lobsters*
by Chicken House, London, in 2014.

Delacorte Press is a registered trademark and the colophon is a trademark of
Penguin Random House LLC.

Visit us on the Web! randomhouseteens.com

Educators and librarians, for a variety of teaching tools, visit us at
RHTeachersLibrarians.com

Library of Congress Cataloging-in-Publication Data
Ellen, Tom, author.
[Lobsters]
A totally awkward love story / Tom Ellen and Lucy Ivison. —First edition.
pages cm
Originally published in paperback by Chicken House, London, in 2014, under
title: Lobsters.
Summary: "Hannah and Sam are each searching for The One—but over the
summer, a series of hilarious misunderstandings prevent them from realizing
that they're It for one another" —Provided by publisher.
ISBN 978-0-553-53732-1 (hc) — ISBN 978-0-553-53733-8 (ebook)
[1. Love—Fiction. 2. Dating (Social customs)—Fiction.]
I. Ivison, Lucy, author. II. Title.
PZ7.1.E44To 2016
[Fic]—dc23
2015011783

The text of this book is set in 11-point Berling.
Interior design by Trish Parcell

Printed in the United States of America
10 9 8 7 6 5 4 3 2 1
First Edition

For Christina, Kate and Alexie . . .
The Original Dream Team
—L.I.

For Carolina
—T.E.

1

HANNAH

Grace burst into my bedroom with such force that she nearly fell over.

"Freddie isn't in France!" she announced triumphantly as Tilly came crashing in behind her.

I sat up in bed, where all morning I had been watching videos of baby sloths and tutorials on how to do cat-eye eyeliner flicks.

"Are you *sure*?" I asked.

"Yes!" Tilly yelled, and started doing a little victory dance on the spot.

"But I stalked him this morning," I said, "and there's a picture of him actually standing in front of the Eiffel Tower, holding up a baguette and pretending it's a mustache. He literally couldn't be more in France if he tried."

"Yeah, he *was* there," Tilly squealed, "but then the most amazing thing happened: his house got robbed and they had to come home early!"

"Obviously, it's really bad about his house and everything," Grace cut in dutifully.

"Yeah, yeah." Tilly nodded. "Obviously . . . but the point is . . . he's coming to Stella's tonight. Fact."

"Fact," Grace repeated. "And you are totally going to get with him. Tonight is the night. . . ." She crinkled her nose and smiled.

I kicked off the comforter and swung my legs out of bed. "What? No . . . I'm not ready."

"You *are* ready," Grace soothed. "You are totally in the right place. He's so the right person."

"No, I don't mean *emotionally* ready. Obviously, I'm *emotionally* ready. I mean I'm *literally* not ready. I haven't gotten out of bed for three days. I look like an absolute mess."

"You look like you always do," Tilly said.

"Thanks, Tills."

"Seriously, Hannah," said Grace. "You've always said Freddie was the one you'd lose it to. The only reason it hasn't happened yet is because you've been on exams lockdown for, like, the last four months."

"Fate was keeping you apart," said Tilly grandly.

"And now fate's brought you back together," said Grace. "Have you got any food?"

"Excuse me, I thought we were talking about the role of fate in my life?"

"Yeah, but I'm hungry—I can't contemplate fate on an empty stomach."

I slumped back into bed. "Go downstairs and have a look, then. My mum hides the snacks above the microwave."

They clomped down to the kitchen. Grace was right.

I'd put losing my virginity on the back burner until after my College Board exams. Although "losing" is such a random word for it. It's not like you're gonna find it under your study guide, is it?

I used to dream about losing it to someone fragile and kind. Someone who understood me and was really cool but didn't care what other people thought of him. Someone with dark, curly hair who tanned really well and spoke Italian. Or maybe *was* Italian.

Freddie Clemence is not fragile, kind *or* Italian. He's not the love of my life. At least, I *hope* he's not, or I won't have much of a life to look forward to. But surely, if everybody held on to their virginity until they found the love of their life, there'd be a lot more virgins roaming around.

Half the problem is that I do the same thing with boys that I do with clothes: I imagine an outfit before I go shopping rather than just waiting to see what's in the stores when I get there. I daydream scenarios that will never happen. I think about boys falling in love with me who in real life wouldn't look at me. And it's not even me in the daydream; it's this sort of celebrity version of me, all glossy and poised and sexy. I imagine being invited to parties where events play out perfectly. How I'll meet the love of my life and he'll be inexplicably drawn to me and say things like, "I would die for you, Hannah." And then we'll have sex in a car like in *Titanic*.

In reality I'm either making out with Freddie in a corner or cleaning up someone else's puke because I feel bad for the person whose party it is.

But maybe Stella's party will be different. Everyone's

finished their exams now, so it's going to be massive. Ninety people have accepted the invite on Facebook. And now that Freddie is back early from France, maybe it *is* a sign. Maybe now *is* the right time. It's not love, but I just need to get sex over with so I can get on with living my life.

Tilly and Grace stomped back up the stairs and flopped onto my bed, clutching two packets of Ritz crackers and a jar of peanut butter.

"I hope you never take Zac down," Tilly said, staring up at my ceiling. "He's been there as long as I've known you."

She was looking at the sticker of Zac Efron I'd put there when I was twelve so he would be the first thing I saw every morning.

"It's *never* coming down," I said. "Zac is my first love. I may have moved on—"

"To Freddie," Grace interrupted.

"—but he will always have a place in my heart."

"And your wardrobe," Tilly said. "Do you still have that T-shirt with his face on? That was crazy."

"Says you in the Aztec-print harem pants."

Tilly swung her legs in the air to show them off. "I have nothing else to wear. My mum isn't doing any laundry because she's on strike. She wants me to learn how to do stuff before college."

"Well, you'd better learn quickly," I said. "You're never going to meet a boy and get out of no-man's-land dressed like Aladdin."

Tilly is in hymen limbo. She's the walking undead. A sex zombie. Max Lawrence *did* go inside her, but not all the way and only for a few seconds. She said it hurt too much, so he stopped. And then he got off with Amber Mason at a party, so Tilly dumped him. She couldn't have known at the time that it was her last-chance saloon. She might have given it a better go if she had known. But Tilly's a wimp when it comes to that kind of thing—she almost fainted when she got her HPV shot.

How can we live in a world where they can identify serial killers from their DNA but we can't figure out if Tilly's a virgin or not? We've Googled it a hundred times, but the more you try to research it, the more philosophical the whole thing gets.

Like, what *is* losing your virginity, anyway? When your hymen breaks? But that can happen horseback riding or doing gymnastics, or even *swimming*, apparently. I could have lost my virginity to Acton Municipal Pool, for all I know. If it's just the hymen thing, then what about gay people? It must be the act of someone else being inside you; after all, boys lose their virginity even though nothing breaks. So maybe it's a mystical, intangible thing? Like the Holy Spirit.

Out of all of us, Grace is the only one who has lost her virginity. She fell in love with Ollie last year and they've been inseparable ever since. I don't know how they're going to cope when they go to college. Grace hasn't told us what having sex actually feels like, though. It's like once you've done it you become unable to speak about it. Can anything be *that* amazing? Maybe nothing feels epic when you're actually living it.

We sprawled out across the bed and started rambling on about other things: what we'd wear to the party and what color we would dye our hair if we had to pick one color for the rest of our lives (me: chestnut; Tilly: platinum; Grace: stay the same). And then conversation inevitably turned to the missing member of the group.

"Do you *really* think she's at his house?"

Tilly was sitting on my bed with her legs crossed, eating the peanut butter straight out of the jar with a spoon. She had added my Duke of Edinburgh hoodie to her Aztec look, and her long red hair was wound into a topknot.

"Well, she's not here, so . . ." Grace shrugged, as if Stella could only be with us or with Charlie. Maybe that was actually true. It did feel weird that Tilly and Grace were here and she wasn't.

"Of course she's with him," I said. "He got back from college last night. I've been with her every day since exams, but I haven't heard from her today."

"Well, I think it's a toxic relationship," Grace said.

I laughed. "A 'toxic relationship'? What do you think this is, *Dr. Phil*?"

"You know what I mean," Grace tsked. "He's really bad for her. Stella, of all people, could do way better."

"Yeah, I know," I said. "Shit, I'd better tell her about Freddie." I wrote Stella a text:

Where are you? Freddie is back from France and I think tonight is the night!

SAM

It all felt wrong. Totally, utterly, terribly wrong. What the hell were we doing? I decided to ask Robin.

"This feels wrong, man," I said. "What are we doing?"

He was kneeling on the wet grass beside the big steel bucket, pressing one final textbook into the mangled mass of textbooks already squashed inside.

"What are you on about?" he muttered, holding the books in place with one hand while he used the other to retrieve a cigarette lighter from his pocket. "I think it's pretty obvious what we're doing."

He sparked the lighter twice to check if it was working. It was.

"Yeah, what I mean is, it feels wrong to be doing this after what happened this morning," I said.

"We're celebrating, you idiot."

"That's my point!" I yelled as Robin stood up, swatting bits of damp soil off the front of his trousers. "There's nothing *to* celebrate. I already told you how badly I fucked up French. So if we're celebrating, then we're celebrating defeat. Who celebrates defeat? It's illogical."

Robin snorted. "We're not celebrating defeat *or* victory. We're celebrating *the fact that it's all over*. It doesn't matter how we did—it's the fact that we never have to think about those exams ever again."

He was way off, there. I'd thought more about that French exam since finishing it that morning than I had in the last six months. Which, to be fair, was probably why I screwed it up so badly. Fucking pluperfect tense. Who needs to go that far back into the past anyway?

Robin clicked the lighter again. "Right. Let's do this then, shall we?"

This had always been the plan. We'd agreed that the

day we finished our College Board exams we'd celebrate by incinerating all our textbooks. It was supposed to be a cleansing thing; a glorious cathartic bonfire that marked the end of childhood and the start of . . . well, not adulthood, exactly, but definitely a step in its general direction.

But, in reality, it was just the two of us standing over a mop bucket in Robin's backyard. If this was the road to adulthood, I was considering turning back.

Robin knelt back down and plunged his hand deep into the bucket to pull out my French textbook. He placed it carefully on top of the pile and held the lighter up to me.

"Here, come on, man. Show those French pricks what you're really made of."

I shook my head. "No. I don't feel like it."

He shrugged. "Suit yourself."

He sparked the lighter and held the flame against the corner of the book's cover.

"Why isn't it burning?" he demanded. "Nothing's happening."

"It's laminated, you dick."

The flame was just about managing to turn the plastic-coated corner a faint browny-black color. If we were going to use this method on every book, we'd be here all day.

"Why the fuck do they laminate them?" snapped Robin, letting go of the lighter.

"Probably to stop people like us burning them in buckets."

"Those bastards," he murmured. "They're always one step ahead. Maybe we could just burn the inside pages. They're not laminated."

"Then we'll be left with a bucket full of empty book covers. What are we going to do with all those?"

Robin chewed his bottom lip as he considered this. "We could cut them up into little pieces and bury them? Or put them in a box and throw them in the sea?"

"The sea? We live in London. The sea is at least an hour away."

"So? I could get my mum to drive us to Brighton when she gets back from work."

"This is beginning to sound like more hassle than it's worth, to be honest."

Robin groaned and stood up. "You need to perk the fuck up, Sam. If you're still like this tonight, then I'm ditching you as soon as we get through the door. End-of-exams parties are the best parties ever; that's common knowledge. I'm not having you ruining this one for me by whining all night. This might come as a surprise to you, given your lack of experience in the area, but girls don't exactly get turned on by constantly complaining about French exams, you know."

Maybe he was right. Maybe I could look at the French Fuck-up as a positive thing. The beginning of an entirely new and unplanned chapter in my life. No university, no job, no real conventional future: I could totally reinvent myself, starting this evening.

Robin only heard about the party tonight through his friend Ben, who knew about it via a friend of a friend. So there was a good chance we wouldn't know *anyone* there. I could become someone else. I could start introducing myself as "Samuel." That might make me sound deeper and more intelligent. I could be Samuel the mysterious drifter;

Samuel, who wears long coats and hand-rolls his own cigarettes and gazes off into the middle distance enigmatically during conversations. Rather than plain old Sam, who fails French exams and tries to burn plastic books.

The problem is, you have to have done something with your life before you can start going around calling yourself Samuel. You have to have *achieved* something. Samuel Beckett; Samuel L. Jackson; Dad's friend Samuel, who drives a Porsche and used to go out with Nigella Lawson: they've all earned the right to those extra letters. What have I ever done? Won an essay contest when I was fourteen and fingered Gemma Bailey in a gazebo. I'm hardly in line for a knighthood.

I'd always thought that getting into Cambridge would be my big achievement. But now that I'd screwed up French—and I definitely *had*—I was going to have to find something else instead. I just had no idea what.

You won't find many virgins called Samuel, that's for sure. You remain a Sam until you get past fingering, I reckon. Or at least past gazebos.

Robin picked up the bucket and stomped off toward the house.

"Right, let's just give the fuckers to Goodwill and be done with it," he muttered.

HANNAH

Stella and I were sitting at the bus stop where we had sat hundreds of times before. Except this time I was in extreme pain.

"I've been mutilated. I think I'm in medical shock," I said. "Have you got any sugar?"

Stella handed me a bag of mixed gummies. "It's just hair," she said. "You don't say you've been mutilated when you go to the hairdresser, do you?"

"Yeah, but what happened to me *in there* was not like what happens at the hairdresser."

Stella had booked me in to have my bikini line waxed as soon as she had found out Freddie was not only back but coming to her party.

"Hannah, honestly, it's just because it's your first time. Shit, all your first times are happening at once," she announced slightly too loudly.

The lady next to us shot a disapproving glance in our direction, and I winced.

Across from the bus stop is a gigantic H&M poster of a model in a neon-pink-and-white string bikini. She looks amazing, all impossibly long and brown and perfect. The poster has been there forever. Looking at it used to make me feel quietly excited. Because that was going to be me. I was going to go running and do my mum's Davina DVD and wake up having morphed into an H&M campaign version of myself. But obviously, none of that had happened, and I looked just the same as always.

"I'm going to buy that bikini for Kavos," Stella said.

We were going away to Greece together in a week, and I wasn't prepared at all.

"She's definitely had her bikini line waxed," I said, nodding at the poster, "and it *definitely* wasn't her first time."

11

Stella shrugged and got out her phone, probably to text Charlie. She wasn't intimidated by the model in the bikini because she is effortlessly cool. She's petite, olive-skinned, naturally sexy and mysterious, and boys always love her. She loves video games and movies like *Pulp Fiction* and *Scarface*. Her dark brown hair is dyed with random bits of lilac, and last summer she got a snowflake tattooed on her wrist. You can't see it in winter, but it appears when she tans. Out of all of us, she is the closest to the H&M girl.

Me, Tilly and Grace don't even come anywhere near. Tilly is tall and willowy with freckles. Her hair is her best feature. It's straight out of a Pre-Raphaelite painting, auburn and flowing with curls at the end. Grace used to be plain until her sixteenth birthday, but like my mum says, she has "really blossomed," especially since she stopped wearing huge shapeless sweaters as her everyday look.

I think it's really hard to see yourself how other people do. I have naturally blond hair, pale blue eyes to match my pale skin and a totally average body. On a good day people might call me pretty. On a really good day.

The bus came and Stella strode to the back while I waddled slowly behind her, trying to keep the burning pain around my lady parts to a minimum.

"You're walking like an old person," Stella said as we sat down.

"Well, it hurts."

She rolled her eyes.

I wanted to ask her about Charlie Allen, about *her* virginity and what was going on between them. She is a virgin *by choice*, which is a distinct category from just being a virgin. She has done everything *but* with Charlie. He is her fuck buddy without the actual fucking part. Or the blow job part because that totally grosses Stella out. He's hot, but behind her back we all say he's a prick who's using her. We know he deals drugs but we don't talk about it. She says she's happy with the way things are between them, but I don't think that's really true.

I can't ask her, though, because the whole her-and-Charlie thing is a no-go area. She'll never admit there's a problem, so we all have to pretend there isn't one. She can ask any of us anything, but we are not allowed to do the same back. Stella is just different like that; she's a closed book.

She is also the kind of person who just has house parties and is relaxed about it. Her parents have gone to France for the whole summer. You would think she would want to go with them, but she never does. This is the second summer they have let her stay home alone. They get her Marks & Spencer food delivered every week and send her allowance by Venmo.

"Are you still getting a bob?" Stella asked.

"I don't know. I don't know if I'm brave enough."

"You are way too uptight about hair."

"Yeah, well, I need to do a lot of things before college."

Stella got out her phone again. "Shall we consult the list?"

Last month, deep in study hell, we had made an action plan of all the things we had to do before college.

" 'Hannah,' " Stella read out. " 'Fall in love and lose virginity.' Well . . . one of those is getting ticked off pretty soon. . . . OK, next we've got, 'Get an amazing body. Get good at fake tanning. Get a new look. Get a bob. Practice having slow mannerisms to appear more enigmatic. Be less giggly and more intellectual.'"

I groaned. "Oh god, there's so much to do. Can you add 'Cope with failing history' to the list?"

"OK, you might need to prioritize. What about just getting a bob and sleeping with Freddie?"

I sighed and fished a gummy fried egg out of the bag. I don't know when everything got so complicated. Eighteen is supposed to be the age when you become an adult. When you are complete. How can anyone feel finished by now? I don't even feel started. I haven't done anything, I haven't been anywhere. Everyone around me seems to have figured it all out. It feels like suddenly it's the norm to be in a long-term relationship. To be having sex like it's no big deal, and have had your bikini line waxed to do it. It's like so much has changed since I was fourteen, but then at the same time nothing has. Sometimes I wish I could be that age again and just not worry about all this stuff. About what people think of me, and how I come across in social situations. When every weekend we used to sleep over at Stella's house and eat ice cream and drink cups of tea. I hate it that now people are constantly expecting me to have become something. And like I'm a failure because I just haven't. Everything seems like it was easier in *Pride and Prejudice*. My nan was married at eighteen. Married. I can't even operate an iron.

When we finally got to Stella's house, I went straight up to the bathroom to fully assess the horror beneath my underwear. As if it wasn't enough having pale red legs with veins showing through and weird albino blond hair and generally looking like a hobbit wife, I was now also deformed.

I didn't tell Mum where I was going because that would have been weird. I know for a fact there are some things she would never do. Like blow jobs and polyester clothing and KFC. I would bet a lot of money she has never had her bikini line waxed.

I can see why people become feminists now. All those years in health class learning about crabs and condoms and consent. Why didn't Miss Smart just get up and say, "As well as voting and learning to drive and being a good citizen and not getting pregnant out of wedlock, one day you will have to go into a room and put on a pair of underwear made of tissue paper and let a woman you have never met before pour hot wax on your cha-cha."

It looked like a raw, bloodied chicken with a Mohawk. And I was supposed to be losing my virginity *tonight*.

SAM

Chris bounded up the stairs two by two. We heard him coming about a minute before he opened Robin's bedroom door. He stood in the doorway, beaming at me with his arms outstretched.

"Yes, Sammy! The boy's finally all done and dusted!" He yanked me toward him and gave me a lung-busting bear hug.

He and Robin had both finished their final exams three days ago, so Chris was clearly eager to have another "last day" to celebrate. He hadn't yet heard about the French fiasco. I almost couldn't face telling him.

It was a few hours after the (attempted) book-burning,

and the three of us had agreed to meet at Robin's before heading to the party. I'd gone home to change but hadn't actually done much more than put on a fresh T-shirt. I was still wearing my busted-up Vans with gaffer tape holding the soles in place. On answering the door to me, Robin had looked me up and down, groaned and told me that girls didn't usually respond well to the "hobo vibe."

Chris, on the other hand, looked annoyingly good, despite the fact he'd also clearly made no effort whatsoever. He was wearing a shabby checkered shirt and the same jeans he'd had for ages. His bushy black hair was even wilder than usual, and he hadn't even bothered to shave the patches of stubble that were dotted across his cheeks. When you're as good-looking as Chris, you don't have to bother with decent clothes or a hairbrush. You're beyond all that.

"So what time are we off?" he asked, releasing me from the hug and slapping me hard on the back once more for good measure.

Robin wrinkled his forehead disdainfully. "Chill out, man. It's only half past five."

"Yeah, but we need to buy booze first."

"Yes," said Robin, reaching into his closet and flinging practically every T-shirt he owned onto his bed. "But before that, I need to decide what to wear."

Chris exhaled loudly and collapsed into a nearby chair. Robin stood over the mountain of clothing with his hands on his hips, like a soccer manager about to pick his first eleven players.

"So how we all doing, then?" said Chris as I slumped down into the chair next to him.

"I'm doing fine," Robin replied, selecting a garish green polo shirt from the pile and sniffing it gingerly before tossing it away. "But Sam's being a thumb-sucking nutsack."

Chris frowned and put his hand on my shoulder. "Oh dear. It's not Jo again, is it?"

I shook his hand off. "No, of course it's not Jo. I haven't talked about her in weeks."

I saw Robin and Chris exchange raised eyebrows. I had talked about Jo almost all of yesterday. And the day before.

"It's his fucking French exam," said Robin.

Chris clicked his tongue against his teeth and turned to me. "Shit, man. What happened?"

"I just screwed it up, that's all." I shrugged. "Like I knew I would."

"Come on, man." Chris smiled. "It can't have been that bad. And anyway, it's over now. Tonight you need to forget about exams and Jo and *everything*, and actually try to enjoy yourself for once."

"Thank you," said Robin, gesturing at Chris but looking at me. "That's what I've been trying to tell you, you grumpy asshole. Now"—he held up a purple T-shirt bearing the slogan THE LIVER IS EVIL AND MUST BE PUNISHED —"shall I stick this one on the 'maybe' pile?"

"If 'maybe' is short for 'maybe burn immediately,' then yes," I muttered.

Robin sighed. "Christopher, perhaps you'd like to join me over here by the closet, and we can leave Sam to sulk in peace while we select an appropriate shirt."

Chris laughed and slouched over, leaving me to sit

grumpily in the corner, trying—and failing—to forget about exams and Jo and *everything*.

Jo. I sometimes wonder if I actually liked Jo. I mean, obviously I liked her enough to talk about her a lot (probably too much, in hindsight), and write that poem (also, admittedly, a mistake), but I'm still not sure if I *liked her* liked her, you know?

Sometimes I think I was only obsessing about her because it's just nice to have someone to obsess about. Every time I got the slightest suspicion that she might like me back, I started to focus on the things that made me question how much I liked her. Like the fact that she's ever so slightly cross-eyed, or that when I first asked what her name was short for, she looked confused and said, "So I can remember it, I guess."

Then, as soon as she lost interest in me and started flirting with Jeremy Marsh again, I was straight back to imagining what it would be like to wake up next to her. It's all a bit of a cliché, really. But then, I suppose clichés wouldn't be clichés if they weren't based on some sort of tediously predictable truth.

This was all moot now anyway, since she'd started going out with Toby McCourt from the year ahead of us. *Toby McCourt. Toby.*

Let's not beat around the bush: Toby is a dog's name. I've known at least three dogs called Toby. And not even good dogs, either; I'm talking crappy, ratty little Paris-Hilton-handbag ones. I don't think I'm overreacting when I say that kissing someone with a dog's name is bordering on bestiality. It's only a short step from dating a boy called Toby to marrying a man called Fido.

Anyway, fuck it. It was only four months of my life wasted. Thank god I never showed her the poem. If Robin's reaction was anything to go by, she would have laughed vodka out of her nostrils and fallen on the floor.

On the other side of the room, the "maybe" pile was down to just two items: Chris's vote was for a plain white Lacoste polo shirt. Robin was gunning for an unspeakable turquoise T-shirt emblazoned with a picture of an evil clown holding his middle finger aloft. And, since it was Robin who had the final say, the clown shirt won.

"Why did you even ask for my advice if you weren't going to take it?" asked Chris, flopping back into the chair beside mine.

"It's always useful to have a second opinion," said Robin, hurling the nice, inoffensive Lacoste shirt back into his closet. "Even if that second opinion happens to be totally wrong."

Chris shot me a glance through narrowed eyes, which I duly returned as Robin unloaded half a can of Axe Hot Fever over his horrendous clown shirt. I don't really know why I listen to Robin sometimes. He's my best friend and everything, but he can be a bit of a jackass. He applied to Loughborough, but he doesn't seem to care whether he gets in because he's taking a year off to "focus on his beatboxing."

I especially don't know why I listen to him about girls. He has some fairly odd theories. He's always banging on about ears for some reason. He reckons ears are the best bits on a girl. He once rejected Vicky Parker on the grounds that she had "shit ears." His words, not mine. Her ears look all right to me, although I prefer her face and body and tits. Obviously, her tits are part of her body, but I feel they deserve special mention. Vicky Parker is ridiculously hot. I told Robin he was bullshitting me about all this ears stuff, but he just laughed smugly, did a sort of faraway look and told me I wouldn't understand.

When it comes down to it, that's the worst thing about not having done it yet. The fact that everyone who *has* done it suddenly thinks they're Russell fucking Brand. They think they can literally say *anything* about sex, and us wide-eyed virgins have to humor them because we can't even begin to imagine what it's like.

Robin got with a French girl with a shaved head from the lycée around the corner from our school. He only did it once. He got a lot of shit for the shaved head thing, but he dealt with it quite well, I thought. I suppose he liked the confidence she showed in fully displaying her ears rather than covering them up with hair like most girls. To be fair, she *did* have pretty amazing ears.

Chris has done it three times. With three different girls. But then, he is six weeks older than me. And about ten times better looking. I know for a fact he's known as Cute Chris among most of the girls in the neighboring schools. Even my mum's friends giggle and go red when they see him. And they're in their forties. It's ridiculous. Before he lost his virginity, though, Chris was never worried about it. Nothing bothers him, really. He's the most laid-back person I know.

"Right," said Robin, pulling his triumphant T-shirt over his head and checking his reflection in the mirror. "That's that settled."

"Finally," said Chris, springing back up. "Shall we go and get the booze now?"

"Are you joking?" laughed Robin, reaching into his closet and hurling two armfuls of sneakers across his bed. "I've still got to decide on my shoes."

Chris crumpled back down into the chair, head in his hands.

2

HANNAH

We fantasized for so long about our exams being over. It was our drug. All we had in the no-man's-land between studying and feeling guilty because we weren't studying. We would sit in the library, with our heads on the desks, whispering about days we would waste rummaging for vintage clothes at markets, or not getting up at all and eating ice cream in bed all day. The post-exam world was hazy, idyllic and always sunny. We were going to step out of the school hall and into an American teen movie.

Except in reality, on the day they were finally over, we walked out onto the main street in the rain and Grace said she had to go to the optician. So instead of anarchic celebrations and dancing like mad, we all just went with her and tried on glasses while she waited for her lens prescription.

Stella's party was a key player in the dream—it always had been. And now, after three days in which all I had done was peel History study maps off my wall and watch twenty-five episodes of *30 Rock* back-to-back, it was actually happening.

Just after six, Tilly and Grace got to Stella's. We put up bunting and made punch, and on Grace's orders cleared out everything really valuable, put it in the laundry room and locked the door. Tilly had brought cupcakes but Stella said it wasn't baby's first bake sale, so we ate most of them before it started. We talked about who we wanted to come and who we hoped wouldn't turn up.

Charlie definitely fell in the latter category for all of us except Stella.

"Is Charlie back from college?" Tilly said while sitting on the kitchen counter, picking the icing off a cupcake. She tried to sound offhand. We all knew he was back, and Stella knew we knew.

Stella turned and grabbed a box of cereal out of the cupboard. Tilly shot a look at me and Grace.

"Yeah, I think so." Stella shrugged, shaking the box and picking out the chocolate bits.

"Do you think he'll come later?" Tilly asked. The air tightened just a fraction.

"I don't fucking know. I'm not his secretary, Tills."

This left the question of what exactly she *was* to him, but all of us knew the answer. It just annoyed me that she had to make out she was fine with it. If she just admitted she was in love with this douche bag who was using her, we could all be sympathetic, make her tea, watch *The Princess Diaries* and agree that boys are mean.

She shook the box again but couldn't find any more chocolate bits, so she put it back. "As long as Carmen doesn't come." The name "Carmen" came out of Stella's mouth as a long groan.

"You always say that, but you invite her because you know she'll come and then you can bitch about her afterward," I said, laughing.

"Yeah, I know. I'm kind of sad she's not coming to college with me, actually. I'll need to hold an audition for a new nemesis."

We went out back to take a picture of us all, and Stella climbed onto the trampoline, held up the camera and screamed, "The last known picture of Hannah Audrey Brown as a virgin. May she rest in peace."

Tilly and Grace bowed respectfully.

"I'm not committing suicide, you freaks," I shouted, climbing onto the trampoline and bouncing.

"You sort of are," Stella shouted between bounces. "Your youth will be over. You're killing your youth."

"Was that in *Breaking Amish*, too? Will you please stop taking life advice from that show?" I said.

Stella is so overdramatic. She has to turn everything into a life-changing moment.

"Anyway, it's about time I killed it off. I'm eighteen." Saying it out loud felt odd.

We bounced in silence for a bit. Stella had been joking around, but suddenly it did feel like *something*. I had been a virgin for eighteen years and later I would cross a line. Whatever *it* actually was, I wouldn't have it anymore.

Just before seven, we went upstairs to get ready. When we were eleven, I had been so jealous of Stella's room, with its purple princess canopy over the bed and lilac fairy lights around the window. Now every wall and surface was covered with pictures and posters and makeup. Stella collected nail polish. She had so many bottles that they spanned the entire circumference of the room, lined up against the walls like dominoes.

When we were fourteen, we had a sleepover and painted the door with a little bit of every color and then painted the names of boys we liked onto it. It had become a tradition. Stella called it the Lobster Door: an ever-growing record of every boy we'd ever considered The One. Once a name was up there, it could never be removed. I studied it for a second, picking out memories from the sprawling chaotic jumble of boys' names. Luke Adams from St. Joseph's, who I crushed on for three weeks when I was fifteen because he had hair like Zac Efron. Below him Guillermo, the superhot Spanish boy we'd met on a ski trip who I kissed for five minutes even though I couldn't understand a single word he said, and to the right of him in huge green sparkly capital letters . . .

Oh *shit*. Shit, shit, shit.

"Stella!"

Stella was lying on her unmade bed beneath her princess canopy.

"I'm asleep," she replied.

"Guys, come in here!" I shouted to Grace and Tilly, who were getting ready in the guest room.

A minute later we were all staring at the door.

"You can't really notice it," Grace said.

Stella nodded. "Yeah, when Freddie and Hannah are doing it in here, Freddie *definitely* won't notice that his name is written in massive green letters on the door."

"Well, maybe he'll just think Stella wrote it—it is her room. It makes logical sense," Tilly said.

"Yeah, and Freddie did do advanced math. So he's probably really logical," Grace said helpfully.

"It doesn't matter who he thinks wrote it, it's still weird," I said. "What if he sees it? What will I say?"

"You could just tell the truth," Grace said. Stella rolled her eyes.

"Or we could prop the door open so he can't see it," Tilly said.

"What, so anyone walking past can see . . . you know"—I lowered my voice—"me having sex."

"Why are you whispering?" asked Stella.

"I don't know. 'Cause it feels weird saying it," I said.

"Well, get over it, 'cause in, like, two hours you'll be doing it," she replied.

"She's got a point," Grace said.

Stella picked up a bottle of white nail polish and opened it. "I've got an idea. Why don't we just paint over the F and the R?"

"What?" I said. "So it'll say Eddie Clemence?"

"Yeah," Stella said, beaming. "Problem solved."

"How is that solving the problem? If anything it'll be weirder explaining why there is a very similar name to his on the door with two white blotches in front of it."

Stella shrugged and put the cap back on the bottle.

"Guys, I'm nervous enough already," I said. "And my bikini line is bright red and now his name is written on the door. Maybe it's not meant to be."

"Trust me," said Stella, "it always goes like that after you get it waxed . . . it'll be gone in, like, an hour, and it *is* meant to be, or his house wouldn't have got robbed and his name wouldn't be written on the door. His name is on the door, Hannah. How much more meant to be can it be?"

"Yeah, but *we* wrote it," I said.

"*You* wrote it."

"Like a premonition," Grace said, looking upward.

We finally decided that the only option was to paint over the whole name.

"Isn't it weird that the only person we've ever erased from the Lobster Door is your *actual* lobster?" Tilly said.

"He's not my lobster." I laughed. "It's not like I'm going to marry him or anything."

"I dunno," said Stella, shaking her head knowingly. "Maybe it'll be so good that tomorrow you'll want to."

As we all worked away deleting different letters of Freddie's name, I thought about how long I had liked him and how it felt right that it should be him. The person I had wanted for so long and then got with. And even if we never went out, and it wasn't some big Romeo and Juliet thing, it was the right time and he was a nice person.

"I totally think it's good that you're getting it over with before we go to Greece," Stella said.

"Why? Do you think I'm going to go all sex crazed as soon as I've done it once?"

"Probably," she said. "Remember how you used to hate rice pudding and then you had it that time at Grace's and now you love it?"

Stella spent forever doing my eyes and lent me her blue bandage dress. It was almost nine when she realized she hadn't got ready herself. I looked good, I thought. For me, anyway. Me and Tilly and Grace went downstairs to put the music on and make cocktails, and ten minutes later Stella appeared. She was in these tight black trousers, flat, distressed boots and this baggy cream boy's T-shirt that she had cut across at the arms and stomach. You could see her black bra through it, and she was wearing bright red lipstick. Next to her I just felt prim and boring and pale. Like the paintings of women you see in stately homes. All pink and chubby and wholesome. Not sexy. How can I have sex when I'm not in the least bit sexy? Aren't the two things related?

SAM

We played rock-paper-scissors to decide who would buy the booze. I lost. As usual.

"Let's play again," I said. "Best of three."

Robin snorted. "Fuck off."

Chris put his hand on my shoulder and pointed toward the liquor store. "The universe has decided that you'll be getting the alcohol tonight, Sam. You can't argue with the universe."

I shrugged his hand off. "Yeah, but the universe should realize that I'm crap at buying booze. I hardly ever get past the cashier."

Me, Robin and Chris are pretty much the youngest in our year. Chris doesn't turn eighteen until July, and Robin and me both have to wait until August. Consequently, buying beer is still a major hassle. The trip to the liquor store can determine a night; if we don't get by, a black cloud hangs over the entire evening. If we do, it seems like a sign that anything is possible.

"I look the youngest out of all of us," I said, still trying to worm my way out.

"Nah," said Robin, sparking up a cigarette. "You're tall. Tall equals old."

"Yeah, but I've got shit facial hair. That always gives me away."

"Well, if the dude in the store asks about your facial hair, just tell him you got burnt in a fire. That's why it doesn't grow right."

"Brilliant. He'll definitely believe that."

"He's not going to ask about his facial hair, Robin," Chris said with a sigh. "He's a dude in a liquor store, not a fucking barber. Anyway, the trick to getting served is not worrying about getting served. Real adults don't worry about getting served, do they? You just have to inhabit a real adult frame of mind."

"What do real adults think about?"

We all considered this.

"Taxes?" suggested Robin. "My dad's always stressing about taxes."

"Taxes are good." Chris nodded. "Or Pink Floyd? My dad talks about Pink Floyd a lot."

"Who the fuck is Pink Floyd?" demanded Robin.

"It's a band. A band that old people like."

"Oh, OK." Robin nodded, satisfied. "Great. So in summary: use your height, say you were burnt in a fire and talk about taxes and Pink Floyd. You'll be fine. I'll have six Red Stripes."

"And I'll have a bottle of red wine," said Chris.

"Fine."

I turned and walked toward the liquor store.

"Use your height!" yelled Robin as I opened the door. I stood up as straight as I possibly could and entered.

The store was empty except for a bored-looking man behind the counter. He was watching soccer on a tiny TV. The door tinkled as I let it shut it behind me.

"Evening," he said without looking up.

"Evening," I responded.

I did two circuits of the shop before I even looked at the beer and wine. I was psyching myself up.

The man looked up. "Can I help you with anything, pal?" he asked as I was preparing to embark on my third circuit.

"No thanks," I said, and taking a deep breath, I grabbed the cheapest bottle of red wine and a twelve-pack of Red Stripe and marched up to the counter. I tried to affect an adult indifference to the whole process. I smiled confidently and whistled as I plonked the booze down.

"Just those, please, man. Cheers."

The man looked at the alcohol, then at me.

"How old are you, pal?"

I gulped. "Nineteen."

"Nineteen?" He didn't sound convinced.

"Yep, nineteen. Just turned nineteen."

He studied my face. I noticed his eyes rest on my hairless chin. I panicked.

"I was burnt in a fire," I blurted.

There was a pause.

"You were what, pal?" asked the man.

"I . . . if you were wondering about my lack of facial hair . . . it's because I was burnt in a fire. That's why it doesn't grow properly."

The man looked confused. "I'm sorry to hear that."

"Yeah, it was pretty awful. Not as awful as taxes, though. God, I hate taxes. Don't you just *hate* taxes?"

The man narrowed his eyes. "Yes, I suppose they can be a bit of a pain in the ass."

Words kept coming out of my mouth. I had no control over them. "Sure can. Still, there's no better feeling than figuring your taxes out and then kicking back with a bit of Pink Floyd. Am I right?"

The man opened his mouth to answer, but at that moment the TV exploded into life. Someone had scored a goal.

"Oh, bloody hell!" he yelled, squinting at the tiny screen. "You've just made me miss a goal."

I saw my opportunity.

"Sorry, man. I'll get out of your way." I slammed a twenty-pound note on the counter. "Here you go—keep the change."

The man didn't take his eyes off the screen as he watched the goal he'd missed replayed from six different angles. "All right, no worries; cheers."

I gathered up my booze and made for the door. Robin and Chris bear-hugged me as I emerged, triumphant.

We jumped on the bus and arrived at Stella's just after ten p.m. The house was actually more like a mansion; a massive three-story palace that looked like it should have servants' quarters.

We got there way too early. If there's one thing I've learned about going to parties thrown by people I don't know, it's that you should always arrive as late as possible. That way, the host and his/her friends are usually drunk enough that they won't notice a load of people they've never seen before raiding their fridge, vomiting in their pantry and fingering Gemma Bailey in their gazebo.

If you get there early, you end up being greeted by some incredibly uptight, sober girl who demands to know how you know the person whose house it is. Which was exactly what happened to us. At one point I honestly thought she was going to ask us for ID. Seriously, nightclubs should forget employing massive bald dudes as bouncers and just get in a few rich teenage girls instead. They'd probably be cheaper and they're twice as scary.

It was just lucky that Chris was with us. As soon as she spotted him at the back, she started giggling and opened the door, saying she hoped we'd brought some booze. Chris's face could get us into any party. He doesn't seem to realize it, though, so it's impossible to resent him. If I was really good-looking like that, I don't think I'd ever get anything done. I'd just walk the streets all day, enjoying being stared at. Not that I ever get anything done anyway.

HANNAH

In the end, loads of people came. Underclassmen and people from the year ahead of us, who are at college now. People from other schools and people we don't even know. People we do know but don't even like. The house was full. The yard was full. People were sitting under the trampoline and on the trampoline, and there were even some boys sitting up a tree.

I felt proud of Stella and happy she was my best friend, but I also felt a bit sick. I don't think the crotch mutilation and the cupcakes and the bouncing had helped, but I was definitely nervous.

Every time a new group of boys walked in, my stomach would lurch in case one of them was Freddie. I kept going into the bathroom to check my cha-cha. I'd go in there and pull down my underwear and stare at it. I covered it with some of Stella's mum's expensive cream and put a cold hairspray bottle against it to encourage the redness to go away, but nothing happened.

Back in the yard, Grace even asked me if I was OK. And then she gripped my hand and squeezed it and said, "This is *so* exciting!" and threw her arms around me. Everyone thought it was my night. I did, too, I suppose.

A bit later, me and Stella were dancing in the living room. Charlie and his stupid hipster hair had just arrived, and Stella was doing her best to dance sexily so he would come over, while I avoided eye contact with him to show I thought he was a prick. Then, out the window, I saw Freddie. I actually felt faint, as if all the blood had drained from my body. For a second I couldn't move. Stella hadn't seen him and for some reason I felt relieved.

I didn't know what to do, so I just went back up to the bathroom. I sat there for the longest time, just looking at myself in the mirror. Psyching myself up for it. I think I might have spoken to myself out loud and said, "Come on, Hannah."

When I walked out of the bathroom, this boy was standing right there with an odd look on his face. He was probably thinking I was a freak who spends ages in bathrooms giving myself pep talks and holding hairspray against my cha-cha. Imagine if he had been looking through the keyhole. Or maybe he thought I was sick and talking myself through it.

I panicked. "I wasn't throwing up," I said.

SAM

By midnight, the party had livened up considerably. By one a.m. it was absolutely jammed. You couldn't move for people dancing and shouting and trying to get off with each other. Me, Robin and Chris were out in the yard, smoking a spliff with Robin's friend Ben.

Ben is only a few months older than us but he DJ's in nightclubs, which automatically makes him around sixty percent cooler. Robin pretty much worships the ground he walks on, but me and Chris aren't totally sure about him. He's all right, but he sometimes wears a fedora.

"Decent party, isn't it?" said Ben, gesturing around the crowded yard as some guy nearly broke his neck leaping off the trampoline.

We all nodded in stoned agreement.

"It's got nothing on The Greatest House Party of All Time, though," said Robin.

Me and Chris nodded our agreement again.

"When was that?" asked Ben.

"Two summers ago," I said. "There was a swimming pool in the yard. Chris let Rosie Moss wax his legs and—"

"And I had a threesome, obviously," Robin interrupted.

Me and Chris groaned.

"You did not have a fucking threesome, Robin."

Ben looked impressed. "Did you?"

Robin nodded smugly.

"No he didn't," said Chris. "He was getting a blow job from Sophie Kendry in one of the bedrooms and some girl interrupted them halfway through to try to find some rolling papers."

"Exactly," said Robin. "I was in a room with *two* girls and there were sexual things going on. That's a threesome."

"It is *not*," I fired back. "It's a twosome with someone looking for rolling papers in the corner. Everyone in the room has to be directly involved in the sexual goings-on for it to qualify as a threesome."

Robin wasn't backing down. "It was a sexual encounter that featured me and two girls. You do the math."

"Right," said Chris, waving his empty wineglass at Robin. "So when my mum burst in on me screwing Laura that time, that was a threesome with my mum, was it?"

"It depends how long she stayed in the room," said Robin diplomatically. "If she just popped her head in the door and then left immediately, then no—it's just an embarrassing interruption of a twosome. However, if she stayed in the room for thirty seconds, rifling through your sock drawer while you were fucking, then yes, I'm afraid you were part of an incestuous three-way."

"You're a jackass."

"A jackass who's had a threesome."

I handed Chris my beer and stood up. "I'll leave this debate in your hands. I'm going to take a piss."

I wound my way through the yard, dodging the bodies flying off the trampoline, and wandered upstairs. The bathroom was locked, so I waited outside. The hallway was lined with black-and-white, professional-looking photos of a middle-aged couple (the owners of the house, I presumed), smiling with their arms around each other. I couldn't imagine myself being that comfortable with another person.

I thought I heard a female voice from inside the bathroom. I figured I'd be waiting awhile—girls always take forever when they're in the bathroom together.

But when the door finally opened there was only one girl standing there—a pretty blond girl with a slightly panicked look on her face.

"I wasn't throwing up," she said.

3

I can't believe I said that.

He stood there smiling at me for a second and then said, "Yeah, me neither."

We both laughed, and I felt a surge of relief as I decided he probably hadn't been spying through the keyhole at me pressing Stella's mum's Tresemmé against my cha-cha.

"Good," I said. "Neither of us has vomited at this party."

"*Yet*," he said, raising his finger and putting on a mock-stern face. "Neither of us has vomited at this party *yet*. There's still plenty of time left. Don't write us both off so easily."

We laughed again. You don't usually laugh two good *authentic* laughs within a few seconds of meeting someone. I looked at him closely. I had definitely never seen him before. Not at a party, not at school, not on Facebook. Not anywhere.

He was tall, really tall, in fact. He looked as though he

hadn't quite grown into his height. As if he was a bit apologetic about people having to look up to speak to him. He put his hands in his pockets and slouched to try to minimize the issue. He had brown curly hair that fell in front of his brown eyes. I noticed his Vans were really battered and had been bound together with gaffer tape. There was something gentle about him. He looked kind. And cute. Really cute. In a scruffy, cool sort of way.

He nodded toward the bathroom and said, "Well, I guess I should . . . you know."

I jumped out of the doorway. "Oh yeah, sorry. Of course."

He smiled at me shyly, then looked down and ruffled his hair. I didn't want that to be it—I wanted to keep talking to him.

"Watch out . . . it's quite . . . intense in there," I said, because it was the only thing I could think of to say.

He stepped inside the bathroom and held the door open as he looked around. "Oh my god. Yeah. Seriously. It's like a James Bond villain's toilet."

He was right. The entire room was painted dark purple, with little flecks of gold dotted here and there, and there was a massive mural of a stag on one of the walls. Stella's mum got this woman in to paint it specially. The shower in the corner had no curtain or wall around it. You just showered in the room.

"It's called a wet room," I said, and blushed because the word "wet" is rude when you say it within five feet of a boy.

"It's a bit like standing inside a blueberry," he added.

"Yeah. It's purple, though, not blue, so it's more like standing inside a Welch's bottle."

"I *love* grape juice." He said it like he'd just remembered that grape juice existed.

"Me too," I said. "Hot grape juice's even better."

"Yes!" His eyes widened like he was having a mini-epiphany. "With cloves and cinnamon! Hot spiced grape juice is amazing. I can't believe I've met someone who knows about hot grape juice."

We grinned at each other, and I felt that warm, tingly feeling you get when you find something in common with someone you like.

Suddenly, there was a roar of laughter and commotion from the backyard. The boy walked over to the bathroom window and, without thinking, I followed him inside, letting the door click shut behind me. I was alone in a wet room with a boy I'd just met. Ordinarily, this kind of situation would have required at least two weeks' preparation with Stella, Tilly and Grace, planning out exactly what I should wear, what I should say, how I should act. We'd have probably even practiced. Without a dress rehearsal I was feeling slightly panicked.

We stood side by side at the window and peered down at the chaos in Stella's yard. My arm was inches away from his. Two massive, troll-like boys were having a drinking competition while everyone around them cheered and chanted.

"Oh my god," I said as we watched one of them pour a whole pint of beer into his mouth before putting the glass on his head, burping loudly and getting thumped on the back by all his friends. "That's insane. I don't think I could even down a pint of *water*."

"It is quite impressive," the boy agreed. "I'm not sure how that skill could ever come in handy in life, though—being able to drink a lot of liquid very quickly."

"Maybe if you were drowning in a really small pond?" I suggested, and he laughed.

It was so weird. Even though he was hot and funny—my dream combination—I didn't seem to need a dress rehearsal.

On the other side of the yard a boy and a girl were greeting each other with a kiss on the cheek. The girl pulled back after one kiss, but the boy leaned in for a second. There was an awkward moment where the boy tried to play off his mistake without the girl noticing.

"Oh, I hate that," I said, pointing. "When you do one kiss and the other person tries to do two and then you both try to make out that it's fine. It's so awkward."

"Yeah," he said. "I always manage to get that wrong. I seriously think there should be a law that says once and for all how people should greet each other. We should just decide on one thing and stick to it. I'm sick of going in for a handshake and having the other person go for a hug, or doing two kisses when they've already pulled away after one. It makes life unnecessarily complicated."

I nodded. "You know they do *three* kisses in Italy?"

He sighed and shook his head. "That's just fucking with us."

"And who's got the time?" We both squinted down at the couple, who were now exchanging cheek kisses with each other's friends. "I kind of miss the days when we didn't have to pretend to be adults all the time. It seemed to change so quickly from us being kids and acting stupidly to kissing each other on the cheek and having to know which clubs are cool."

This was the type of statement that Stella would never have permitted me to say in front of a boy. She would have died if she knew I'd said something like that. But he didn't look embarrassed or weirded out in the slightest. He was smiling back at me.

"Definitely," he said. "I remember the exact moment it all changed. I went away on vacation the summer I was thirteen, and when I came back all my friends were kissing girls on the cheek. That was it—we were all suddenly grown-ups. I remember going to a party and everyone messing with me because I tried to high-five one of my girl friends."

"I actually really like a high five," I said. "It's friendly and informal but there's also not much risk of embarrassment. Unless your hand-eye coordination is really bad, and you slap the other person in the face or something."

"OK, well, that settles it," he said. "The new law will decree that *everyone* must greet each other with a high five. No hugs or handshakes or multiple cheek-kissing."

"Sounds good."

"Or," he said, "if it's a really important occasion—like two prime ministers meeting or something—a high ten is acceptable."

"Agreed," I said.

"Shall we high-ten on it? I think this qualifies as an important occasion."

"Definitely."

We slapped hands. In Stella's bathroom. With the door shut. For just a couple of seconds we stood there, grinning at each other.

Then I heard footsteps outside in the corridor and someone knocked on the door.

"Hello? Excuse me? Is anyone in there?"

Grace's voice. I love how Grace is polite even when she's drunk.

"Yeah, Grace, it's me," I called back through the door.

"Oh my god! I've been looking everywhere for you! Is everything OK?" Then she affected a sort of preschool stage whisper. "It's not your vag again, is it? It can't be *that* bad. Do you want me to come in and check it out?"

A wave of utter mortification shot through me. The boy slapped his hand over his mouth to suppress a laugh before giving me a sideways this-is-unbelievably-awkward-isn't-it? sort of smirk.

Before Grace could divulge any more highly personal, cha-cha-based information, I quickly yelled back, "No! Grace, please . . . I'm fine. I'll be out in a sec. Are you all right?"

"Yeah, fine, but you need to come downstairs *now*. Freddie's here! He's asking where you are."

Freddie. I'd totally forgotten about him. I'd been thinking about him all night, but he'd completely disappeared from my thoughts since I opened the bathroom door. At the mention of Freddie, the boy's embarrassed grin dissolved and he just blinked and looked down at the floor. I tried to think of something to say, but nothing came.

"Come on, come on! It's time for you and Freddie to get

jiggy with it!" Grace finally lost all patience and rattled the door handle. It swung open and she gasped as if she'd found me with a hippopotamus.

"Erm . . . hello," she said to the Toilet Boy.

"Hello," replied the Toilet Boy.

"Sorry, I . . . thought it was locked. I didn't realize there was . . . anyone else in here." She said that to me rather than him. "It's just that . . . *someone's* downstairs waiting for you, that's all." Her eyes were bulging like a lunatic.

"OK," I said slowly. "Cool." I turned to the Toilet Boy. "Sorry, I'm supposed to . . . I said I'd . . ." No real sentences were forming, so I left it at, "I'd better go."

He nodded and put his hands back in his pockets. "Cool. See you."

As we marched down the corridor, leaving Toilet Boy in the bathroom behind us, Grace reached down and held my hand. "Oh my god. I am *so* sorry," she hissed. "Who is *he*?"

"I'll tell you later," I said. I'd just caught sight of Freddie at the bottom of the stairs.

SAM

Freddie. Of course there was a Freddie. There's always a fucking Freddie.

In films and books you're allowed to meet pretty girls in bathrooms without any Freddies popping up to ruin it, but in real life, you *always* get Freddied. Or, at least, I do.

She—the Grape Girl—just muttered something about having to go, and then walked straight out the door. I didn't even get the chance to introduce myself—Samuel or otherwise.

I listened to her friend whisper excitedly to her as they disappeared down the hallway. I just stood there, staring at that stupid fucking stag painting on the wall, and wondering what had just happened.

Nothing had happened, really. Not in a tangible, something-I-could-brag-about-to-Robin-and-Chris kind of way. All their stories with girls involved actual physical activities—kisses, bra removals, hand jobs or threesomes that were technically not threesomes. They certainly didn't involve high tens and discussions about hot spiced Welch's.

All that had happened was that I'd had a conversation with a girl in a bathroom. Why did *that* feel like a big thing when, in Robin's eyes, it wouldn't even have warranted a text message?

Maybe because it was all so . . . *easy*. Talking to girls is usually a nightmare—trying to find the perfect balance between saying things they want to hear and saying things that don't make you come across as an utter dumbass. There was none of that with the Grape Girl. It just . . . flowed.

But it was more than that. She was, undoubtedly, really pretty. That was what made the whole easy, funny, flowing conversation thing so weird. She had blue—*really* blue—eyes and soft, straw-colored blond hair, strands of which she would occasionally absentmindedly unfurl from her ponytail and chew on. It sounds odd, but it was actually really sweet.

Her smile seemed to cover her whole face, and she smiled a lot. I only got a brief glance, but I was pretty sure she had a really good butt, too.

Basically, she was hot. And in my (admittedly limited)

experience, hot girls do not do easy, funny, flowing conversation. They only do standing around sulkily, pouting, and waiting for someone like Toby McCourt to come and talk to them. Toby McCourt. He was a Freddie, too. He was probably a bigger Freddie than Freddie.

My not-particularly-productive train of thought was finally interrupted by the door being thumped open by a dude in a gray hoodie swaying drunkenly in the doorway.

"Oh, sorry, man," he mumbled, looking slightly confused to find me standing in the middle of the bathroom and staring intently at the wall. "Are you finished in here? Because we're not allowed to piss in the rosebushes anymore, apparently."

I nodded, not entirely sure why he'd felt the need to impart the rosebushes information, and stepped out into the hallway. I slunk along it feeling glum. Somewhere downstairs Grape Girl was with Freddie. Probably, in the words of that Grace girl, getting "jiggy."

It seemed like everybody in the whole world was getting "jiggy" except me.

HANNAH

Freddie looked exactly how he has always looked. Stella says he looks like he's in a boy band, and I suppose he does a bit. Like he's thought about what he's going to wear for a long time and is really pleased with how it turned out. He's quite small, with blond-brown hair and blue eyes.

"Sorry I'm late." He smiled. "We went to a bar first and then we had to go to this random girl's eighteenth because Amir's trying to get with her."

45

"That's OK. Nothing's really happened." Actually, it felt like a lot had happened already.

"Do you want to go outside with me?" He smiled slightly as he said it. Like it was a euphemism. Up close, I could see the gel in his hair. He was wearing a vest.

"Yeah, all right. We can go on the trampoline."

I walked outside ahead of him, climbed onto the trampoline and started bouncing. He clambered on after me but almost immediately shouted, "Stop" and lay down on his back.

"Are you OK?" I asked, and sat down and crossed my legs.

"Yeah, I'm fine. Just a bit . . ." He suddenly sounded much drunker than he had before. "You look really hot, Hannah."

I didn't know what to say. "You do, too" would have sounded strange, and "Thanks" a bit cold. I stared up at the house and all the people in all the different rooms. The light was on in the bathroom and I wondered where Toilet Boy was now.

And then, from out of nowhere, Freddie sat up and said, "I'm really pleased you want to do it with me, Hannah."

And with that, he lurched forward clumsily and kissed me. I was too busy trying to process what he'd just said to stop him. Stella must have told him. Why? Why did she have to control everything everybody did? She just *has* to get in there and be buds with everyone. It was OK for it to be my night, but only if she said so. What was the point of getting all dressed up to seduce Freddie when she had given me to him on a plate already?

I pushed him back gently. I'd kissed him loads of times

before, but this time felt different. Wrong. His mouth was really wet, and he tasted like beer and cheese puffs.

He smiled, his eyes half shut, as he swayed backward. "We could do it here if you like," he murmured.

As if. There was no way it was happening now. I looked around the yard at the clusters of people smoking weed, getting off with each other or looking ill. Yup, this was just how I'd pictured losing my virginity—being publicly de-flowered on a piece of exercise equipment. I suppose the only advantage was that it didn't have his name written across it in huge, sparkly letters.

"Erm, yeah, we *could* do it here," I said. "That *is* an op-tion. But there are about a hundred people out here and you aren't coping very well with moving or staying con-scious."

Freddie's eyes were now fully shut. He didn't even look like he was interested in being awake, let alone with me. This wasn't really how I had imagined it. A half-asleep Freddie Clemence, deigning to do me a favor by murdering my youth on a trampoline.

SAM

I couldn't find Robin or Chris anywhere. I wandered through to the kitchen. Grape Girl wasn't in there but her friend was, the one who'd summoned her down to meet Freddie. She and another girl were staring out the French windows into the yard and giggling. I saw what they were staring and giggling at, and immediately I felt a bit sick, like I'd just done a shot of Jägermeister on a full stomach.

She—Grape Girl—was sitting on the trampoline, kissing

a guy I can only assume was Freddie. Freddie had apparently come straight to the party from a Jonas Brothers tribute band rehearsal. He had one of those Mr. Men T-shirts on (he'd gone for Mr. Messy) and a blond quiff that laughed in the face of gravity.

Most appallingly, though, he was wearing a vest. A fucking *vest*. Unless you're a pool player or a magician, wearing a vest outside your own house is surely not an acceptable thing to do. If you're the sort of person who can get up in the morning, put on a vest and walk out the front door, what other atrocities might you be capable of? It doesn't bear thinking about.

I suppose it was strange to feel jealous over someone I'd just met, but I did. Or, I don't know, maybe not *jealous*, exactly. It's not like we had some major moment or anything, but we got along well and what are the odds of getting along with someone you bump into outside a bathroom? What are the odds of getting along well with *anyone*? Especially when most of your conversation revolves around spiced grape juice.

I couldn't watch anymore. I turned around and pushed my way out of the kitchen. I was about to head into the living room to try to find Robin and Chris when I heard what was unmistakably Robin's high-pitched cackle coming from inside the cupboard under the staircase.

I opened the door, and a cloud of weed smoke hit me full in the face. I peered through it to see Robin and Ben crouched inside, smoking a spliff the size of an ice cream cone. This probably makes the spliff sound impressive. It wasn't. It had major structural design flaws.

Robin threw his arms up in greeting. "Yes, Sam! We're hotboxing Harry Potter's bedroom." He laughed, clearly not realizing that any credibility he hoped to gain from talking about hotboxing was immediately wiped out by his encyclopedic knowledge of the Harry Potter franchise.

"Come on in!" said Ben, a Cheshire cat grin splitting his face in two. He was very, very stoned.

I shuffled inside and shut the door behind me.

HANNAH

Freddie was out for the count. I think I even heard him snore. I sat next to him thinking about Stella and what the fuck she was playing at, and wondered whether other people had this much trouble losing their virginity. I suppose Bella Swan did have the whole potentially-being-killed-accidentally-in-the-moment thing. But at least they were on that tropical island, not a goddamned trampoline. And I bet Edward didn't taste like Cheetos.

That was it: Freddie and me were dead in the water for tonight. I decided to just leave him to sleep it off and stood up, but the movement woke him. He opened his eyes.

"Freddie, do you want a drink of water?"

"OK, let's go inside," Freddie said, sitting up. He had drool coming out of the corner of his mouth. "We can find somewhere quiet."

I wondered whether he actually still thought we were about to have sex. Really? I linked arms with him, as he clearly needed support, and we went into the kitchen. All of a sudden he seemed to get this fresh wind of energy and he went to kiss me again. I pushed him back firmly.

"Freddie, why don't you have a glass of water and a nice sit-down?" I sounded like my mum.

I wasn't sure if he heard me; if he had, he didn't care. His eyes stayed closed.

"I think I'm going to puke," he said.

"Oh my god, can you get to the toilet?"

But he was already heaving and I knew the answer. I looked wildly around the kitchen, snatched the kettle and took the lid off. But it was too late. Freddie grabbed my waist in an effort to stabilize himself. And then he vomited. All over Stella's blue dress, down my legs and onto my shoes.

I heard a group of boys laugh and some girls "oh my god"-ing. Freddie lurched out toward the bathroom. Grace and Tilly, who'd been watching the whole thing, ran over to me in a fluster. Grace had a kitchen towel in her hand and started to hurriedly wipe me down.

"Do you want me to find you something else to wear?" she asked.

"I'll go and get a mop," Tilly said, and darted off into the corridor.

"I just want to go home," I said to Grace. "Right now. Let's just go."

She nodded. "Why don't you stay at Tilly's? You can just walk there. It's really late and people will start leaving soon anyway."

"Will you get my bag from Stella's room?"

Grace nodded. "Yeah, of course. Do you think Stella will mind us leaving?"

"I don't really care," I shot back. "She's acted like a complete bitch tonight."

"What? OK, tell me about that in a second. I'll just go and let her know we're leaving."

Tilly rushed back in, mop in hand, and started trying to wash down my lower legs.

After we had finished rinsing out my shoes and I had decided to walk home barefoot, Grace returned with Ollie in tow. "Stella's upstairs in her room with Charlie."

Great. Stella was going to go ahead and lose her virginity the night I was supposed to. Grace was clearly thinking the same thing.

"They weren't *doing* anything. They were just sitting on her bed, talking, so I left them to it."

I don't really know what I had thought would happen that night, but I know it didn't include a bald, puckered cha-cha and carrot-speckled vomit running down my legs.

As we walked up Stella's street, Grace stopped suddenly in the middle of the road and held out her arms like a crossing guard so none of us could take another step.

"Hang on a minute! Hannah, who was that BOY you were locked in the bathroom with?" She looked at Ollie as if she was apologizing for what she was about to say. "That HOT boy you were locked in the bathroom with?"

Tilly whistled. "Barf-legs-red-muff has still got it!"

"Maybe that should be your Native American name," said Grace.

"First of all," I said, "I told you that no one is allowed to mention Native Americans or anything from my history exam ever again. And secondly, who cares about Freddie Clemence or any of these other hopefully transient issues? Because I have officially found my lobster."

SAM

"Do you want to hit this shit, man?"

Ben waved the poorly constructed joint under my nose.

"No, I'm OK; cheers."

Just *being* in the cupboard was getting me stoned. I didn't need to double the effect. I could barely see Ben for all the smoke, and he was crouching right next to me.

"Where've you been, then?" asked Robin, his smile implying more than his words.

"Just speaking to someone."

"Someone male or someone female?"

"Someone female."

"Ooooooh! Someone female!" This came from Robin and Ben simultaneously.

"Don't," I said. "It wasn't anything like that. She definitely doesn't like me."

Robin groaned. "Fuck's sake, Sam. You've only known her ten minutes and she's already managed to break your heart. It's the same with every girl you meet."

"No, it's not," I said. Even though he sort of had a point.

"It fucking *is*. Me and Chris had to hear about what happened with Jo again and again. You gave yourself such a hard time over her but I don't reckon you even really liked her that much in the first place."

"He liked her enough to write that poem," said Ben.

I turned to Robin, distraught. "You told Ben about the poem?"

Robin had "accidentally" opened the poem upon spotting it on my computer desktop. Once he'd stopped howling with laughter, I'd made him promise not to tell another soul.

"I didn't tell him about it in any great detail," said Robin.

"I loved that line about her 'raven hair dancing in the autumn breeze,'" Ben said. "That's some deep shit, man."

I glared at Robin. He exploded into laughter. Ben joined him.

"You're both pricks."

I grabbed the joint from Ben and took a drag. It made my head swim.

Robin wiped his eyes and composed himself. "Look, Sam, Jo fucked you around. It's a shit thing to happen, but you can't just assume every girl is going to do the same. You've got to get on with your life."

I considered this as I stared up at the thick spirals of smoke circling the lightbulb. Ben took the spliff back and inhaled deeply, causing most of its contents to fall out in the process.

Suddenly, the cupboard door was wrenched open to reveal a flustered-looking girl in a plaid dress. She coughed and waved her hands about as the cloud of weed smoke engulfed her.

"Who are you?" she demanded. "What the hell are you doing in here?"

"We're hotboxing Harry Potter's bedroom," said Robin enthusiastically.

Ben held the joint up to her. "Do you wanna hit this shit?"

The girl tutted and leaned into the cupboard to grab the mop that was resting by Robin's shoulder. "I haven't got time for that. It's an emergency," she said before slamming the door.

"She needs to chill out," said Ben. "What kind of person chooses a mop over a spliff?"

Robin ignored him. He wanted to return to the matter at hand. "So tell us more about this new girl, then, Sam," he said.

"You don't know her," I said. I could see him flicking through his mental Facebook database.

"How could you possibly know that I don't know her? I know about two thousand people. Probably about two thousand one hundred if we're counting people over forty."

"Was she over forty?" asked Ben.

"Obviously not, no."

Ben whistled and turned to Robin. "Shame. That would have narrowed it down loads. Like in Guess Who when the other person's got a woman or a redhead."

"Was she a redhead?" asked Robin, clearly enjoying himself.

"No! She wasn't a redhead or over forty and you don't know her. I didn't know her until about twenty minutes ago."

"All right, all right," Robin said, laughing. "So where is she now?"

I hesitated. There was no way I could tell them about Freddie and the trampoline. "I'm not sure where she is."

Robin handed me the spliff. I took another drag and it finally caved in, breaking open at the seam and depositing large clumps of burning tobacco and weed onto the bottom of my previously spotless white T-shirt.

"Fuck!" I leapt backward, smacking my head on the ceiling in the process. "Ow!"

Ben panicked and hurled the dregs of his Guinness at my T-shirt to put out the smoldering debris. Robin collapsed in a crumpled heap of laughter on the floor. I looked down at my T-shirt. The burning tobacco had been extinguished, but a murky brown stain was spreading quickly across the bottom.

"Brilliant. What am I going to do now?"

Ben laughed as he slipped off his red Kanye West T-shirt and handed it to me. "Just put this on over it. I'll be all right in my undershirt."

Ben goes to the gym a lot. He will gladly take *any* opportunity to strip down to his A-frame.

"I'm not wearing that. I don't even like Kanye West."

"It's either that or spend the rest of the night looking like a cat's shat in your lap," said Robin.

"Give me the T-shirt, then."

Robin stood up as I pulled Ben's T-shirt over my own. "Well, since the spliff's gone out, let's see if we can find her," he said.

He and Ben clambered out of the cupboard.

"Come on!"

There was nothing I could do but follow and hope Freddie and Grape Girl weren't still making out on the trampoline. We squeezed our way through the crowd—waving at

55

Chris, who was being chatted up by three different girls at the same time—and into the kitchen.

"So," said Robin, scanning the room. "Which one is she?"

She wasn't in the kitchen. I peered out into the yard through the window. Neither Grape Girl nor Freddie the Quiff were out there. Relief surged through me.

"She's not here. I guess she left."

Robin's eyes widened. "Oh my god. What did you do to her? Did you literally bore her into leaving a party?"

"No!"

"Then what? Please say you didn't tell her about how you're not on Facebook?"

"I didn't do anything! We just talked and then I guess she had to go."

Robin didn't look convinced, so I added another lie into the mix. "She mentioned something about another party."

"Two parties in one night? She sounds a bit out of your league, Sam."

I told Robin to shut the fuck up and walked out of the kitchen and back into the hallway. And then, one of the strangest things that has ever happened to me happened to me. A girl strode up—a properly, like, *seriously* hot girl—and put her arms around my waist.

"Hi, I'm Stella," she said.

And then she kissed me.

4

HANNAH

Ollie was the only one who didn't seem overwhelmed with excitement about me potentially meeting the love of my life.

"You should be pleased," I said. "At least now I won't have to come and live with you and Grace in the granny apartment."

"Now it'll only be me," Tilly said brightly.

"All I've heard is something about mashed-up sneakers and grape juice. And a guy whose name you don't even know. You can't like him that much if you don't know his name." The way Ollie made his case sounded rational.

"That's all you've heard," Grace said, "because you weren't really listening. I love you, but at times you are emotionally deaf."

"Deaf? I fucking wish I was deaf with the amount of random shit you all are going on about."

"She said *emotionally* deaf. But because you're emotionally deaf, you didn't hear it," I said.

Me and Tilly said goodbye to them and started to walk down Tilly's road. We linked arms. "Stella told Freddie I was going to do it with him."

Tilly's mouth dropped open. "No. Are you sure? What?"

"He told me. We were on the trampoline and he was all, like, 'Oh, Hannah, I'm glad you want to do it with me.'"

"Ugh, that is so embarrassing."

"I know. It's like . . . what was the point of the whole thing? It's like she thinks I'm not good enough to get him by myself. Like she has to seal the deal beforehand by telling him he's going to get sex out of it. What was she thinking?"

"She'd probably say she was just trying to help."

"Yeah, but we both know it's not that. It's her way of controlling everything."

"Yeah, I don't like how she always says she's pals with Ollie and Freddie. I still think it's weird the way she talks to Ollie on the phone all the time. He's Grace's *boyfriend*."

"I know. But it's like you can't say anything to her because she'll say you're being weird or a bitch."

"Yeah."

"When actually it's *her* who is being a bitch. A massive fucking bitch. I love her but I hate this side of her."

We psychoanalyzed Stella all the way down Tilly's road and into her house, and then continued the psychoanalysis in whispers while we made tea and toast and crept up to her room.

Tilly's room is tiny. She is the only person I know who

58

still has bunk beds. The bottom bunk was covered with piles and piles of laundry, so we just climbed up to the top. We talked about how even though Stella is rich and beautiful we wouldn't want to be her. How it is weird that her parents leave her alone. How the whole Charlie thing shows how fucked-up she must be. I felt bad bitching about her, because she *is* my best friend. Because she *is* loyal and has always stuck up for me. I love hanging out with her, but it's like as soon as boys get involved she just can't resist making everything weird.

We sat opposite each other on the bunk and talked about Toilet Boy. Tilly got out her phone to try to find him on Facebook.

"There's a band called Toilet Boy," she announced, squinting at the screen.

"Tills, his name isn't *actually* Toilet Boy, you know."

"I know, but that's all we've got to go on right now. I think it's romantic. Like Cinderella. Toilet Boy Cinderella."

"All right, Nancy Drew. Calm down. But, actually, don't calm down. Who *is* he?"

We talked endlessly about how we would find him. How it would be our summer project.

"I really wanted a summer project," Tilly said. "And it's way better than knitting or . . . Actually, I really want to learn how to do tarot readings."

"I bet my nan would teach you. She's very into it."

"Yeah, but a romantic mission is way better."

"Maybe one will lead us to the other?"

I told her again how Toilet Boy looked. About his curly hair and brown eyes. About how funny he was. We even acted out the high-ten conversation, with her as me and me as Toilet Boy.

"It's giving me goose bumps!" Tilly squealed. "I believe in love at first sight. Do his voice again!"

She started braiding her hair. She has the longest, thickest hair of anyone I have ever met. She looks like how I imagine Ginny Weasley. And then, finally, Tilly's mum yelled, "It's five in the morning, girls. Some people have to work and others have a *lot* of chores to do tomorrow."

We lay down head-to-tail and Tilly whispered, "We *will* find Toilet Boy."

I fell asleep thinking about him. I love having someone to think about.

As I turned the key in the lock the next day I could hear Mum and Nan in the kitchen.

"Do you want a cup of tea?" Nan called.

"Yeah."

I walked in, and they were both poring over Nan's iPhone. She is doing online dating. My mum definitely disapproves but Nan loves it. She's addicted. She's always checking out potential dates. My nan and my mum are not really the same kind of people. Sometimes I wonder how my mum came out of her. My nan thinks my mum is the most boring person ever.

"He looks nice," Mum said. "He's got a KitchenAid mixer—look."

Nan took the phone and looked at it closely. "Oh no. He looks so old."

"Mum . . . ," Mum said.

"Don't say anything," Nan said. "You're only as old as you feel."

On Mum's birthdays and at Christmas, Nan buys her ridiculous things that she knows she will never use. Like really expensive perfume or sparkly tights. And Mum takes them back and exchanges them. Usually for saucepans or a new school uniform for my little brother, Joe.

Nan is visiting for the summer. She's lived in Spain ever since Granddad died, when I was eleven. She's got an amazing apartment with a swimming pool and two best friends named Annie and Jean. She came back to spend some quality time with us, but she's getting on my mum's nerves already and it's only June. She's staying until September. I like having her here, though; it diverts Mum's attention, and she's fun.

Nan handed the phone back to Mum and turned to me. "I've been waiting for you. You've got to come and help me buy an outfit."

"How was the party?" Mum said.

"Really good, thanks." I kept it brief. Me and Mum only communicate by her asking me questions and me giving the simplest answer possible. "I'm going to have a bath and then we can go."

"A bath at two p.m.?" Mum said.

"Very Elizabeth Taylor," Nan said, and handed me a cookie.

I put my head under the water and lay at the bottom of the bath. I wasn't going to call Stella. She could call me. And when she did, I wouldn't answer.

Me and Nan looked a bit ridiculous standing on the crowded bus. She likes to dress in themes. And she likes lots of sparkle. We were only going to Westfield, but she was dressed in lemon-yellow trousers and matching lemon-yellow sandals and a T-shirt with an enormous sequined parrot sitting in a palm tree. She wears pretty much every item of jewelry she owns every day.

"I know I don't look it," she said to some poor man who was sitting down, listening to his iPod, "but I'm actually a senior citizen."

He got up awkwardly, and she sat down and immediately reapplied her lipstick.

"We could look at some things for your trip?" Nan said. She loves buying me clothes but she thinks I can wear things I can't. I try to tell her that I'm self-conscious but she just ignores me, like I'm insane.

"Not if you make me try on a leather crop top again."

"If I had that stomach I'd wear leather crop tops every day of the week. You're eighteen. You're beautiful."

How are those two things connected? My nan presumes I've already lost my virginity. She thinks I'm some sort of crazy teenager with a life.

While we were eating sushi in the food court, she leaned in. "So, any nice boys there last night?"

If my mum asked me that I'd cringe and leave the room, but with Nan it's different. She's not trying to extort information, she just likes good gossip.

"Well . . . nothing really went to plan."

"Oh, so there *is* a boy, then? I knew it. What's his name?"

"Well, one of the boys' names is Freddie, but—"

"More than one, eh?" Her eyes sparkled.

"No, not like that. Nothing . . . *happened* with either of them."

She leaned in even closer. "Is it your time of the month?"

She's really matter-of-fact. As if, in her book, having sex with multiple partners is an acceptable party agenda.

"Nan! No."

"What? Sister Melanie's not here." She looked around in an overdramatic way just to check. She calls my mum "Sister Melanie" because she thinks she's a prude.

"I'm not a slut, Nan."

"Of course you're not. But you're young and beautiful. Live while the living's good, babes."

"I'm not beautiful."

She just looked at me. There are some things she knows not to push.

"Well, which one do you like, then?"

"I thought I liked Freddie. I've known him forever and I used to really . . . want him."

She nodded knowingly. "Is that the one you had a scene with before?"

How does she even know this stuff?

"Erm, kind of. Anyway . . ." For some reason I couldn't bring myself to tell her about the puke. "I think I've sort of . . . grown out of him. And there was this other boy there." I didn't know what to say after that.

"Is he a looker?" The way she said it made me giggle.

"He's really tall and he's got dark brown hair. He's really gorgeous, actually. I just . . . I don't know, there was something about him."

She nodded to show that she absolutely definitely understood. "I love a tall man. Too bad when you get to my age they're all shrinking or dead."

That made me collapse in hysterics. For the rest of the afternoon, everything seemed better. We went through all the shops and Nan bought a bright pink-and-green shirt with a dolphin playing the guitar on the front.

On our way to look at shoes, we walked past the store with the dress. Or as Stella calls it, *my* dress.

"Look, Nan, isn't it beautiful?" We stood for a second, staring at it shimmering in the window.

It was cream and gold and made entirely of sequins, except for the rows and rows of cream feathers that made up the bottom of the skirt. It had a drop waist and was lined in pale turquoise silk. A dress Daisy in *The Great Gatsby* would wear to a party, or Tallulah from *Bugsy Malone* would appear in for cocktails. A movie-star dress. I want to be the kind of person who thinks dresses like that are made for her and knows everyone will look at her but doesn't care.

"Now, *that's* a dress," Nan said. She linked arms with me and we went in. She walked over to the rack and picked it up, looked at the price and put it back on the rail. It was £250. The most expensive thing I own is the dress I wore to my eighteenth birthday, and that cost £140.

But then she picked up one in my size and said, "Go on, try it on. For fun."

"Nan, it wouldn't look good on me. You try it on."

"I'm seventy years old. Don't be so damn cheeky."

So I took it into the fitting room and shut the curtain while Nan sat on the fancy armchair outside. What I didn't tell her was that I had sat on the exact same chair weeks ago, in the middle of a study break, when Stella and I had snuck out of the library because we couldn't bear it anymore.

Stella had picked out the dress and marched into the fitting room, and I had waited outside. When she came out, of course she looked amazing. As she did the Charleston around the shop, the gold sparkled against her olive skin, then she draped herself across me and said, "I *will* get it. It *will* be mine. I just have to convince my mum."

There had been no question of me trying it on. It was Stella's dress, all the way. Not for mere mortals. Even taking it into the fitting room now felt like crossing an invisible line. I carefully put it on and looked at myself. I felt giddy. It made me feel how it looked. Confident and cool and sexy. I didn't want to show Nan in case she got carried away, but she shouted at me, so I opened the curtain. I stood inside the changing room, not wanting to step out into the store.

Nan looked at me and smiled. "Don't tell Sister Melanie how much it cost," she said. And that was it.

The next thing I knew, we were at the register and she had her credit card out. She handed me the glossy bag with the dress inside, all wrapped up in pink tissue paper.

Walking out with it felt thrilling. I knew I had started a war with Stella, but right then I didn't care.

SAM

At first I thought the Stella thing was an accident. Girls like her don't just come up and kiss guys like me. It goes against the natural order of the world. Even as she was kissing me, I kept expecting her to suddenly break away and say, "Oh, shit, sorry—I thought you were someone else." But she never did. She just kept kissing me. Out of the corner of my eye, I could see Robin and Ben gaping at us from the kitchen doorway, probably wondering if they were both hallucinating after the Harry Potter's bedroom hotbox. They're also well aware that girls like Stella don't just come up and kiss guys like me. Robin gave me a double thumbs-up and mouthed, "You lucky fucker!" as Ben dragged him into the front room.

When Stella finally stopped kissing me, she started talking to me. Or, talking *at* me is probably more accurate. She was a tiny, perfectly formed ball of energy, rattling off sentence after sentence, flapping her hands dramatically to emphasize certain words. She explained how this was her house, and how her parents were out of the country, and how she absolutely *loved* throwing parties here when they were away (the word "loved" came accompanied by a particularly dramatic sweep of the hands). I complimented her on the decor of her upstairs bathroom, but I don't think she even heard me. She just kept jabbering on and on about what a great night she was having and how she hoped everyone else was loving it, too. She was at that lively, fiery stage of drunkenness that usually comes just before vomiting or falling over, or both.

As flattered and nonplussed as I was by the fact she'd kissed me, I noticed that she would rarely hold my gaze for more than a few seconds. Her eyes were constantly pinballing around the hallway, as if to check whether there was someone more important she should be talking to. Finally, there was.

"Oh my god, there's Carmen!" she screamed, pointing

behind me into the kitchen at a tall, dark-haired girl. "I didn't think she was coming. Listen, Sam, I'd better say hi. I'll see you later, yeah?"

She gave another final glance around her and pulled me back in for one more kiss.

"Why don't you give me your number?" she cooed. "We could meet up sometime."

I recited my number as she jabbed it into her iPhone. "This is me," she said, and I felt my phone buzz in my pocket as she dropped me a missed call. "Give me a call, OK?"

With that, she disappeared into the kitchen and left me standing in the hallway, wondering what the hell had just happened. I popped my head into the front room to find Robin, Chris and Ben all deeply stoned and very much ready to go home.

I didn't see Grape Girl again. I guess she had already left with Freddie. Kissing Stella had been a weird—and, to be honest, quite nice—diversion, but I still couldn't get Grape Girl out of my head. I kept replaying the way she chewed her hair and then pushed it back behind her ears when she laughed.

The next day me, Robin and Chris were sitting around the computer in Robin's bedroom. We'd met up with the intention of sorting out our trip to Woodland Festival in Devon later that month. But we ended up just going over and over the events of the party.

Robin was obsessed with Stella. He'd never seen anyone so fine.

"She's hot, she lives in a massive house *and* she's named after a beer. She's basically the perfect woman."

"I don't think she's actually named *after* the beer, Robin."

"Yeah, you're right. The beer's probably named after her. I bet some French dude fell in love with her and invented a beer just so he could name it after her as a romantic gesture."

Chris Googled "Stella Artois." "It was invented in 1926. And it's Belgian."

"Look, whatever," said Robin. "That's not important. What's important is us figuring out why the hell she got off with Sam."

"Thanks, bud. Appreciate that."

"No, no offense, man. But Stella is next level. She's one of those girls who should be going with a professional athlete or an ugly billionaire or something."

"Why would the billionaire have to be ugly?"

"All billionaires are ugly. Why do you think they become billionaires in the first place? Do you think if Mark Zuckerberg looked like me he would've bothered to invent Facebook? No, he would've been too busy banging hotties."

"You've pegged one girl, once," said Chris.

"Whatever. All I'm saying is, Stella is out of Sam's league." He turned to me. "No offense, man, obviously."

I wasn't offended. It was true. I was as confused as he was. Me and Stella definitely didn't fit. Me and *Grape Girl* fit. Or, at least, it had seemed like we did before she went off with Freddie the Quiff.

"So should I text her, then?" I asked.

"Do you like her?" asked Chris.

"I don't know," I said. "I mean, she's really hot. So I guess I do. It would be stupid not to like her, wouldn't it?"

Chris shrugged. Robin nodded.

"Right. So, yes. I guess I like her."

"OK," said Chris. "So text her."

Robin shook his head in despair. "Don't listen to this dickhead. *Obviously* you shouldn't text her."

"Why not?"

"Because you'll look like a desperate freak. I usually leave it at least a week before I text a girl. Sometimes I don't even text them at all."

"What happens then?"

"Well, I don't see them again, do I? But at least I keep my dignity intact."

Chris and I exchanged glances.

"We can *compose* the text now, if we must," said Robin. "But you'll have to promise you won't send it for another five days, *at least.*"

"All right, I promise," I said, fully intending to send it the minute I left Robin's house. I couldn't imagine waiting a week to text someone. It seemed rude. And anyway, Stella would surely have found someone else by then. A professional athlete or Mark Zuckerberg, probably.

"OK, let's brainstorm this carefully." Robin grabbed a pad of paper and a pen from his bookshelf and began pacing the room like a caged animal. Chris had lost interest. He was reading the rest of the Stella Artois Wikipedia entry.

Finally, I broke the silence. "What about starting with 'Hi, Stella'?"

Robin stopped pacing and stared at me. "Do you want her to text back?"

"Yes."

"Right. Well, let's have some serious suggestions, then."

"What exactly is wrong with 'Hi, Stella'?"

Robin sat down heavily on the edge of the bed and sighed. "Listen, Sam. Do you know how many texts Stella has probably received in her life that began 'Hi, Stella'?"

I assumed this was a rhetorical question. It was. Robin continued.

"There are probably at least ten guys from the party last night all sending her texts right now that start with 'Hi, Stella.' You need to stand out from the crowd."

"Fine. How?"

Robin nibbled his bottom lip. "Start with a joke," he said finally.

"A joke?"

"Yeah."

"What, just any old joke?"

Chris looked up from the computer screen. "My uncle tells a good one about an Irish lighthouse keeper."

Robin jabbed the notepad with his pen like a judge calling for order. "Can we concentrate here, please? I mean a *private* joke. A callback to something funny that happened last night between the two of you."

"Nothing funny happened last night between us!" I said. "I told you. She just came up and kissed me, jabbered on at me for ten minutes about how much she loved hosting parties, kissed me some more and then we left."

"It's not exactly comedy gold, is it?" said Chris.

"Yeah. How am I going to make a joke out of that?"

I idly started composing a private joke-laden text to Grape Girl in my head. It would have been a five-screen message, at least.

Robin folded his arms and frowned. "Look, I'm trying to help you out here, man. I don't have to do this. I'll be in Florida in a couple of days, beating the women off with a stick."

"You're going to the Harry Potter theme park."

"Yeah, only because my little sister wants to," Robin snapped back. "She literally begged my parents to take us."

From across the hall we heard Robin's little sister yell, "You're the one who begged them! I hate Harry Potter—it's for babies!"

Robin leapt up and shouted back across the hall. "I'd like to see a baby grasp the complexity of Dumbledore's relationship with Snape!"

He slammed the door and then sat back down as if nothing had happened.

"Yeah, my sister's obsessed with Potter. She's been on my parents to take her for years. Fucking annoying. I'd rather go and check out the Florida club scene."

He noticed Chris and I smiling down at the Voldemort wand under his bed. He gently pushed it out of sight with his foot.

I felt my phone vibrate in my pocket. I took it out. I had a text. From Stella.

"I've got a text from Stella," I announced.

"What?" yelled Robin, leaping up from the bed. This did not compute for him.

"What shall I do?"

Chris sighed. "Open it."

"No!" shouted Robin. "Don't open it! You'll look like a desperate freak. Wait at least two days to open it."

"She can't tell whether or not he's opened it, Robin," Chris said wearily.

"She might be able to." Robin peered out the window, as if Stella might be standing in the street outside. "You don't know what girls like Stella are capable of."

"Open it, Sam," said Chris.

I opened it and read it out.

See u at 7 tonight at the cafe opposite the popcorn counter in westfield cinemas? I'll bring a friend . . . Do u have a friend for my friend?

Chris never stood a chance. Robin jumped into the air. "Fuck yeah!"

When he'd returned to the ground, he added, "Stella's friend better be as hot as she is."

HANNAH

When I got home I had six missed calls from Stella and one text:

I need to talk to you. Where are you?

That's the thing with Stella. She had no idea how angry I was about her using my virginity for social point-scoring. And I know if I said something, she'd act like I was crazy and turn it around so I'd seem immature and silly. Nothing touches her. She's impervious.

My phone started ringing again. It was her. I considered not answering, but, of course, I did.

"Where are you? Are you OK? Honestly, Han, Freddie feels awful. I spoke to him for hours this morning and he literally wants to buy you a house in the Caribbean and give you everything he owns including his cat to make up for it."

I didn't speak for a second, then all I said was, "Uh-huh." So she would know I knew what a bitch she had been.

"He really feels bad."

Why did he call *her* to say sorry? Why didn't he call *me*? There was a pause and I gave in. If I had even tried to say something, she would have just managed to turn it back around on me.

"Good. I had puke all over me. It was the grossest thing that's ever happened. It had carrots in it. Wait, *Freddie* has a cat?"

And just like that we both got silly and everything was back to normal. Well, it always had been for her. I just felt angry with myself for giving in like I always do.

She told me about the rest of the party. How Freddie had fallen asleep on top of the washing machine and how she found people eating dog treats out of unlabeled Tupperware.

"Freddie will be heartbroken that he's been replaced by someone else."

Even though she had already heard the whole Toilet Boy story from Tilly, I told it again. It seemed even more romantic now. We went over the grape juice exchange. His old white T-shirt and battered Vans and how he looked like a beatnik poet.

"I am totally in on the quest to find Toilet Boy," Stella said. "One hundred percent in. I'm going to dedicate my life to it, in fact." There was a pause. "Hang on, I'm putting you on speakerphone. I'm writing him on the door to make it official. What color do you want?"

"But we don't know his name."

"I'm just writing 'Toilet Boy.' I'll write it in black. Because he is obvs your lobster, and black is classic and doesn't date."

"He probably didn't even like me, though. Honestly, Stell, he was so cute."

Stella responded to this concern in song form. "You're insecure/Don't know what for/Right now I'm writing 'Toilet Boy' on the do-or-or. . . ."

"Stell!"

"Don't need makeup/To cover up/'Toilet Boy' on the door is en-ou-ou-gh . . ."

"Stop singing!" I screamed.

But she was off and running. Freddie was forgotten. In the memory bin with all the other boys we've been obsessed with and would get hysterical over if we ever saw them by accident on the bus.

"Where is Toilet Boy?" I asked. "Where have you written him?"

"Over Freddie. Freddie was so a life phase, not a life stage." That is a classic Stella thing to say. As if she were a therapist letting you in on the fact she always knew how things were going to turn out.

"Yeah," I said. "Toilet Boy is the future."

"Definitely. Listen, are you busy tonight? You've got to help me." Stella didn't usually admit she might need assistance with anything.

"Well, I'm supposed to have dinner with my family but—"

"Cool; well, basically, we're meeting these two random boys tonight."

"WHAT?" Boys were suddenly popping up with no appropriate warning. Where had they all been for the last five years when we were actively hunting them?

"I made out with this random boy last night," she said.

"What? What happened with Charlie?"

"Nothing. We're both free to see other people." The tone of her voice altered slightly, as if she was repeating something he had said to her. No one else would have picked up the hurt, but I could hear it.

"Are you OK, Stell?" I said softly. I felt sad for her because when she makes out with someone who isn't Charlie, it's usually just to cover up how much she likes him.

Stella sighed, pretending to be bored by the whole conversation. "Yeah, I'm fine. It just pisses me off. He was the one who was acting like we should be exclusive and then last night he was all, like, 'Oh, I'm seeing this girl from school. I don't know if we should be doing this.' So I was, like, 'Fine, fuck you,' and I went off and had a bit of fun on my own."

"OK," I said. "What was this bit of fun called?"

"He's called Sam. And, well, I can't really remember anything else about him except that he was wearing this cool, red Kanye West T-shirt."

Poor guy, I thought. Totally unaware he was just another pawn in Stella and Charlie's never-ending game of fuck-buddy chess.

"So why are you meeting up with him?" I asked.

"Because Charlie's being a dick and I just want him to know what he's missing, that's all. So I arranged for us to go for a drink with Sam and one of his friends."

"And how is that going to teach Charlie a lesson? Are we going to live stream this double date or something?"

"No, we're meeting the boys in the café opposite the popcorn counter in the Westfield cinemas."

That was where Charlie worked during the summer.

"Are you being serious, Stell?" I said. "So you're going to sit there and flirt with this random guy while Charlie watches?"

"No. Well . . . yeah, maybe," she said.

"Yeah, but why do I need to come, too? This is clearly going to be so awkward. And anyway, I thought we'd just established that I should focus my energies on finding Toilet Boy?"

"Hannah, be realistic. There are a lot of boys in the world. Obviously, Toilet Boy is your lobster, but equally, you probably won't ever see him again."

"Great, thanks, Stell. For someone whose favorite film is *Dirty Dancing* you're not exactly giving true love a chance."

Stella laughed. "Look, Hannah, it's one hour of your life and I'm your best friend. Just come along and help me out. You never know, his friend might look like Channing Tatum."

"Urgh," I said. "I hate Channing Tatum. He looks like the missing link."

"Oh god," groaned Stella. "Well, OK, Oscar Wilde, then."

"*Oscar Wilde?* Stell, do you even know who Oscar Wilde is?"

"That boy you love. The one you always go on about."

"Yeah, I love his *writing*. And he's not a boy, he's a man who's been dead for about a hundred years."

"Whatever. Either way, you're just there to help me out. If you don't like Sam's friend, we can always say you've got a boyfriend or something."

It was done. We were going. She was already talking outfits.

"I need to go shopping for a whole new wardrobe before Greece. I wonder if my dress is still in that shop," she said.

That was my moment. To make up a lie and say my nan had bought it for me as a surprise. To tell her it was sitting in a bag at the end of my bed. But I didn't. The chance to make it right swam past and all I said was,

"Yeah, that dress is so amazing."

"I know," Stella said. "OK, see you outside Westfield at ten to seven."

This was crazy. Why was I going on a blind date when all I wanted to do was find Toilet Boy?

5

SAM

Me and Robin both agreed that the café opposite the pop-corn counter in the Westfield cinemas was a pretty weird place to arrange a double date. But then, when a girl like Stella tells you to be at the café opposite the popcorn counter in the Westfield cinemas, you don't ask questions. You just go to the café opposite the popcorn counter in the Westfield cinemas.

Robin, for all his apparent dedication to playing it cool and not coming across as a "desperate freak," had insisted we arrive early so we could settle in and formulate a good "game plan."

So at 6:45 p.m. we sat in the café opposite the popcorn counter in the Westfield cinemas, waiting for Stella and her girlfriend. Robin picked at a raspberry-and-white-chocolate muffin while he checked his reflection in the back of a tea-spoon.

"How can you possibly tell whether you look all right

by doing that?" I asked. "Your reflection's all mangled and tiny."

He looked up. "I've looked in enough teaspoons in my time to know whether this mangled and tiny reflection is a good one."

"And is it?"

He checked again. "Yes."

"You could just ask me if you look all right."

Robin snorted. "You're *clearly* not qualified to say whether or not someone looks all right. If you were, you wouldn't have worn that shirt."

I looked down at my shirt. It was light blue, from the Gap. You couldn't find a less offensive shirt if you tried.

"What's wrong with my shirt? You couldn't find a less offensive shirt if you tried."

"Exactly," said Robin, waving his teaspoon at me. "You're playing it safe. Light blue. Boring and safe. This is a first date. You need to shock her. You need to show her you're an unpredictable, crazy, exciting guy."

"But I'm not an unpredictable, crazy, exciting guy."

Robin sighed. "I realize that. I am well aware of that. But *she* doesn't need to know that, does she?"

"You can hardly talk about being unpredictable, crazy and exciting when you're wearing a plain gray hoodie."

"Oh, really?" Robin smirked. "Is that so?" He unzipped his hoodie to reveal a T-shirt with the slogan FBI—FEMALE BODY INSPECTOR on it.

"Oh my god," I said.

Robin beamed proudly down at his chest. "I bought it last week. It's good, isn't it?"

"No, it's not good. It's literally the least good thing I've ever seen."

"It says 'unpredictable, crazy and exciting.'"

"If it said that it would be fine. But what it actually says is 'Female Body Inspector.'" I reached over and pulled up the zipper on his hoodie. "Just keep that zipped up. Even if we end up going to a sauna, I want you to keep that hoodie on."

Robin unzipped it again. "We're hardly likely to end up in a sauna with these girls when you're wearing such boring clothes. Look, Sam, as the only person here who has actually had actual sex with an actual girl, I think I'm more qualified to say what will or won't turn a woman on. And this"—he indicated his T-shirt—"is basically a one-way ticket to a lady's bedroom."

"A lady who can't read, presumably."

"Whatever." He glanced into the teaspoon again. "Oh, fuck this, I need a real mirror." He jumped out of his seat and headed toward the bathroom.

Left alone, I started to daydream about how the date might go. I tried to conjure a few possible conversation topics in my head, but I kept drawing blanks. This was largely because I knew literally nothing about Stella (except that she had a James Bond villain bathroom and she loved throwing parties), and thus I had no idea what she'd want to talk about.

It sounds weird but I couldn't even really remember what she looked like. I knew she was really hot—mainly because Robin had been reminding me every fifteen seconds—but when I actually tried to picture her face in any sort of detail,

I couldn't do it. Whereas every freckle and dimple of Grape Girl's was still imprinted on my mind in HD.

It seemed ridiculous to be thinking about Grape Girl this much. I guess, for her, that ten minutes in the bathroom had just been a weird stopgap between going to the bathroom and getting "jiggy" on a trampoline with a jackass called Freddie. But I couldn't help it. I wanted to see her again. So badly.

I made a mental note to stop calling her Grape Girl, though, as it made her sound like a crap superhero.

Robin returned from inspecting his reflection and plonked himself back into his chair.

"I just got a text from Ben," he said. "He's DJing tonight at a club in Camden. We should have a few drinks here, then head there with the girls."

"I'm not sure . . ."

Robin groaned. "What's there to not be sure about?"

"Well, firstly, we might not get in. Secondly, if Stella sees me dance, then any chance I've got with her will immediately go out the window. I look like I'm having a very polite epileptic fit."

Robin groaned, louder this time. "You don't *dance* at clubs, Sam. Only idiots *dance* at clubs."

"What do you do, then?"

"You stand around the DJ booth and nod your head."

"Sounds pretty crappy."

"Well, it's not. Seriously, if I see you dancing instead of nodding at the Woodland Festival, I'm going to ditch you. I'm telling you now out of courtesy."

"Thanks, man."

"This is what you get for spending all your summers in . . . what's that stupid place you go with your mum and dad? That stupid island?"

"Sark."

"Yeah. You better get all your uncoolness out of your system when you're there next week so you don't embarrass me at Woodland."

I glanced at the clock above the popcorn counter. Stella was now two minutes late. "Let's just hope she actually turns up, first of all," I said, "before we start making plans to go clubbing with her afterward."

"She'll be here," said Robin. But he didn't sound one hundred percent confident.

"You might not even want to go clubbing with them. What happens if you don't like Stella's friend?"

Robin chewed his bottom lip. "Good point. Maybe we should establish some sort of code so I can let you know whether or not I want to make the move."

"Oh, god. Do we *really* need to establish a code? Isn't this going to be stressful enough without throwing a *code* into the mix?"

"No, come on. It'll be fun," said Robin, reexamining his chin in the teaspoon. "How else are you going to know if I think Stella's friend is cute?"

"Because I'll also think she's cute. I've got eyes too, Robin."

Robin exhaled loudly through his nostrils. "Sam. Come on, now. Seriously. You told me when we were fourteen that you had a crush on that art teacher, Mrs. Flynn."

I wrinkled my forehead, offended. "She's all right."

"She looks like Jack Black. So no, she's not all right, and yes, Sam, yes, we do need a code. How about if I—" He broke off and stared up at the ceiling, spinning the teaspoon between his forefinger and thumb. "How about if I tug my right eyebrow three times, like this."

He tugged at his right eyebrow violently.

"That looks like you're having a seizure."

"OK . . ." More staring at the ceiling and spoon-spinning. "Tell you what; when the waiter comes around, if I dig Stella's friend, I'll order a lemonade. If I *don't* like her, I'll order a Coke. Cool?"

I sighed and glanced at the clock again. Five past seven. "Yeah, whatever, cool. And cover that T-shirt up."

"Fine." Robin reluctantly zipped up his hoodie. "But if I sense they're getting bored or restless at any point, I'm unzipping it. And remember, lemonade means I'm up for it, Coke means she's a dog."

"Yes, Robin. Understood."

Suddenly, we caught sight of Stella. She was marching up the escalator, grinning broadly and wearing a bright red strappy top that showed off her ridiculously tanned shoulders. Even thirty meters away she still looked hot.

Robin gaped at her. "Even if her friend is half as hot, I'll be ordering lemonade," he muttered.

Stella's friend was about three steps behind Stella on the escalator. Me and Robin watched her emerge—first head, then shoulders, then body. . . .

At first I thought it was my mind (or my long-outdated contact lens prescription) playing tricks on me. I figured that because I had just been thinking about Grape Girl, I was actually imagining her, too. But as she got closer to our table, it became clear that I wasn't going crazy. Grape Girl was here. She was Stella's friend. She was Robin's date. My heart started trying to punch its way out of my chest.

"Hi!" Stella beamed down at us as she and Grape Girl arrived at our table.

My brain was still too busy trying to process Grape Girl's presence to respond. What the hell was she doing here? Apparently not content with spending last night fondling Freddie on a trampoline, she was also partial to the odd double date, too.

Grape Girl looked just as shocked as I was. She had turned redder than Stella's top and she hadn't closed her mouth since she materialized at the top of the escalator. She looked completely mortified. And, I couldn't help thinking despite my blinding bewilderment, really pretty. Even prettier than in the bathroom. She was wearing a thin white cotton top and faded blue jeans. I tried desperately to catch her eye, but she seemed extremely interested in the carpet pattern.

Robin only let about two seconds go by before he jumped in and responded to Stella's greeting for me. Robin is not one for an awkward silence.

"Hi! How are you doing?" he offered. "I'm Robin." He tried to kiss her on both cheeks, but she pulled back after only one, leaving him hanging awkwardly in the air for a moment, with his lips still pouted.

"Sorry!" He laughed nervously.

Grape Girl and I locked eyes for a split second. If this

hadn't been potentially the most awkward and confusing moment of my life, I would have burst out laughing. I was sure I saw a flash of a smile across her face, too.

"Erm . . . cool," said Stella, plonking herself down on a chair and shooting me a wide, toothy smile. "Hi, Sam. How are you?"

I finally found my voice, quivering behind my tonsils.

"Hey. Good, thanks," I said, sounding slightly more high-pitched than I would have liked.

"This is my friend, Hannah," Stella said, pulling The Girl Formerly Known as Grape down into the chair next to her.

"Hi, Hannah, you all right?" said Robin, raising one hand in salute. He'd clearly decided non-contact greetings were the way forward after the two-kiss fiasco.

Hannah cleared her throat. "Erm . . . yeah," she croaked. There was a pause, and then she looked down at the carpet again.

Stella was clearly unhappy with this as her dating partner's opening conversational gambit.

"Don't mind Hannah," she said, looking as if *she* minded Hannah quite a lot. "She's just kind of . . . kooky."

I was thankful for Robin's flawless social skills, because I was still unable to do anything more than blush and try to make eye contact with Hannah, while he took charge of the conversation for all of us.

"Wicked party last night, Stella," he said. "I mean, seriously—in the top ten parties I've been to. And we've been to some serious blowouts, haven't we, Sam?"

"Yeah," I said, almost on autopilot. "Serious blow-outs, yeah."

"Did you have fun last night, Sam?" Stella asked me, cocking her head to one side and smiling. I noticed her eyes dart quickly to the left and right of me.

"Yeah." I nodded, struggling to take my eyes off Hannah. "It was great."

A waiter approached the table. "Can I get you some drinks, guys?" he said.

"Skinny latte for me," Stella said, smiling.

"The same, please," muttered Hannah.

"And you gentlemen?" asked the waiter, turning to Robin and me.

"I'll have a coffee with milk, please," I said.

"And I will have a *lemonade*," said Robin slowly, narrowing his eyes at me and nodding, not particularly subtly.

"We're out of lemonade," said the waiter. "We've got Coke."

Robin looked nonplussed. "Erm . . . well, it's just quite important I have a *lemonade*, that's all."

"Well, I'm sorry, we've not got any," said the waiter impatiently. "I could get you a Coke."

Robin sighed and raised his eyebrows at me. "I'll have a Coke, then," he said, still staring at me with his eyebrows raised so high they nearly met his hairline. "But I'd like it to be clear that I wanted a *lemonade*. My initial order was *lemonade*."

"Right," said the waiter, rolling his eyes. "I'll make sure to note that down."

He turned and walked off.

"Wow," said Stella, looking, understandably, a little confused. "You *really* like lemonade."

"Yes." Robin smiled at me and nodded. "Yes, I do."

We lapsed into silence, leaving Robin the space to deliver a lengthy monologue outlining his thoughts on the music selection at Stella's party, which basically amounted to "It needed more dubstep."

I couldn't form coherent sentences. I just wanted to talk to Hannah. I wanted ten minutes alone with her to find out what was going on. Was she with this Freddie douche bag or not?

Clearly unimpressed by my lack of conversational skills, Stella kept glancing over at the popcorn counter, where a lanky, bored-looking guy with a hipster haircut was dishing out overpriced snacks.

Robin was not having much luck, either. Since Hannah didn't appear to have any strong opinions about the current state of dubstep, he gave up.

"Were you there last night, too?" he asked her.

She nodded.

"Have fun?"

She nodded again.

"You don't say much, do you?" said Robin.

"No," said Hannah. "I guess not."

"The silent type." He smirked. "I like it. Not to worry—I can do the talking for both of us."

Hannah laughed uncomfortably. Stella was still gazing at the popcorn counter, with a faint smile on her face. She seemed to have forgotten the three of us were even there.

Robin shuffled his chair slightly closer to Hannah's, making an unholy scraping sound that rang out across the café. The noise drew Stella's attention back to the table.

Robin's focus was fixed on Hannah like a laser. He leaned in toward her conspiratorially—a classic Robin move I've watched him perform countless times at countless drunken house parties—and added what he presumably thought was a seductive glaze to his voice.

"You know, a friend of mine's DJing at a pretty cool club in Camden later. Maybe we could go and check it out together? Could be fun."

I winced. It was bad enough watching Freddie hit on Hannah from a distance; seeing my best friend do it right in front of me was something else.

"I'm . . . not sure," said Hannah, her eyes bulging desperately in Stella's direction. "I was supposed to be doing something tonight already, I think."

Stella nodded and stepped in breezily to take the conversational baton.

"Yeah, erm, to be honest, I think Hannah's meeting someone after this," she announced. "You see, she sort of . . . hooked up with someone at my party last night."

"Oh," said Robin, visibly crestfallen. "Right."

Hannah fixed her big blue eyes on Stella. "Stell, I don't think they want to hear about—"

But Stella had clearly found her stride. Having struggled to get any sort of dialogue from me and Robin that didn't involve either lemonade or dubstep, she seemed quite pleased to be back at the center of things, fully in control. She shushed Hannah with a flick of her wrist and continued excitedly.

"Yeah, she got talking to this boy at my house last night, and now she's, like, literally in love with him."

I felt a thin line of sweat prickle my forehead. We were all going to hear about how much Hannah loved that boy band dipstick, Freddie. I just prayed Stella would miss the part where Hannah got trapped in the bathroom with a weird scruffy dude with crappy shoes.

Stella continued. "Yeah, basically, this stunning guy just appeared in the wet room and they totally had this connection, and it was immense and then he just *disappeared*. Like a boy Cinderella. Toilet Boy Cinderella."

I blinked. I felt waves of confusion crashing against me.

Hannah tried again to interrupt. "Stella, please—"

"Oh, come on, Han!" Stella laughed, waving Hannah's protestations away. "They don't care."

She was in full flow now, dramatic hand gestures accompanying every third or fourth word.

"She hasn't stopped talking about this boy since. They bonded over hot grape juice, can you believe that? Well, not literally *over* it—but by talking about it. Isn't that just *too* cute?"

This time, it was me who turned bright red. Not to be outdone, Hannah went a shade darker. I was actually sweating now, and I had to bring my sleeve up to stop the perspiration rolling down my forehead. I went through it again in my mind to make sure I hadn't misunderstood.

Hannah hadn't stopped talking about the boy in the wet room. Hannah was literally in love with the boy in the wet room. The boy in the wet room. Not the boy on the trampoline. I was the boy in the wet room! I WAS TOILET BOY CINDERELLA! My whole body felt like it was smiling.

Robin was less pleased. "Right," he muttered, shifting his

chair back to its original position with another deafening scrape of the floor. "Hot grape juice. Wow, I didn't even know that was a thing." He turned to me. "Is hot grape juice a thing?"

I was still desperately trying to catch Hannah's eye but she wouldn't give up her red-faced stare-off with the carpet. She looked as if she might start crying. I suddenly realized how embarrassing this must be for her. As amazing as the moment was, I wanted it to end.

"Not many people know about hot spiced grape juice," I said quietly. "But yes, it is a thing."

The waiter arrived and slammed our drinks down. Stella's phone beeped and she pulled it out of her bag to read the message. As she examined the screen, her eyes twinkled, and she glanced eagerly back up at the popcorn counter.

She took one sip of her latte and stood up abruptly. "I'm just going to the loo. Han, do you want to come?" Hannah stood up automatically. "We'll just be a sec." Stella smiled sweetly.

As they marched off, Robin leaned across and clamped a hand on my shoulder.

"Look, this clearly isn't going anywhere. My one's quite hot but if she's already obsessed with this wet room grape juice nerd, then I'm wasting my time, aren't I? I say we just fuck off; make our excuses and go to Ben's."

All I could think of was getting Hannah alone. Freddie was out of the picture, and I was Toilet Boy Cinderella. Against all odds, it seemed that a girl I liked *actually* liked me back.

"Why don't you head off to Ben's?" I suggested. "I'll

come and meet you afterward. If these two want to come, I'll bring them along."

Robin frowned. "You sure you don't mind?"

"No, man, of course not."

He shrugged. "OK, cool. See you in a bit."

He sloped off. Halfway across the café he stopped and turned back.

"Sam!" he yelled. "If it turns out Hannah was interested, though, you can give her my number."

I gave him a thumbs-up. He turned around and started walking again. Two steps later he turned back.

"Sam! Same goes for Stella."

I shooed him away and watched him disappear down the escalator.

HANNAH

I have never been so relieved to walk into a public bathroom. I sat on the toilet seat for ages, just staring at the stall door. I didn't really want to process what had actually just happened. My cheeks ached from burning so much. It felt like I was getting the flu. This was the worst. Worse than Freddie's vom running down my legs. Even worse than the time I got my period on the back of my skirt during the middle-school production of *Fiddler on the Roof*. There was no getting away from this being the worst thing that had ever happened to me. Literally no getting away. I stayed in the stall until Stella shouted.

"Are you having a baby in there or what?"

When I came out I washed my face to try to cool it down.

"Are you sick?" Stella did sound a tiny bit concerned.

"Maybe."

"Well, you must be, because you were acting like a fucking lunatic out there." She looked at me for some kind of explanation and then started to rummage through her bag. She found her phone and started texting.

"I wish you hadn't told them about Toilet Boy." I tried to make it sound casual.

"Why not? You clearly aren't into that Robin boy, who, by the way, is actually quite hot. Anyway, how are we going to find Toilet Boy if we don't actually try to look for him? He's not just going to *appear* in front of us, you know."

She got her lip gloss out of her bag and carried on talking as she applied it.

"I'm totally behind the mission to find him. But you know, we have to be practical. He could be foreign or have a girlfriend or . . ."

"He wasn't foreign."

"Anyway, I'm just saying in case we don't find him, you should still keep chatting to boys, or at least not act like you're a man-hater." She sounded a bit tired of the whole evening. "Right, I'm going to meet Charlie. He just texted me. He's finished his shift."

It was the happiest she'd looked all night. Her plan had worked.

"Stella, are you kidding?" I pleaded. "You organized this date! You can't just leave. What about Sam?"

"Well, can't you stay and talk to him and say I'm sick or something?"

"But I *am* actually sick."

"Hannah, you're being so weird. You're always saying we

should try to meet boys and then I introduce you to some and you just act like a freak show."

"I just . . . Please don't leave me with him. He obviously really likes you. I can tell by the way he looks at you." It made me feel flat saying the words out loud. "He'll be crushed if he's left with me."

"He's a boy, he'll get over it. . . . This doesn't have to be so complex. I'll call you tomorrow." She kissed my cheek. "Bye, babe. Shit, your cheek is burning."

And then she left.

I stood in the bathroom. I wanted to leave, too. But the thought of Sam waiting and waiting and Stella never appearing seemed so cruel. I had daydreamed about bumping into him when I was wearing the Gatsby dress and him falling in love with me. But the dress was wrong for me and so was he. Toilet Boy was just a fantasy. Sam was the reality, and just like every boy on earth, he wanted Stella.

I walked out slowly. He was still sitting at the table, ripping little pieces off a napkin. He looked lost. I shuffled over to the table, and he looked up and smiled at me as I approached. He opened his mouth to speak, but I beat him to it.

"I'm really sorry, Stella had to leave. She's . . . hungover. She got so drunk last night, and it's just hitting her now."

"Oh, right," he said. "Poor her."

I suddenly realized how that must have sounded. That she had kissed him because she was so wasted. I didn't want him to think that. I stared down at the carpet.

"Not *really* drunk," I mumbled. "I mean . . . I guess she's a bit burnt out from exams. She wanted to stay."

All of a sudden I was just babbling lies. I was painting Stella as some kind of workaholic geek who was in love with him. He looked up from the floor and I met his eyes, then he looked down again. Neither of us spoke. He sat staring at the table and I stood staring at the floor.

"I really hope Stella's OK," he said with a smile.

"I'll tell her to call you."

I put my bag over my shoulder. He stood up, too.

"So what are you doing now?" he asked.

Going home to make a wax effigy of you to worship? Getting a giant tattoo of your face across my torso? Going to check myself into a mental institution? He would probably think all these answers were perfectly possible given the last ten minutes.

"I'm meeting my boyfriend."

The words were out of my mouth before I had time to think about them. It was totally involuntary; a knee-jerk reaction.

Maybe it was a last desperate attempt to convince him I was a normal person. This way he might think there was some boy somewhere who thought I was sane enough to go out with.

His eyes widened. He opened his mouth to speak but nothing came out, so he just blinked up at me. I knew he didn't believe it. He knew I was bullshitting. *Of course* I didn't have a boyfriend. I was a lunatic who was obsessed with him.

Even last night I hadn't realized quite how cute he was. Girls like Stella are probably just his average hook up.

"I'll tell Stella to call you," I said.

And then there was this weird moment where we just looked at each other. He lowered his head and his hair fell over his face, hiding it from view.

"See you around, then." I held my hand up and waved on the spot like a five-year-old.

And then I walked away. I felt a momentary relief that it was all over, and then the full horror of it hit me.

I had spoken to him for five minutes and gone and made out like he was the love of my life. He had spoken to me for five minutes and gone and made out with my best friend. My cheeks were still red-hot when I walked through the front door at home.

My nan could sense something had happened. She probably thought I was worried about my scores. Which I am. But she didn't know about Sam and Stella.

I decided to start packing for the trip to Greece to take my mind off it all, and she came into my room to see if everything was OK.

I wanted to tell her about how weird and awful everything had got but I didn't know how. And she might have told Mum. I felt like I didn't have solid reasons to feel bad. It's not Sam's fault he wants Stella and not me. It's not Stella's fault she wants Charlie and not Sam. It's not that boy Robin's fault that he obviously wants Stella, too. I'm not even fucking in it. I'm just the puke-covered anomaly on the edge of the experiment.

Nan was looking at the hundreds of photos that cover my wall, ignorant of the fact that my life was in free fall.

"You can't worry about things like exam results," she said. "It's in the hands of the gods now, babe."

I just smiled at her weakly. "I just really want to go to a good college, Nan. I feel . . . ready."

But I didn't feel ready. The words were just generic ones that she could understand.

"Let's just cross that bridge when we come to it. Are you excited about your trip? Can't believe the four of you are all so grown-up now. Where are you going again?"

"Kavos."

"Greece? I don't like Greece myself. I like my food piping hot."

I had no idea what that meant. Nan went to my closet and took out the dress, handling it like a newborn baby. Looking at it didn't make me feel excited or beautiful anymore—it just reminded me of everything I want to be that I'm not, and just won't ever be.

Nan smiled at me. She doesn't see I'm ugly and pale and ludicrous. She's deluded. "Let me teach you how to fold this so it doesn't crease."

She folded it and laid it gently next to the suitcase.

"'Night, babe," she said, smiling. Then she left me in my world to cope with it all.

I leaned down and picked up the neatly folded square Nan had made. I was surprised at how heavy it felt in my hands, the rows of sequins weighing it down. I tried to keep it perfectly folded as I opened the zip compartment inside the suitcase and slid it in.

It was like I'd put a bomb in there. The thought of Stella finding out made my heart beat double speed.

I shut the suitcase quickly and zipped it up.

6

HANNAH

Four days later, by the night before Kavos, everything was back to normal. At least to some extent. Stella had been spending all her time with Charlie and I'd been watching chick flicks with Nan. I had buried the party, the Westfield date and the way that whole twenty-four hours had made me feel as far down in my being as possible.

We were all staying at Stella's so we could go to the airport together the next day. I'd already fake tanned and painted my nails five different pastel colors.

When I got to her house she ushered me in, all excited. Tilly and Grace were there, and so was Ollie.

They are so in love. It makes me jealous because I think Grace is normal, like me, and she's got someone who likes her so much he can't even bear for her to go away for a week. When he left, she made an excuse just so she could walk him down the road.

As soon they left the kitchen Stella rolled her eyes and whispered, "He's been here *forever*."

Tilly just laughed, but it annoyed me because she just *has* to be bitchy.

When Grace got back, we made tea and went upstairs to talk about what clothes and makeup and hair stuff we'd all brought. Our suitcases were lined up in a row in the bedroom, with Stella's right next to mine. The dress was lying less than six feet from her but she had no idea. Every night since putting it in there I had lain in bed, telling myself I had to take it out. That it was weird to bring it because, obviously, I could never wear it. But I hadn't.

As we lay on the floor, staring up at the glow-in-the-dark stars that have been there since we were eleven, things felt a bit more like how they used to be.

"Are you in love with Ollie?" Tilly said into the darkness.

We all know Grace is, but she's never announced it or anything. She laughed a bit awkwardly, almost shyly.

"Yeah, yeah, I am."

We all aahed together.

"At least one of us is in love," I said. "One out of four isn't that bad an average."

"I'm in love, I'll have you know." Tilly makes me laugh.

Stella was straight in giggling.

"Yeah, but it doesn't count if they're not in love with *you*."

Stella was talking about Jake. Tilly's loved him since she was thirteen, but we all know he wants Stella. It's an unspoken rule among us that we never mention it.

"I think it still counts," I said. "Look at me and Zac Efron.

I mean, no one can say I didn't want him. I had the perfume and everything. Unrequited love exists. You can totally want someone without them wanting you."

I wondered if the others were thinking about Stella and Charlie, too.

"I think only loving someone because they love you is selfish," I went on. "It's spineless. It's like only admitting you want someone once you know they want you."

Stella must have realized I was aiming that at her. She never admits she likes anyone in case they don't like her back.

"No, I know what you mean." Grace is so nice all the time. "I think you can, but it's a different kind of love."

"Yeah," I said. "Like, if someone dies you don't stop loving them because they aren't there to love you back anymore, do you?"

We were all quiet for a bit, partly because we were almost asleep, but I think we were all wondering what the closest thing to love we've ever felt is.

I guess Freddie is mine, by process of elimination, based on the events when we were fourteen and fifteen. That's depressing. Thinking about Freddie reminded me of the buried party night, and I went cold for a second. I thought about the double date, too, and Sam's face when Stella was talking about me being in love with him. Whenever I thought about it I got this guilty feeling. Like I'd done something wrong. Like I should have told them all that Toilet Boy was Sam. Stella still had no idea. Her getting with Charlie had diverted it all. Sam and that boy Robin were just a weird few minutes opposite the popcorn counter in Westfield cinemas. We didn't know anyone who knew them, and Sam wasn't even on Facebook—I'd checked. There are nine million people in London. It was pretty unlikely we'd randomly bump into them.

In my daydreams, I went to college and Sam was the person in the room next to me in the dorm. But he didn't recognize me at first because I had my bob and my new clothes. So he fell in love with me. And we moved to California.

It was like Stella could read my thoughts by osmosis.

"Do you ever think about Toilet Boy?"

"No. I think I was just drunk."

"And you call *me* fickle? *You* said he was your lobster. What happened to you hunting him down?"

"*Us* hunting him down," Grace interjected, all slow and sleepy. "I was totally up for it."

"All for one and one for all."

That's our motto. We've been saying it since we were kids. There's a photo of us dressed as musketeers and we've each got a key chain with it.

"Yeah, and about that," said Tilly, sitting up for dramatic effect. "When is this blow job lesson actually happening?"

Tilly was phobic about doing it wrong and had been begging Grace to give her lessons.

Grace just rolled over. "Not now, that's for sure. I'm tired."

"You are so not a team player. You are the only one who is actually having sex and knows how to do stuff and you just lie there and keep all your sex secrets to yourself," Tilly said.

Stella sat up. "Well, she's not, actually."

Stella and Tilly sitting up in the dark made me feel like I should sit up, too, to mark the occasion.

"What?"

"I did it with Charlie yesterday."

That made Grace leap up as well. And there in the dark, Stella had her moment. Which left Tilly in limbo and me as officially the last virgin on earth.

SAM

Every summer, me and my parents go to visit my gran in Sark. Sark is one of the Channel Islands—in the English Channel just a few miles north of France—and it is absolutely tiny. You can walk from one side of it to the other in about twenty minutes.

There are no cars and there is no cell phone reception. It's an idyllic haven of unspoiled, pebble-strewn beaches and sweeping, majestic cliffs. The dusty roads throng with cheerful, ruddy-cheeked men on horseback, pulling carriages full of elderly, camera-wielding American tourists. The lush, verdant fields are lined with huge, old chestnut trees that bend and dance crazily in the blustery ocean wind.

Basically, what I'm saying is, Sark is beautiful. However, like many other beautiful things—Kate Middleton, for example—it is also *massively* fucking boring.

There are about two hundred people living on the island and two hundred is also their approximate average age. My dad (forty-nine) is frequently called "young man" by the old women who run the village shop.

The majestic cliffs and dancing trees kept me entertained

for about ten minutes when I was eight. Now that I'm seventeen they've lost their appeal completely. There's no Internet. You can't even get Channel 5. Not that anyone watches Channel 5, obviously, but it's like a life jacket—you might not need it but it's still reassuring to know that it's there.

Anyway, this year's visit to Sark promises to be even more massively fucking boring than usual because it represents my crazy, hedonistic post-exams summer holiday.

It's a real shame that me, Robin and Chris didn't organize a real trip together. Back in January we decided we'd go to Crete in July for a two-week-party bender. Every day one of us would ask, "Has anyone looked into flights yet?" or "Any news on accommodations?" Then July came and no one had looked into flights yet and there was no news on accommodations.

So I ended up bound for Sark, as usual. Robin was in Florida (for purely Potter-related reasons) and Chris was visiting Berlin with his parents.

Still, at least we had the Woodland Festival coming up. Two days of music, camping and getting drunk in a field in Devon. That was going to be our real chance to celebrate.

As I sat in the kitchen with my parents, waiting for the taxi to take us to the airport, I started thinking about Hannah. It wasn't the first time I'd thought about her since that awful evening in Westfield. I don't know why. She said she had a boyfriend, so I guess that's that. But if she was so into this boyfriend, why did Stella say she was "literally in love" with *me*?

I was wrestling internally with these questions when my mum, who doesn't cope well with travel anxiety, interrupted my train of thought by starting to polish the mantel-piece so hard I was worried it would collapse.

"Isn't the house cleaner coming later?" I asked.

"She is."

I waited for further explanation but nothing came.

"So why are you cleaning, then?"

"Because I don't want the place to look like a pigsty when she gets here," she replied, scrubbing some invisible dirt off an old school photograph of me. "I don't want her thinking I can't keep my own house tidy."

"The very reason you employ her suggests that you can't keep your own house tidy. What's she going to do when she gets here and finds that's everything's already clean?"

"That's her business," she said, dusting a drawing of a giraffe that I did when I was five. "Now, have you packed all your books?"

My mum was becoming increasingly obsessed with my Cambridge reading list. For her, any moment I wasn't staring intently at *Paradise Lost* was a moment wasted.

"I'll do it now," I said with a sigh, and went upstairs to squeeze half my bookshelf into a backpack.

A cab ride, a flight and a stomach-churningly rough boat trip later, my parents and I stepped out onto Sark's cobbled harbor.

As we climbed the hill that leads up to the village, I noticed a hot girl ahead of us. This was a pretty big deal, as she was the first hot girl I'd seen on Sark since the village shop mistakenly ordered a few copies of ZOO *Magazine* six years ago. Which made her the first three-dimensional hot girl I'd *ever* seen on Sark.

She had long black hair and a delicate, doll-like face. Her lips seemed to be frozen in a permanent Instagram pout. Even though they were partially obscured by the straps of her extremely large backpack, I could tell her tits were amazing. She was lagging behind her parents, looking even less happy to be on this tiny island than I was. As her mum pointed out a particularly attractive clump of flowers, she turned and caught my eye.

She flashed me a smile and carried on walking.

My stomach bubbled. I watched her as she disappeared over the top of the hill, her backpack bouncing gently against the top of her butt.

I felt the splat of raindrops on my hair and yanked up the hood of my coat. There is only one thing more boring than three days on Sark, and that's three days on Sark when it's raining.

HANNAH

Going to Kavos was supposed to be all about us doing a last special thing together before college. But like all things always, it just turned out to be about boys.

Greece was not how I thought it would be. I knew the others were only bothered about clubs and the pool and getting tanned, but I thought it would be beautiful. With donkeys decorated in flowers and old women dressed all in black and brilliant white buildings with blue roofs. I don't know why Odysseus was so bothered about coming back here. He probably thought it was going to be like *Mamma Mia!* It's not.

Kavos is basically just one street with a beach. Our hotel was exactly like the hostel we stayed in when we went to Dartmoor in middle school. Just two single beds in the room and a tiny en suite bathroom. There was no air-conditioning. We got in at one a.m. and went straight to bed. All I could hear was booming music from the million bars that lined the street. They played it all night. That's what they do to prisoners of war. I couldn't sleep. *Maybe I'll get used to it*, I thought. But they played it all day, too. I could hear it underwater in the swimming pool.

It was my idea to go on the boat trip. A man came up to us by the pool and told us about it. You sail all around the island and can dive off the boat into the sea and explore caves. And they cook fresh fish and serve cocktails. It sounded glamorous and more along the lines of what I had thought this trip was going to be. We were all up for it.

Tilly said she'd gotten seasick on the ferry when she went to Ireland, but Stella said small boats are different and don't make you seasick, so we booked. It was quite cheap, considering all the stuff you got.

When we got to the meeting place and were waiting in line, we could see all the other people going on the trip. I think everyone there was our age or maybe a year or two older. Loads of people who had just finished exams, too.

The last people to arrive were a group of boys. There were four of them and they all had scruffy hair and looked like they had just gotten out of bed. They were all brown and casually perfect, carrying towels and not a lot else. They were above worrying about sunscreen and a top in case it got cold. In fact, they were exactly the kind of boys you daydream about being in a group of friends with. Because they were just unbelievably HOT.

As soon as they arrived, the atmosphere changed ever so slightly. All the girls became more affected, fiddling with their hair and trying but failing to check the boys out without anyone else noticing.

I knew without even looking at her how Stella would be feeling now. Because this is exactly the type of situation she loves. I can't imagine being attractive like that. Knowing that without even doing anything, just by *being*, boys will be drawn to you.

She got onto the boat and walked straight to the sun deck, where she laid out her towel, stripped off her white sundress and stretched out. She was wearing a gold bikini and gold earrings and enormous sunglasses. By herself with the sea behind her, she looked like Cleopatra. Even sex-face H&M bikini girl would have been jealous.

We laid our towels next to hers. I kept my dress on. I'd brought *Mansfield Park* from my York reading list but I couldn't face taking it out of my bag. So I just lay there, feeling hot. Not *Stella* hot—*sweaty* hot.

The hottest of the scruffy-haired boys wandered over and sat down by us. Boys who are that hot don't need to think of any excuse to talk to you. He didn't even try to make one. I knew he would start hitting on Stella, so I took my book out of my bag and shuffled over to be nearer the others. But it was me he spoke to.

"I've got that book. Is it good?"

I could see Stella looking at me, inscrutable behind her

sunglasses. I knew she would be pissed off that he hadn't spoken to her first.

"I don't know. I'm only on page one. It's on my college reading list."

He took off his sunglasses. His huge green eyes were flecked with amber bits. He was the most beautiful person I had ever seen in real life. He was tall, but not gangly like most boys our age, just lean and muscular. The tips of his brown hair were blond where the sun had lightened them.

"Can I see?" he asked.

Passing him the book made me feel self-conscious. He looked at the back cover for a bit.

"It's pretty weighty to carry around."

I laughed and didn't know what to say. I was sort of bowled over by the situation; by his eyes and his love of books and the fact that he was talking to *me*.

I was almost relieved when Stella sat up and started speaking. I didn't mind that she'd gotten his attention. Because I could keep quiet and observe him talking and laughing. I could look at his brown belly and see the white line where his tan ended.

I was constantly dreaming about sensitive, intellectual boys to fall in love with. Maybe they *did* actually exist.

As Stella started telling him about where we were staying, Tilly tapped me on the shoulder. Her eyes were watering. She looked awful.

"Han, will you please come to the bathroom with me?"

She said it almost desperately. I took her hand and helped her up. Stella didn't even notice as we wobbled off the sun deck to the inside of the boat. The bathroom was tiny and stank so badly of piss that I had to breathe through my mouth. I held Tilly's mass of hair back as she puked her guts out.

"Sorry, Han," she spluttered between heaves.

"It's not your fault," I said. "Clearly, Stella was full of shit about seasickness and small boats."

The boat rocked suddenly. Tilly missed the toilet bowl and a fresh jet of vomit hit my foot.

"Sorry," she whispered.

I bent down and closed my eyes and wiped it off as quickly as possible, laughing. "Don't worry. What is it with me and vomit lately?"

I led Tilly back to the deck and sat her in the shade. Stella was now lying horizontally with her head on the cute boy's belly.

A part of me felt jealous, that it was *always* her. But it made me proud, too. If she could do this now, what might she be capable of in a time of national emergency? The other boys in the group were talking to a different group of girls. Obviously, Tilly, Grace and me didn't make the grade.

The crew brought out shots for everyone. And more shots. And punch. And then there was a drinking contest. I felt a bit out of place in my dress with my book. I looked like my mum on vacation. I could still smell the puke on my foot. When the boat stopped, Hot Boy got up and went to get his friends. I sat down next to Stella. She grabbed my arm and pulled me toward her.

"He's called Pax," she whispered excitedly. "It means 'peace' in Latin. Is my makeup running?"

"I can't believe you're wearing makeup."

I bent over and blended her foundation with my thumb. Hot Boy—or, rather, Pax—walked back over with his friends in tow. Tilly and Grace shuffled their towels over. Everyone was standing up except Stella. She was laid out before us like the main attraction.

"Are you feeling better?" Pax was looking at Tilly, all concerned. I hadn't even realized he'd noticed us leave.

"Yeah, honestly. I wasn't really sick that much at all."

I looked at the splashes on the bottom of my dress and smiled at her.

Other people on the boat started to dive into the water. Pax's friends took their phones out of their pockets and Stella offered them her bag to put them in. They started to peel off their clothes and leap into the sea.

"Come in!" they shouted.

Stella looked like she was thinking about it for a moment. "No, I want to lie in the sun. I'm more of a pool swimmer."

Tilly wouldn't risk it after being ill and Grace was a bit drunk. I couldn't go in alone. And I couldn't go in with the boys. I didn't know them. I wouldn't know what to say.

Pax looked at me. "Come on, Hannah."

How did he know my name? Hearing him say it made my stomach flip. It was like no one had ever said my name out loud before.

"There aren't any sharks, you know." He smiled broadly. His teeth were perfect.

I wanted to tell him that I was actually a really good swimmer. That I swim in Cornwall in massive waves every year with my brother, and I can hold my breath underwater for nearly a minute.

But I didn't have time to do that because he just walked to the edge of the boat and dived in. He didn't even hesitate. It was one movement. He looked up at me from the water.

"Come *on*!"

He bobbed up and down in the water, smiling at me. I had been looking forward to swimming off the boat all day and there was literally no logical reason—or at least none I could explain to him—why I shouldn't.

"OK, just a second."

He stayed there, treading water, and I realized I had no choice but to take off my dress with him looking at me. I knew I was going red. Taking my clothes off suddenly seemed complicated, and I felt a new and instant respect for strippers. I just wanted to get in the sea as quickly as possible. I felt exposed in my bikini. I was still so pale. I clambered down the ladder and he swam across to meet me.

Swimming next to him was weird. I kept expecting him to try to find his friends but he didn't. We drifted away from the rest of the swimmers and started treading water.

"Are you going to major in English at college?"

"Yeah. York is my first choice and Sussex is my second."

"No way! I'm going to York. But I deferred for a year, so we'll be starting together."

Except that we probably wouldn't be starting together because I think I fucked up History.

"You're the first person I've met who's applied there," I said.

"Me too. But now we know each other."

He said it in such an offhand way. He *wanted* to know

me. There was a chance he would be in my life, even if only to look at, for longer than just today, or this trip.

We swam a bit farther and talked about English classes and what texts we'd covered and our exams and where we were from. He told me about his year off and how he went to a Full Moon Party in Thailand. I nodded like I knew what that was.

Then he told me about the town in Devon where he grew up. I suppose even really attractive people were just kids once, like everyone else. His looks didn't seem to affect him. They were just part of him.

By the time we swam back to the boat the sun was starting to go down.

Stella was lying exactly as she had been before. Resplendent, copy of *Cosmopolitan* in hand, sunglasses still hiding whatever she might be thinking.

I went to the bathroom and when I got back, Pax was talking to her and it was as if the last half hour had never happened. When it comes to boys she doesn't have to try to win, she just does automatically. Not that it's a competition. But her always winning sort of makes it one, whether you want it to be or not. Like you've inadvertently entered the Olympics when you know you're shit at P.E.

Grace was deep in conversation with one of Pax's friends. She kept laughing and touching his arm. Tilly started feeling sick again as soon as the boat moved. I went back to the bathroom with her.

Between hurls, she said, "What is Grace *doing*?" Her voice echoed around the toilet bowl.

"Just flirting. She won't do anything. She's in love with Ollie."

But when we came out, Grace had her arms around the boy's waist. Tilly and I instinctively looked the other way.

Stella looked up at us from her towel.

"We're all set for dinner," she said. "The boys know a really nice place, apparently."

Before I could stop myself, my eyes flicked straight to Pax.

SAM

After a day and a half on Sark, I felt like I was getting cabin fever. A day and a half of torrential rain, marathon Monopoly games with my dad and endless cups of Earl Gray all drunk while listening to my gran shouting at the TV during her stories.

"Don't marry her, you fool! She's just after your money!"

"He can't hear you, Gran."

"I know, dear. He doesn't listen, does he? He's hopeless."

At least my mum was happy; I'd pretty much finished *Paradise Lost*. Not that I'd understood much of it, of course.

After lunch, when the rain finally let up, my mum asked me to go into the village to buy a newspaper and some milk. Since it was either that or spend the rest of the afternoon out in the front yard helping my dad unblock the drains, I gladly accepted the assignment.

I charged through the deserted lanes on my rented bike, past the glistening muddy fields that flanked them and the bored-looking cows and sheep they were home to.

The village newsstand was empty. No one was even at

the register. The idea of theft doesn't really exist in Sark; people regularly leave their houses and bikes unlocked. In that respect, I suppose it qualifies as a utopian paradise. If so, utopian paradises are vastly overrated.

I picked up a newspaper from the rack and spotted the six-year-old copies of ZOO Magazine, which were still up on the top shelf, untouched by the looks of it. I suppose the elderly women who run the shop were simply too terrified to take them down. I grabbed one and flicked through. Megan Fox—and her breasts—featured heavily.

"Wow. She's got great tits."

I swiveled around to be confronted by the black-haired girl I spotted on the walk up the hill yesterday. She was holding a basket full of bread, eggs and bacon and had obviously been peering over my shoulder at the magazine.

She had a thick, ridiculously sexy American accent. Her long black hair was pulled back into a ponytail and a tight Rolling Stones T-shirt showed off her impossibly tanned arms and belly. And never mind Megan's tits—hers were even more amazing up close and without the backpack straps impeding them.

"Do you think they're real?" she asked, pointing to the breasts that Megan was trying (not very successfully) to contain with only her bare hands.

I hastily jammed the magazine back onto the rack.

"Yes—no," I stammered. "I mean—it's a horribly sexist magazine, isn't it? I was just going to . . . complain, actually."

"Oh, no, don't do that." She smiled, taking the magazine back off the rack and placing it in her basket. "You need all the excitement you can get in a place like this."

We walked out of the shop together—leaving our money for the food, newspaper and soft-core pornography on the counter—and continued talking as we wandered toward our bikes.

It turned out she was not American but Canadian—from Calgary. Her name was Erin. She had come to Sark with her mum and stepdad. She's didn't get on particularly well with either of them. She was twenty-two and studying Fashion and Design at a college in Toronto. She had no qualms about admitting that she found Sark interminably dull, and she told me she was really pleased to have met at least one person around her own age.

She talked *a lot*. By the time we had wheeled our bikes to the road that leads to my gran's house, I had barely said five words.

"Where are you staying?" I asked, boosting my verbal total up to nine in the process.

"In the big house down by the windmill," she replied. "Do you know it?"

"Yeah—that place is massive."

"Mm," she said, nodding. "I've basically got a whole wing of it to myself, which is kind of cool because my mum and Martin can't keep checking up on me."

She stopped suddenly in the middle of the road and studied me closely. "How old are you?"

I decided honesty was not the best policy here.

"I'm . . . twenty. Just turned twenty."

She examined me intensely for another second or two, as if deciding whether or not she believed this. I considered telling her I was burnt in a fire but decided against it. Finally, she smiled.

"You know, you should come over and check the house out. What are you doing tonight?"

This was *huge*. I was being invited to a deserted wing of a mansion by a hot twenty-two-year-old Canadian fashion student with large breasts. This was bigger than huge. This was *massive*.

"Nothing," I said, trying to remain (outwardly) calm.

"Cool. Well, why don't you stop by the house at, say, nine? Come around back. I can let you in through the window."

"OK, great," I said, starting to feel anxious already.

She hopped onto her bike. "See you tonight."

She cycled off. I climbed onto my bike and was about to head back to my gran's when I saw her stop about ten yards down the road.

"Hey, Sam," she shouted, unflapping the copy of *Zoo* from her bike basket and pointing to Megan Fox. "I hope I can live up to your high standards."

I hadn't realized it was possible to feel sexually aroused and slightly terrified at the same time. I laughed and gave her a thumbs-up. A fucking *thumbs-up*. Who am I, the Fonz? I am literally the least cool person on the planet. She smiled and rode off.

I cycled back slowly, thinking over what had just happened. I figured I should be happy. I was potentially about to lose my virginity to a hot Canadian girl during a supposedly dull family vacation. However, the problem was that "I lost my virginity to a hot Canadian girl during a supposedly dull family vacation" is every virgin's classic default lie. No one would *ever* believe me. And, in the end, losing your virginity isn't really about you—it's about everyone else. It's about telling everyone else that you've done it so you can get on with doing it again. Properly this time.

I could just see Robin's face when I told him "Oh yeah, I slept with this really hot twenty-two-year-old fashion student from Calgary." He'd have none of it. He'd want proof. Even a photo of me and Erin together wouldn't be enough. He'd want a full-length HD sex tape.

I considered signing up for Facebook. Maybe I could friend her and then ask her to publicly confirm that we had sex by posting a signed declaration on my wall. That wouldn't be awkward at all.

Anyway, maybe the "I lost my virginity to a hot Canadian girl on a supposedly dull family vacation" line is now so clichéd that it's actually become believable again. Because no one would have the audacity to tell such an obvious lie.

By the time I got back to my gran's, though, the fact that no one would believe me seemed totally insignificant. I couldn't pass up an opportunity like this. It was happening. It had to happen. Tonight.

7

HANNAH

Meeting new boys is something we talk about constantly. It's always on our to-do list. But the problem is, meeting new boys is actually really hard to do. Living in London makes everything worse because it seems like everyone else is doing all this cool stuff that we're not doing. There is this whole world of bars and clubs and cool scenes that we have no idea how to infiltrate.

Tilly isn't even eighteen yet so she still can't get in anywhere. We are relegated to house parties and sleepovers and sometimes going to birthdays at boat clubs, and that's about it, really. It's supposed to be the time of our lives, but it doesn't feel like it.

Meeting the boys felt exciting because the last time we met boys we didn't know (apart from the buried Sam night) was in middle school, when Grace met Jake at her Drama class. Secretly, we all hoped this trip would bring us new boys. And for once, something we had wished for had actually happened. And happened in tanned, cool-named, book-reading form. And on the first day we got here.

Getting ready we were all a bit insane. Even Stella wasn't as cool as usual. She had talked incessantly about Pax. About his body, about his year off in Australia and Thailand, about his tattoo and how he played the guitar. She kept changing her outfit and reapplying her lipstick. Grace was on edge, and I could tell things were a bit tense between her and Tilly. None of us had mentioned anything about her flirting with Pax's friend James.

When we left and started taking the obligatory pre-night-out photos, Stella finally called her on it.

"Grace, you need to relax. It's not like you're married to Ollie. I mean, if it's not meant to be, it's not meant to be. Maybe this is, like, the *test*. Like you need to do it to prove your love or something. . . ."

Stella made it sound like Grace *should* hook up with James. Like it was a necessary part of reaching some relationship zenith with Ollie. It irritated me. Grace would obviously regret it if she did it. If we were going to tell her anything, surely it should be that it wasn't a good idea. It grated on me. Because Stella just loves the drama and knows Grace making out with James will bring her closer to Pax.

She talked about Pax in the same way she talked about Charlie when she first met him. Although Charlie hadn't been mentioned once since the boat. You wouldn't think she had just lost her virginity to the person she'd been casually stalking for two years. Although I would pick Pax over that douche any day, so I can't really blame her.

The restaurant the boys picked was not exactly the little taverna I had pictured. It reminded me of the café at my local swimming pool. I felt a bit silly in my white bandage dress, so I put my cardigan on as we walked in.

Stella seemed impervious and paved the way for us all in her sequined hot pants and Kurt Cobain T-shirt. She likes all eyes being on her, and they were. Saying hello was more nerve-wracking than on the boat. Stella was at ease, though, and within ten minutes I heard her asking Harry whether they played dubstep at the club we were going to go to later.

The boys were like all groups of boys. There was Pax, who was the leader. He had to be cool as well as hot because boys don't elect their leaders based on looks alone. Then there was Harry, the second-in-command, almost as good-looking as Pax. Then James, the joker, and Jordan, the not-as-confident one.

And then there was a boy who hadn't been on the boat. He was Pax's cousin, a year younger than them and obviously different. He was slighter than the others, with mousy-brown hair and freckles. He didn't tan like they did or dress like they did or have their easy, outgoing banter. They didn't leave him out or behave nastily to him—I don't think boys really do stuff like that—but there was just an invisible line. You could just tell he wasn't one of them. He wasn't from the same place as them or part of their gap-year in-jokes. He wasn't sprinkled with the same Abercrombie soft-focus haziness they were. He was called Casper.

We drank wine with the meal, like parents at a dinner party. It was like we were all playacting at being adults, and that made me think of Sam and our cheek-kissing conversation. At the beginning it felt awkward, but by the main course everyone had relaxed.

I tried to do my slow mannerisms and to seem mysterious, but it's harder than it looks. James and Grace getting it on was obviously a foregone conclusion. She laughed hysterically at everything he said. At one point everyone was talking about what College Board exams they took and Tilly said, "*Ollie* did Biology" and just looked at Grace. I suppose she has the right to feel loyal toward Ollie; she's had to hang out with him loads. I just didn't understand what the hell Grace was doing when she loves Ollie so much.

After a while I got sick of being enigmatic and slipped back into being my normal self. Grace was telling James about a YouTube clip of a girl who is obsessed with sloths.

"*How* can you not have seen it?" I said.

"Because I'm not a girl."

"As far as I'm concerned, if you don't like sloth videos you don't even have a soul. You are just a sloth-hating death-eater. Haven't you ever seen their little faces?"

To underline my point I did my impression of a sloth waking up, which involves a lot of puffing my cheeks out and screwing my eyes up. James and Grace cracked up, and from the end of the table I could hear Pax laughing, too. Our eyes met, and he shook his head and smiled at me.

I saw Stella catch it. Instantly, she laid her hand on his forearm. "When did you get your tattoo?" she said. His eyes were back on her again.

Pax had a tattoo on his chest of a swallow surrounded by some black symbols that looked like Chinese letters.

"I got it when I was traveling in Thailand," he said. "It's an ancient Thai proverb that means 'The bird that flies highest always avoids the cage.' Basically, it reminds me that I need to keep aiming for the stars if I want to stay free."

I glanced at Grace and Tilly to see if they were also cringing into their napkins, but they were both smiling and nodding politely.

Stella looked suitably awestruck. "Wow, Pax," she cooed. "That's so deep."

She turned her wrist to show him her snowflake glistening against her tan.

"That's *epic*," Pax said. He said "epic" a lot. "What does it mean?"

I knew exactly what it meant—that Stella had seen an Instagram picture and copied it.

"That I'm an ice queen," Stella fired back, and Pax raised his eyebrows and shot her a cheeky smile.

"I bet you are," he whispered.

That was it. I thought they'd probably be sucking face by the time we got the bill, but as we left the restaurant to decamp to a bar, I stopped to change into my flip-flops and Pax hung back to talk to me.

"You came prepared," he laughed.

"Yeah, I hate my feet aching and I don't want to tread on broken glass or something. Although I did bring my medical card so I could go to the doctors."

I have no idea what made me say that. It is one of the most ridiculously stupid things I have ever said. Let alone to a boy.

"Oh, you did? Think that makes you special, do you?"

He was laughing.

"No. It makes me practical. We could get run over."

And then he took his wallet out of his pocket.

"Yeah, but having the card doesn't cure you, does it? You can't use it to administer to the wound. Anyway, you're not so special, I've got a mum, too."

And from out of his wallet he pulled a European medical card. The thought of Pax being connected to anything so run-of-the-mill as a mother seemed weird. He seemed so independent and adult. We laughed about the sort of injuries we'd need our cards for out here: donkey attacks, incessant music-induced comas and poisoned Jägerbombs.

He was actually just a normal person. In the same way celebrities and presidents must be when they're with their mums, eating toast.

We were so far behind the others by now that we had lost sight of them completely. And all of a sudden, although nothing had actually changed, it turned awkward. I could feel we were both aware that we were a boy and a girl alone together.

"You're really nice, Hannah. I hope you get into York." He sounded offhand as he said it. He was kicking a stone along the road, looking down at the ground.

I nodded. I sort of knew saying "I do too" would mean "Yes, I want you."

And I wasn't really sure whether "Yes, I want you" was what I wanted. He was so hot that the answer had to be yes, Stella or no Stella, but then was it?

I stopped walking for a second. "Maybe I should put my shoes back on. We're not far from the club now."

I walked to the curb and sat down, and he sat next to me.

His brown legs stretched out next to my pale ones made me look almost translucent.

"You are ridiculously brown," I said.

"You are ridiculously pale. I burnt myself a bit today, *actually*."

He said it as if he was defending himself. He pulled his T-shirt up and revealed his slightly red stomach. I could see the top of his bright white Armani boxers. They were so bright they looked radioactive. None of my underwear has ever been that white, even when it was brand-new.

"It's *burning*."

He lifted my hand and held it against the red patch. His stomach felt smooth and toned, and I could feel it rising and falling gently with his breathing. He was the most attractive boy I had ever seen, and I was touching him. And it wasn't just an accidental brush of hands. It was so deliberate I couldn't hide from it. I didn't move my hand. Almost like I was daring myself to see what would happen. When I did put it back down by my side again he put his hand over mine and held it. I could hear my heart beating so loudly it drowned out everything else. Stella's face popped into my head, and the way Pax had looked at her after dinner. And then, for some reason, I thought of Sam. Next to his gentle shyness, Pax seemed a bit too confident somehow. A bit too socially at ease and perfect.

"We should catch up with them," I said.

I took my hand away and we both got up. And then he was standing in front of me. He stepped toward me, to the place you only step for one reason. I knew he was trying to get me to look at him, so I just kept looking at the ground.

"Hannah."

I had to look up. I could see the amber flecks in his green eyes. He leaned toward me and kissed me on the cheek and whispered in my ear.

"Can I kiss you?"

I put my arms around his waist and pulled him closer. He smelled like chlorine and salt and coconut after-sun lotion. We stood there holding on to each other really tightly.

And then he pulled away just enough to hold my face in his hands.

His lips were so gentle when they met mine.

SAM

I told my parents I was going for a long bike ride after dinner. They seemed suspicious. Their suspicion was heightened when I drained three glasses of white wine during the meal. My mum, clearly concerned by the fact I couldn't get up from my chair without steadying myself on the table, insisted I wear a helmet and a gigantic luminous poncho.

This was exactly how I imagined I would look on the night I lost my virginity—like a safety-conscious cowboy.

As I cycled the short distance to where Erin was staying, I could hear my heart beating in my ears. I was more than a little bit drunk. At one point, I turned a corner at full speed and nearly swerved into a blackberry bush.

After a few minutes cycling, the house by the windmill emerged ghostlike out of the darkness. It was huge: not really a house, more a mansion.

I rode straight past the front door—noticing that all the

lights in the main house were out—and dumped my bike by a tree near the back window. I left the helmet and poncho there, too—no one was going to steal them in Sark. Although I doubt anyone would have stolen them in London, either.

I knocked on the window. There was no answer and after about thirty seconds I decided to just leave. It surprised me how relieved I felt as I turned to go—I could say that I had given it my best shot, but nothing happened. Oh well. Better luck next time.

And then suddenly . . .

"Hey, British Boy!"

Erin swept back the curtain, hoisted up the window and kissed me roughly on the cheek as she helped me into the living room. It was the size of the entire ground floor of my gran's house.

"You didn't have to use the window, in the end. You could have come through the front door. My mom and Martin are out for dinner."

She was holding a glass of clear liquid that her behavior suggested was alcoholic.

This was confirmed seconds later when she poured me one. Just vodka—no mixer. My head felt heavy as I took a swig.

We settled down on the sofa and started talking. Or, rather, Erin started talking. And once Erin started talking, it was quite difficult to get her to stop. I stayed mute, nodding and sipping my vodka, while she confidently held court on everything from music ("If I had to describe a beautiful field of tulips to a blind person I would just play them 'Fix You' by Coldplay") to what she thought of the Kardashian sisters ("Whores, every one of them").

As she talked, I began to feel more and more nervous. Not just about the potentially impending sexual stuff, but also about the creeping suspicion beginning to solidify in my mind that Erin was actually a bit of an idiot. That's the problem with hot girls—their otherworldly attractiveness can often blind you to the fact that they're also really irritating.

For instance, when I asked her why she didn't get on with her mum and stepdad, she just threw her head back and sighed and said, "Listen, Sam, I'm just a fucked-up chick trying to find my feet in this crazy old world."

That's what she *actually* said. Like a shit character in a shit film.

After a twenty-minute monologue about what she wanted to do with her life ("Become a kind of cross between Lady Gaga and Hillary Clinton"), she finally asked me a question. Although, admittedly, it was a question about her.

"So how many guys do you think I've been with, Sam?"

Despite my inexperience, I knew this was dangerous ground. If I said zero, I'd be implying she was ugly. If I said four or five hundred, I'd be implying she was a Kardashian sister.

"Erm, I reckon . . . ten?"

She threw her head back again and screeched with laughter.

"Oh my god! You're so cute!"

She took another swig of vodka.

"Yeah. Let's just say ten, then," she said, grinning broadly. "Ten's a nice round number. What about you? How many girls have you fucked?"

I gulped down my mouthful of vodka. This could also be tricky. Telling her I was a virgin would almost certainly end in her laughing hysterically before asking me to leave. And possibly even patting me on the head as I walked out. I decided my best bet was to go vague.

I exhaled loudly and laughed. "God, how many girls have I been with? It's difficult to keep track, Erin, to be honest."

"Really?" She smiled. "That many, huh?"

This wasn't good, either. If she thought I'd screwed more women than I could keep count of, she'd be expecting a half-decent performance in bed, rather than what would actually probably happen—three minutes of confused thrusting and then a long, relieved hug.

"So come on, then," she said, shuffling closer to me on the sofa. "How about a rough estimate?"

I decided I had better rein it in a bit. I made a face as if I was doing a large and complex sum in my head. "Probably . . . two. Maybe three."

There was a pause. Erin narrowed her eyes.

"Two, maybe three?"

"Yep."

"And that's difficult to keep track of?"

"Yep."

"Why?"

"Because," I said, making the word last as long as possible as I wasn't entirely sure which words would follow it. "Because . . . I've just got a really bad memory."

She didn't look convinced. But then, to be fair, it wasn't a convincing answer.

"Yeah," I continued, "my cousin whacked me on the head with a camping stove when I was nine. Haven't really been able to remember anything very well since then."

Clearly, if there was *one* other male on this island between the ages of sixteen and forty, Erin would have politely shown me to the door. Since there wasn't, however, she just smiled and took another swig of vodka.

"Right. So in a week's time, you won't even remember if we fucked?"

I gulped. This was the first time she had explicitly made it clear that fucking was on the table. Not literally. I *hoped* it wouldn't happen on the table, anyway. I'd be nervous enough in a bed.

"No, no. Don't be silly. Of course I will. I'll—I'll make sure to set a reminder on my phone."

Erin smiled. She was now clearly beyond caring about my obvious social ineptitude. She was drunk, I was drunk. I was *really* drunk. She poured us both another vodka.

"Sorry," I said, sipping it. "I don't usually come across as this much of a dick."

"Come on!" she laughed. "It's fine. You're funny. You're my only source of fun on this island, you realize that, don't you, Sam? You want me to have fun, right?"

She shuffled closer to me on the sofa and put her hand on my knee. Oh god. Oh god, god, god.

"How long are your mum and stepdad out for?" I asked.

"Don't worry," she purred as her hand crept up onto my thigh. "They'll be gone for hours. They won't bother us."

Then she kissed me. Actually, "kissed" makes it sound like a romantic experience. What actually happened was that her tongue probed the depths of my mouth with enough force to remove my tonsils.

I started to feel a bit sick. For some reason an image of Hannah at Stella's party popped into my head. When we were in that bathroom together, I didn't feel sick or nervous at all. It was like I was with a friend. But a friend I really wanted to kiss.

This didn't feel anything like that.

Erin unzipped my fly and slid her hand inside the gap in my boxers. She was now literally touching my hard-on. She squeezed it, hard. I felt a sudden surge of excitement pulse through it. Oh please god, no. Let me at least last a couple of minutes.

She squeezed it again. Suddenly, I was right on the brink. One more squeeze and, well . . . the night was over.

Instinctively, I recoiled.

"Erm, sorry . . ."

Erin furrowed her brow. Clearly, no man had ever recoiled from her before. She didn't look happy about it.

"What's wrong?"

I took a deep breath. The tingling excitement between my legs seemed to have died away. I decided it was just a combination of nerves and alcohol. I shuffled back across the sofa toward her. I was OK. I felt good. I had it under control. A weird calm came over me. I had been to the brink of sexual inadequacy and I had survived. I was about to become a man. This was it.

"Everything's fine," I whispered, craning in for a kiss. "Let's do it."

Erin smiled and wrapped her fingers around my dick again. And that's when I came. All over her hand. And her sleeve. And the arm of the sofa.

Time stood still. For a few seconds we both stayed frozen in our positions—me with my arms around Erin's neck, reaching in for a kiss, Erin with her hand on my dick, her mouth hanging open in shock. Only her eyes moved, flicking madly back and forth between my face and my penis, as if trying to process what had just happened.

Finally, she let out a squeal of disgust.

"Ewww!"

She jumped up and ran to the kitchen.

"Ew! Ew! Ew!"

I heard her turn on the tap and frantically scrub her hands.

"EWWWWW!"

I stared blankly at the ceiling while I listened to the running water and the loud, horrified "EWWWs." My head was swimming. Humiliation had swallowed me and spat me back out again.

I realized what had just happened was phenomenally embarrassing, but I also realized that Erin didn't know anyone I knew and, as a result, no one would ever have to find out about it. It was a bit like falling off a tightrope and remembering, in midair, that there's a safety net below you. Strangely reassuring. I was even considering asking Erin if we could have another go. I was going back to London in about fifteen hours—what was the worst that could happen?

I heard her turn the tap off. She stomped back into the room, rubbing her hands frantically. She spotted the sticky stain on the arm of the sofa and let out a little scream of dismay.

"Oh my god! Do you even know how much this sofa is worth?"

"How much?"

"I don't know! But it's a lot! And it's going to be a lot less now that it's got your cum all over it!"

"I'm sorry . . . I didn't mean for that to happen."

"Oh really? Ejaculating on sofas isn't usually part of your seduction technique?"

"Not usually, no."

She sat down in a chair opposite the sofa and shook her head.

"Look, sorry, I think you should go, Sam."

I nodded. She yanked the window open and I clambered out toward my bike, my virginity intact and my pride in pieces on the floor.

8

HANNAH

He opened his mouth slightly to kiss me again and I closed my eyes. I knew if I didn't stop it then, I never would.

"Pax."

I wanted to tell him that I couldn't because of Stella. But was it even because of her? Pax kissing me didn't really feel like I thought it would. It was a movie star kiss, and he looked like a movie star, but maybe it was a bit *too* cinematic. I felt like we were both acting or something. Like it looked really hot but didn't actually feel it. And Stella did seem to really like him. More than Charlie, more than I've seen her like anyone. And yeah, she does some shitty, self-involved things but she wouldn't hook up with someone I had said I really liked.

Deep down I know it's not Stella's fault about Sam. She doesn't know he is Toilet Boy. It's not her fault that he wanted her and not me.

I took a step back and looked at Pax. I couldn't read his face.

"I just—I can't—This isn't—what I want."

Which was sort of a lie. Looking up at him I wanted to kiss him again to see what it felt like. I mean, who could *not* want Pax? He nodded and smiled. I sort of wanted him to fight for it. To not take the rejection. To kiss me again. But he just said "OK" and nodded.

As we walked up the main strip and into the bar where the others were, he talked just as easily as he had before, as if the moment had never happened.

I saw Stella and Tilly first. They were deep in some sort of intense conversation. My cheeks burned because I thought it was about me. Pax went and joined the boys at the bar and I walked over to the girls. I tried to look casual. Stella was focused like a laser.

"She's actually done it."

If she had noticed I'd disappeared with Pax, she didn't show it. I followed her gaze toward Grace, who was on the dance floor, kissing James. I wasn't quite sure how to react. It wasn't exactly a surprise. I just felt sad because Grace and Ollie are such a lovely couple, and this James thing would probably end up ruining it.

"What should I do?" Stella looked at Tilly and me.

What did she mean? What response was she looking for?

"I don't know," said Tilly. "I feel awful for Ollie. He's going to buy her a charm bracelet before they go to college. He told me."

"Ollie is my friend," said Stella. "I'm going to have to tell him. He has a right to know."

Typical fucking Stella, wanting to stick her nose in.

Suddenly, it all just bubbled up inside me. The fact that

it hadn't even occurred to Stella to worry about me being with Pax. That she thinks she is way better than me, that a boy could never want me when she is around. The thought of her kissing Sam. The betrayal of her telling Freddie about my virginity.

She doesn't even like Ollie that much. But Stella always sounds right, even when she couldn't be more wrong. She got out her phone. I wanted to say something, but then the boys came over and she put her phone away.

She told me again how hot she thought Pax was. She was pumped up with anticipation, dancing and drinking quickly. She smiled and hugged me. "All for one and one for all."

And then she strode out onto the dance floor and I knew she would get him. Because she wanted him. By the end of the first song they were kissing. All for one and one for all. Truth is, that isn't really Stella. She's more every girl for herself. I didn't want to watch them, so I walked outside.

I found Casper sitting on the little stone wall outside of the bar. I felt sorry for him. He just looked so alone and out of place, as if he was looking in on the world. I knew how he felt. I went and sat next to him.

"Hey! It's kinda crazy in there, isn't it?"

He looked up from his phone. He was playing a game on it. Probably wanting to look busy, knowing otherwise he would just look weird. I've done that.

"Yeah. I just needed to text my friend."

I wanted to make him feel liked and part of things. We talked about exams and how they had gone. He didn't seem as shy as at dinner. He just didn't belong with those boys, or in Kavos. He looked like he should be drinking coffee in Paris or in the philosophy section of a library in New York. But he seemed like he knew he belonged somewhere and was OK with not belonging here. Maybe he just wanted to be alone and was fine with that; I don't know.

I managed to get a few things out of him. He was staying with his gran in Devon, and she was the one who had bought him the ticket to Greece. I told him about my nan and how weird she is. I told him about her Internet dating and he really laughed. We both did.

And then Pax and Stella tumbled out of the club. They came over and I suddenly felt embarrassed. As if sitting with Casper made me a loser. I didn't want to be on the outside of the group with Casper, I wanted to be on the inside with them. Stella gave Pax a look.

"You two look *friendly*. . . ."

Her eyes sparkled. She knew I would never like him like that. She was just being drunk and overdramatic and stupid. Casper went red. Pax was unreadable. He didn't even catch my eye.

"Didn't mean to interrupt." He caught Stella's hand. "We're just going for a walk," he said, and led her toward the beach.

She turned around and blew me a kiss. "See ya!"

Casper was silent. I just wanted to escape. I hated the fact Stella had brought up the idea that we might like each other when she knew full well that I didn't. I got up.

"I need to go and find Tilly" was all I said, and then I walked back inside.

I found Tilly and we decided to go. She was obviously

sick of it all, too. She went and told Grace, and I could see the awkwardness between them. Walking out, I could see Casper in the corner of my eye. He smiled and waved. I could have walked over and asked him to join us, but I just waved back. My stomach lurched with guilt because I could have made his evening better, but I didn't.

The next day things were awkward. We all sat by the pool, eating breakfast, and even small talk between us all seemed strained.

"I love that swimsuit," I said as a girl in a glamorous white one-piece strutted past. No one responded.

None of us mentioned Ollie, but none of us mentioned James, either. Grace was obviously dying to talk about it but knew she was in the immoral corner. She was the one being judged today. She was the *bad person*. She wore the scarlet letter well and just ate her weird crisp bread toast and didn't say much. The way I had kind of ditched Casper was making me feel bad, too. I wanted to find him and make it better.

Tilly was jumpy. She had taken sides last night with Stella and bitched about Grace. Grace could sense it, I thought. She directed her few comments at me.

Later on, we lay by the pool in our bikinis. Stella flirted with the hotel tour guide and changed her bikini at lunch. She wanted to wear every single one she'd brought by the end of the trip. Tilly and I went and got drinks and talked about neutral stuff—our families, college, celebrities. We wanted to talk about how awkward things were, but some-how we didn't know how.

As we walked back to the pool she said, "Where did you and Pax go last night before we got to the club?"

I didn't realize anyone had noticed.

"We just fell behind. Talking about York and classes and stuff."

She just left it. Everything she wanted to say was sort of hanging there. I wanted to tell her. To boast that Pax had wanted me, but I knew it would change everything. It would be out there and impossible to take back.

Instead, we planned our outfits for the evening. We were meeting the boys again and I was sort of dreading it. It was only the third night and I already wanted to go home. I felt claustrophobic. The reality was dawning on me that apparently we weren't the four musketeers; we were just four girls who didn't seem able to be honest with each other at all. Are there groups of girls out there who can openly talk about how they cheated on their boyfriend or how they made out with a boy their best friend wants? Or is it always loaded small talk and snide comments?

Everything that was unsaid was tainting the memories of the last seven years. Our rooms plastered with millions of photographs, every weekend spent together since we were eleven, but in the end it just amounted to some sort of *Mean Girls*–style survival of the fittest.

We went back to the room and had a nap, and when I woke up Stella was in the bathroom. I could hear Tilly and Grace in the next room, playing *Hairspray* and singing along. They sounded happy. Less strained than earlier, anyway.

Me and Stella have always been friends who pee in front of each other, so I swung my legs out of bed, strode across the room and opened the bathroom door. And there she was, standing in front of the mirror, more brown than the H&M girl and Pax put together.

And wearing the dress. *Her* dress. *My dress.*

I was so shocked I couldn't speak. She didn't turn around, just kept rummaging in her makeup bag before looking up at me in the mirror and giving me a really broad, fake smile. Neither of us spoke. I made myself walk across to the toilet and sit down. I couldn't even pee at first. I just looked at her. Neither of us acknowledged each other. There was silence.

The feathers on the bottom of the dress brushed against her thighs and her gold shoes looked perfect with it. She had piled her hair messily on top of her head. A few strands were left out, just resting gently on the gold sequins. I got up and stood next to her while I washed my hands. Everything felt like it was going in slow motion because of the silence between us. She looked even more perfect than usual. She hummed as she applied her eyeliner. If she felt nervous, it didn't show.

I shut the bathroom door behind me and got into bed. I rolled over and looked at the wall. My hands were shaking; I had no idea how the next few minutes would play out. I felt like doing something dramatic. Something that would change everything. I thought about calling my nan and asking her to pay for me to come home. But she would just say I was being silly. I didn't know who was more in the wrong: me for buying the dress or Stella for taking it. I thought about saying I was sick so I didn't have to go out. But that would just mean staying in alone. I heard Stella putting her things in her handbag and zipping it up. She came back into the room and I felt her sit down on the edge of the bed.

"Hey, are you OK with me borrowing your dress?" Her voice was all breezy, sugarcoated with mock concern. "We always share clothes, so I thought it would be cool."

I carried on looking at the wall.

"Yeah . . . course." I tried to make my voice sound even, but it came out quiet and false.

"'Cause if you want to wear it tonight, I can totally change?"

She was making sure that at no point this could be retold to make her look like a bitch.

"No, it really looks good on you."

"Cool. I'll see you at the bar in a bit."

She left. And I just lay there. I drew my knees up and held them really tight. I could feel tears, but I bit my lip as hard as I could and put the pillow over my head. She had looked so beautiful. It had suited her.

Eventually, I got up and made myself get dressed. I had brought loads of dresses but I picked up the same one I'd worn the night before and shoved it on. Then I went downstairs and made myself smile through the photo shoot.

We met the boys on the strip, and as we were walking to the club I could see that Tilly was going to get with Harry. I walked the same stretch of road as I had with Pax, but this time I was watching Pax and Stella, Grace and James, and Tilly and Harry. Jordan and Casper were nowhere to be seen. I felt invisible. Tilly obviously noticed because she hung back and made Harry walk with me as well, which was even more humiliating. As we walked past the public bathrooms Stella yelled over her shoulder at me.

"Hannah, you better get in there! Toilet Boy might be waiting for you."

"Fuck off, Stella."

I shouted it without even thinking.

It cut the air, and for a split second everyone was on edge. Stella laughed. No one else did and for a moment there was just silence.

"Chill—it was only a joke," she said.

Pax turned around and looked me in the eye. I had no idea what he was thinking. I wanted to know what he thought about what had happened between him and me, but he acted like he couldn't even remember it. We all kept walking. When we got to the club and everyone dispersed to get drinks and go to the bathroom, I turned around and walked back toward the hotel.

For a moment, being alone and walking in the opposite direction felt freeing. As if being brave enough to walk away was taking some kind of stand. I knew I was running away from everything, but at least I wouldn't be in some shit club, posing for pictures like we were having the best time ever. I texted Tilly and said I felt sick and was going to lie down. Her text back was predictably concerned and sweet.

Back in our room, I lay in bed and listened to the sound of Kavos. Girls shrieking and boys being rowdy. Bass from all the different clubs thumping, and random snippets of people's drunken conversations. I pulled the thin sheet up and read *Mansfield Park*. At least my name wasn't Fanny.

I don't know when I fell asleep but I woke up to Stella's

laughter coming up the stairs. As she fumbled with the key I could hear Pax laughing, too, and then they were right there. They sort of fell into the room and he was kissing her really hard, and pulling her dress, *my dress*, up around her waist.

I should have said something then but I thought they would realize I was there. But they didn't. They were sort of walking and kissing. She pulled him onto her bed, and then out of the corner of his eye he saw me. He looked up and at me, and then she did, too.

She mock-screamed and then burst out laughing as if it was the most hilarious thing that had ever happened to her.

"Awkward," was all she said.

"How are you feeling?" Pax said. He was obviously flustered. Well, as flustered as Pax seemed to get. He took a step back from the bed and folded his arms as if we were having a normal conversation over a cup of tea.

"Yeah, I'm fine now. I'm going to go back out and find the others. I'll sleep in Grace and Tilly's room tonight."

He looked like he wanted to say something, but he didn't.

I put my flip-flops on and left the room. As soon as I shut the door I realized I was wearing my pajamas—the ones with hedgehogs eating pancakes and bagels—and that I hadn't even brought a cardigan. I wandered out into the cool evening. I had no idea where to look for the others. I went to get my phone and realized I had left that, too.

SAM

Robin blasted another alien to gooey smithereens and shook his head for the hundredth time that afternoon.

"You didn't meet a single girl?" He sighed. "Not even one? Honestly, Sam, I despair of you sometimes. I really do."

It was Sunday night—about four hours after my family and I had returned from Sark across an English Channel violently swollen by stormy winds—and Robin and I sat in my bedroom. I was supposed to be plowing through the Cambridge reading list, but what I was actually doing was watching Robin massacre an army of extraterrestrial insurgents on my Xbox. I was pretty pleased he was getting some use out of it. I hadn't played on it since I was fifteen.

I was actually tempted to tell Robin about the whole Erin thing. Well, at least everything up until the very last bit. I could even have pretended I got a hand job. Which, technically, I suppose I did. An incredibly humiliating hand job, yes, but a hand job nonetheless. When you're still a virgin, they all count.

But I didn't say a word. It was all starting to piss me off, to be honest. If I had actually slept with Erin, I couldn't have told anyone because nobody would have believed me. And I couldn't tell anyone that I had *nearly* pegged her because they'd just laugh at me for screwing up my opportunity in such an embarrassing way. It was a lose-lose situation. I guess that's why they call it *losing* your virginity, instead of winning your masculinity or something.

Since I had nothing to report (or, rather, nothing that I was *prepared to* report) from my Sark trip, Robin prattled on to me about his week in Florida—failing miserably to conceal his excitement at visiting the Harry Potter theme park ("They had an actual Zonko's Joke Shop!")—while he murdered Martians on the Xbox.

In place of any exciting or uplifting girl-related news, I thought about telling him what had happened with Hannah. About how I was the Toilet Boy Cinderella who Stella had gone on about on the double date. But what was the point? Maybe she did feel that same weird connection I felt in Stella's bathroom, but she had a boyfriend. She'd told me so. It was almost certainly Freddie the Boy Band Dipstick. When someone tells you they have a boyfriend, what else can you do but try to forget about them and move on?

I had to accept that Hannah was just a daydream; a weird, wonderful ten minutes at a party, but not something real or palpable. Certainly not something I could tell Robin about. Telling him would have just made the disappointment worse.

So I kept my thoughts about Hannah firmly to myself while Robin jabbed at his controller and blathered on and on about how a girl in Orlando had taught him how to stand up on a surfboard for more than two seconds.

Suddenly, as if reading my mind, he broke off from his story and gave me a look while a new level of the game loaded.

"You haven't heard from that Stella girl, have you?" he said.

I shook my head.

Robin clicked his tongue against his teeth in disapproval. "It was pretty shit of her, just disappearing like that at West-field."

"She didn't disappear. She was sick. And anyway, you disappeared even before she did!"

"Yeah, but only because I was clearly getting nowhere with her friend. What was her name again?"

I watched the TV screen turn green as it filled with alien blood. "Hannah," I said quietly.

"Yeah, that's it. Literally didn't say a word to me. She's probably an 'introspective intellectual' like you. You should have asked *her* out for a drink when Stella fucked off."

"I don't think so," I said, even more quietly.

Robin was hardly listening. "Yeah, well, we should have known the Stella thing was never going to happen. How many Xs did she put in that first text to you?"

"What do you mean?"

"Exactly what I said. How many Xs, how many kisses, did she put in that text she sent you when she was organizing the date?"

I pulled my phone out and checked.

"One."

Robin's eyes widened. He paused the video game and looked over at me. "One X? Jesus. Sam, that is pathetic. I get more Xs from girls I've rejected."

I stuffed my phone back into my pocket and folded my arms.

"Piss off. Maybe Stella's just not a loads-of-Xs-on-texts sort of girl."

Robin laughed and then stood up, dropping the controller onto the carpet. "Sam. Listen. I know you're young—"

"You're four days older than me," I said. He continued as if he hadn't heard.

"—but you must understand that the number of Xs a girl puts in a text to you is an indication of how much she likes you. I once got a text from a girl that was *just* Xs. Nothing else. Just a screen full of Xs."

"She sounds like an eloquent young lady."

"If by 'eloquent' you mean she gave me a blow job at Matt Farley's eighteenth then, yes, she was."

"I didn't mean that, obviously."

Robin was in full form now and pacing the room.

"You remember Alex Spokes? How into me she was when we were fourteen?"

I nodded wearily.

"She put six Xs at the end of her first text to me. Six."

"Are you counting the one at the end of her name?"

Robin blinked. "Yeah, all right, five Xs. But still. She was fucking nuts about me, and those five Xs proved it. Six if you count the one in her name."

"Which you clearly shouldn't."

"One X in a text from a girl may well be unprecedented, Sam. You may have uncovered a whole new level of female apathy. If you keep this up, by the time you hit twenty you might even get a text from a girl with *no Xs in it at all*!"

I was just about to chuck a pillow at Robin's face when my mum shouted up from the bottom of the stairs.

"Sammy! What are you boys doing up there?"

Robin rolled his eyes, sat down and unpaused the video game.

"I'm looking at Cambridge housing, Mum," I yelled back.

"I can hear that computer-game machine," she responded, her voice wrinkled with concern.

I kicked Robin and he muted the TV.

"Robin's playing on that," I shouted. "I'm looking at housing."

I didn't hear her sigh, but I knew she had. "Perhaps you

should be doing something to improve yourself a bit? Why don't you and Robin look through some of the books on your reading list?"

Robin made it clear how he felt about this suggestion by pretending to fix and tighten a noose around his neck.

"All right, Mum! I'm literally reading *The Waste Land* right now!"

I heard the sigh loud and clear this time as she padded back to the living room.

"Your mum's always going on and on about Cambridge," muttered Robin as he unmuted the TV. "If she loves it so much, why doesn't *she* go there?"

"I don't know what she's going to be like if I don't get in," I said. I was genuinely starting to feel like my parents would be more upset than me if I didn't get the grades.

"You'll get in easily, man. They love bookworm assholes like you at places like that."

"Thanks, pal."

"Plus, you're going to do that work experience thing. What is it again?"

"Dunno really. Just working in an office, I think."

I had a week's work experience lined up in my mum's friend's office. Mum had arranged it for just a few days before I got my exam results, as if she thought it would help convince Cambridge to still accept me even if I didn't get the grades. I hadn't given it much thought. I wasn't even entirely sure what the office *did*.

"The kind of dickhead who *willingly* goes and works in an office during his holidays is exactly the kind of dickhead Cambridge is after," Robin announced.

"That's probably true," I said. Although I wasn't entirely convinced.

"Course it's true," he sniffed.

"How can you be so calm about scores, anyway?" I asked. "Do you seriously not care about getting into Loughborough?"

Robin chewed his thumbnail. "I do, but I'm more worried about what I'm going to do on my year off. Like, these two guys I met in Miami were talking about how they'd spent last year teaching at one of those American summer camps. Sounded pretty amazing. Apparently, *all* the teachers at these places are ridiculously hot American girls."

"Apart from the two guys who told you this, obviously," I said.

"Yes, obviously, apart from them," Robin snapped. "It can't be one hundred percent hot women or they'd get in trouble with the equal opportunities groups."

I nodded patiently.

"So yeah, I might just do that," Robin continued. "Spend six months living in a tent in the wilderness, plowing hundreds of hot American girls by telling them I'm related to Prince Harry."

"What about your beatboxing?"

"There'll still be time to do that in an American summer camp, Sam," he said pointedly. "That's the great thing about beatboxing—it's non-location-specific. You can do it anywhere."

I laughed and lay down on my bed.

"Anyway, look," said Robin, returning his attention fully to the Xbox. "You won't have time to worry about

Cambridge or Stella or your lack of X-based texts next week. Because we will be in a field in Devon, at the Woodland Festival, absolutely wasted, without a care in the world." He cut another alien in half with his virtual shotgun. "What do you think about *that*, you big space prick!"

9

HANNAH

I only became aware of how ridiculous I looked when I turned onto the main street. No one else was walking by themselves, let alone in their pajamas. I pulled my massive scrunchie out and tried to cover my face with my hair.

Boys checking you out and waiters whistling at you when you're in a big group feels exciting and fun, but on your own in the dark, the neon lights and the leery men just seem frightening. The girls weren't in the bar they said they were going to be in, or the one from the night before. They weren't on the beach I had seen Pax and Stella heading to, or in the restaurant. They weren't anywhere. Every time I scanned a new bar or stared through a window my chest felt a little bit tighter. I seemed to get more alone and freakish. I was shrinking into a lost child, biting the inside of my cheek to stop myself from crying.

I couldn't go back to Stella. I wouldn't. Grace was

probably having sex with James; Tilly was probably having sex with Harry.

I reached the end of the strip, where the resort ended. There was just a dark road stretching out into the countryside. Probably the idyllic type of postcard place I had pictured us frolicking in before I got on the plane. Standing there felt like standing on the edge of the world. I had never felt so desperate. I tried to think what my mum would do. Thinking about her and home made me start to cry.

I turned around and started walking back. And then I saw Casper standing outside a bar, holding a bottle of beer. My stomach relaxed. There was something about Casper. His independence or his ability to be OK outside of things that made him strong somehow. But weirdly, although it felt like everything was going to be all right because I had seen someone I knew, it just seemed to make me cry even more. I just stood in the middle of the road, with the music and the clumps of drunk girls and puddles of couples hooking up with each other, and sobbed. He saw me and came over.

"Are you OK?"

"Yeah, I'm fine. I . . ."

But I couldn't stop. Every time I tried to speak it seemed to make it worse. I could feel snot coming out of my nose. I didn't even have a cardigan. I just wiped it with my hand. The crying and the trying and failing to speak seemed to go on forever. He didn't move. He didn't touch me. Not even a hand on my arm. He just stood there in his own little circle of space. Like the moon orbiting the earth. He is the stillest person I have ever met. Maybe he would have stood there all night watching me blubber. In the end, his lack of response became so noticeable that it made me pull myself together. Like he coaxed me out of my hysteria though playing social-nicety "chicken."

"I'm so sorry. I think I'm just tired." The socially accepted excuse for being totally off her rocker.

He nodded. No words. But I saw his eyes notice the hedgehogs with bagels.

"I've lost everyone. And I'm locked out. Do you know where Grace and Tilly are?"

"No. Me, Jordan and Harry split from the others."

He looked over at the bar. I could see the outline of Jordan making out with some girl. Casper was the only one not getting together with someone. He would have every right not to want to hang out with me after yesterday, but I couldn't bear the thought of being left alone again.

"Do you want to get a doughnut? I saw this man selling hot doughnuts."

He nodded, but then I remembered.

"Except . . . I don't have any money."

And then he smiled. Just a tiny bit. He couldn't help it.

I linked his arm and we walked down the street. His quietness seemed to feed my confidence and I started jabbering away. We bought the doughnuts and I told him about messing up my History exam.

Gradually, he talked more and held my gaze. I told him about wanting to see some of the island and he showed me a tree at his hotel with this weird waxy stuff trickling down it. We wondered if it was amber.

From out of nowhere, when we were huddled together

looking at the bark, he said, "If you don't have anywhere to sleep, you can stay in mine and Jordan's room. I mean, Jordan probably won't . . . come back. . . ."

"Thanks."

It wasn't really that weird. Neither of us said "just as friends." It didn't need saying.

The room stank of boys' feet and stale beer, and there was sand all over the floor and in the sheets. I clambered gratefully into bed.

"I'd offer you pajamas but . . ." We both looked down at the bagel-munching hedgehogs and laughed.

We lay in the dark, which wasn't really dark at all because of the lights from the clubs. I felt like it was a "now or never" moment. I wanted to be brave and actually verbalize an unsaid thought for once in my life. I wanted to be someone who actually had guts.

"I'm sorry I kind of ditched you yesterday at the club. I just felt really awkward."

"It's OK."

"I just . . . I don't know what's wrong with me. I'm not really enjoying . . . Everything is going wrong. . . ."

And then I told him. About Freddie and my virginity curse, about Stella and the dress. And Sam and the buried night. And about Pax. And how he had wanted to kiss me. About feeling ugly and pale and fat. About being scared I've failed my College Boards. About feeling guilty that I'm so moody at home sometimes. It felt like I was confessing. But mostly it just came back around to Stella.

"I think I hate her. But if I hate her, then who do I actually *like*?"

We were both just lying there, staring up at the ceiling. We didn't turn to face each other. I thought he wasn't going to say anything for a bit, but he's someone who only speaks when he knows what he's going to say.

"Stella is just one of *those* girls. You keep saying about her being stunning. And she is really hot. But so are you, Hannah. Pax wanted you because you're pretty and smiley and actually nice." He laughed. "Ditching me last night aside. Because you didn't leave your friend to puke her guts up alone. If you want to be Stella so much, then just *be* her. It's not like it would be that hard. Getting boys to want you isn't hard. They already do. You just *think* they don't. You're in her shadow because you choose to be there. Just tell her to fuck off. Or don't. Whatever. Pax might want to sleep with her but it doesn't mean he thinks she's cool."

I just lay there. And I realized he hadn't told me anything about himself, or that I'd rambled on so much he hadn't had the chance. But maybe he didn't want to. We fell asleep as the sun was coming up.

If Jordan was shocked, or even vaguely interested in the fact that I was in his bed when he walked into the hotel room the next day, he didn't show it. He smiled, took his T-shirt off and walked into the bathroom.

"Your friends are looking for you, Hannah," he shouted through the door. "I met them earlier and they asked me if I knew where you were. Can't believe Pax and Stella threw you out. That's *super* harsh. They should have known ol' Casper would come to the rescue."

"He's my knight in shining armor," I shouted back. "You actually are," I said quietly, just to him.

I knew it would be a massive drama. I had a sinking feeling about it in my stomach. Like being in trouble at school. I walked slowly back toward the hotel. I saw them before they saw me. All huddled together, with the rest of the boys. Grace saw me first and ran over. She hugged me. The others followed.

Stella spoke first. Of course.

"Are you alive? We have been looking for you for hours. Literally hours. Where have you been? I thought you were dead and that someone had dismembered your body and fed it to one of those mangy street cats."

"I'm alive." *No thanks to you*, I thought. I didn't say any more. I channeled Casper. I wanted her to work for it.

"Well . . . where *were* you?"

"I stayed with Casper."

Pax narrowed his eyes and stared at me. Then he looked down at the floor. The other boys all started laughing.

"Fucking hell. He's a dark horse." James was clearly shocked, even if Jordan hadn't been.

Pax looked back up at me. I could tell he was surprised. The other boys started messing around, making stupid jokes, but Pax stayed silent, looking at me every so often. Grace, Tilly and Stella were trying to read me. I could have gone into a massive explanation about how nothing had happened, but why should I? They would know soon enough. If Stella wanted a drama, I would give her one. I knew the girls were desperate to quiz me. They would know we hadn't slept together, whatever the boys might be thinking.

I went back to our room. The dress was on the floor in a puddle. I didn't pick it up. I sat on the end of my bed and prodded it with my foot. The image of Stella falling backward in it and taking Pax with her replayed in my mind.

There was a knock on the door.

"Han?" It was Tilly.

I opened it and she walked in, beach-ready, her bikini on under her dress and her stripe-y cotton tote filled with towels and magazines.

"We found a place on the beach. I was just coming to get you so you wouldn't get lost again."

"I didn't get lost. What was I supposed to do? Sit there and watch?"

"We were all really worried."

"I couldn't find you—I looked for you everywhere. Where were you all?" I wasn't that angry anymore, but I didn't want to let it go just like that. I wanted to stand up for myself a little.

"We thought you were asleep, Han. We obviously didn't know you were wandering around. . . ."

"Yeah, but Stella knew. I didn't have my phone. I was in my pajamas. I literally looked like Cathy from *Wuthering Heights* wandering around looking for my long-lost love."

"Come on, you love those pajamas. I swear you wore them on Spirit Day once."

"No, I wore them for the getting-ready-for-bed race for charity. Which is a bedwear-themed event." I looked at her and we laughed together.

"I'm sorry, Han. It must have been really shit. I would have freaked out. So . . . what happened with Casper? All the guys are making out like you slept together."

"Eugh, boys are so gross. Maybe I *should* just sleep with

155

him. At least he's actually interesting. I dunno exactly what I think I'm holding out for."

"Your lobster."

"Well, I suppose we are at the seaside."

We laughed again, and suddenly that memory of Toilet Boy in the wet room flashed across my mind.

"What's Stella doing anyway? She's finally slept with Charlie and now she's getting with someone else." I didn't say Pax's name.

"Yeah, I know. They didn't do it last night, though."

For some reason I felt relieved.

"They did other stuff."

I felt weird again. The word "stuff" can pretty much mean anything depending on how you say it.

I put on my bikini and packed a bag with *Ariel*, *Mansfield Park* and a bag of gummies, and we left.

When we got to the little camp they had on the beach, I walked past Stella and over to Casper, but I didn't sit down.

"I'm going to go look in the tide pools," I said.

"What?" Grace sounded confused.

"I don't like lying on the beach all day. I want to do something. Go exploring."

Casper stood up and put his flip-flops on. "Yeah, I'll come," he said.

Pax looked up. "Sounds good. I love tide-pooling. And you're in safe hands with Casper and me. We've been tide-pooling since birth." He stood up and shook out his T-shirt.

Stella put her magazine down. "Are we all, like, five years old? Pax, maybe the point of their expedition isn't to actually go tide-pooling. Whatever tide-pooling is." She looked at him pointedly, like he was completely thick. She knew there was nothing between Casper and me.

Tilly and Grace didn't say anything but the boys laughed. Pax stood, holding his T-shirt. It was the first time I had seen him look embarrassed.

"Don't be stupid. Anyone can come." I said it to all of them but I was aiming it at Pax. I half wished he'd come just to piss Stella off. "There's a shop up there that sells buckets and shovels and fishing stuff."

"We could get a mask and some flippers," Casper added.

Stella snorted loudly. I knew she felt uneasy.

Casper picked up his wallet. "Come on, cuz," he said to Pax. "You only have a five-minute attention span. You'll get bored lying on the beach."

Pax looked down at Stella. She snatched her sunglasses off and rolled her eyes at him. "Oh my god, Pax, just sit down. You can't seriously want to go off playing with buckets and shovels. Plus, I really need someone to do my back." She tapped her bottle of sunscreen impatiently.

"Yeah, OK," Pax muttered. "See you later then, guys." And he sat down obediently next to her.

As we walked away up the beach, Casper said, "Wow, your friend Stella is pretty intense. Pax is more under the thumb than my dad, and he's only known her forty-eight hours."

I laughed. "Yeah, that's the Stella effect, all right."

Pax was beginning to seem more and more like one of those Greek god statues you see in museums—nice to look at but not much going on inside.

We walked beyond the end of the strip and onto beaches

157

that were deserted except for the odd swimmer or group of Greek kids playing. We bought ice cream and dipped the gummies in it and realized that we couldn't hear the thud of the music anymore.

We saw a family of crabs. Casper said he was going to college to do marine biology. We talked about potential exam-failure backup plans. I suggested Casper could go to work at SeaWorld in Florida, and he said I could be one of those people who dresses up in period costume and shows people around historical sites.

We got to a place where a line of tumbled boulders made the beach impassable. A group of young boys were climbing up and jumping into the sea. A tiny little kid clambered up really high—he must have been thirty feet above the water.

"Oh god, I can't look," I said. "It's actually making me feel queasy. What if there are rocks under the water? Should we stop him?"

But he leapt off, his tiny body clearing the rocks at the base and plopping into the sea. And then he swam back to the surface and heaved himself onto a rock and started scaling the cliff again.

"I can't believe they're not scared."

"Well, it's a calculated risk," said Casper. "He's seen the other boys doing it, so he knows he'll land safely, as long as he clears the jump."

"Yeah, but it's so high and he might not clear it."

"That's why it's exciting."

It felt like we watched them forever. And then they finally got bored and wandered away.

"What's the scariest thing you've ever done?"

Casper shrugged. The sun was lower in the sky, turning it magenta. "To answer honestly, I'll need time to think about it."

I looked at the cliff. "Shall we do it?"

"All right."

Climbing to the top ledge was hard enough. When we were standing on it I started to shake. It was so much higher than it looked from the beach.

"You need to make sure you take a really big, confident step out, OK?"

"OK, OK." I could hear myself getting hysterical.

"Because you have to jump far enough out to clear the rocks at the bottom. As long as you do that you'll be fine." He felt for my hand. "Right, I'll count to three."

"All right."

"One, two . . ."

"Stop, stop! I need more time to psych myself up."

"That will just make it worse. I'm jumping this time, and you either jump with me or you jump alone."

"OK."

We both took a tiny step closer to the edge. He squeezed my hand.

"One, two . . . three!"

And we both jumped at exactly the same time. I held his hand for as long as I could before the descent tore us apart. I screamed loudly as I fell, hit the water and plunged deeper than I ever have before. The water swallowed me up, and then the cold and the dark spat me back out and my head resurfaced. I hadn't been expecting the freezing water, and I made weird gasping, squealing sounds.

As we clambered back onto the beach, I said, "I wish we had got someone to take a picture. To prove to everyone I actually did it."

"Why would anyone think you didn't? It would never occur to me that you wouldn't do that. Stella maybe. I don't think Stella's the cliff-jumping kind."

"Stella is fearless, actually."

"Yeah, I can see that, too. We don't need a photo because we were both there and we can both keep it alive forever."

It felt like an admission that we were going to be friends after the vacation and beyond. He is the first boy *friend* I have ever had.

It felt like the dress night had drawn an invisible line between me and Stella. Or maybe just inside me. But maybe it was so invisible only I had actually noticed it.

We spent the last few days on the beach, swimming and reading magazines. We wandered to the gift shops and all bought matching bracelets. Slowly, Stella and I found a rhythm again. A new, more formal and tentative one, but one that we both knew would be all right. Neither of us mentioned the dress. It had been packed away into my suitcase, along with everything else that had happened that night between us, never to be spoken of again.

I did some things on my own. I finished my books, and went and petted the donkeys, and swam far out to sea with the flippers we bought. We hung out with the boys and, on the day of their flight back, Pax gave Stella his favorite hoodie as a goodbye present, and Grace told James she was with Ollie and that hooking up with him (James) had been a drunken mistake.

Grace had planned to call Ollie to confess all, but it had gone wrong because he'd called her first and offered Stella and me his two tickets to the Woodland Festival. He and his brother had been set to go with Grace and Tilly the week after we got back from Kavos, but apparently they hadn't bothered to check with their mum, who'd told them they couldn't miss their cousin's wedding just to get drunk in a big field.

It's pretty hard to confess all and then accept two hundred pounds' worth of festival tickets, so Grace decided to keep it to herself and, all of a sudden, the four musketeers were going to Woodland. Me and Stella agreed to go because we couldn't *not*, really, and outwardly the four of us were still all the best of friends.

On our last day in Kavos, Stella got stung by a jellyfish and sat on the beach in Pax's hoodie, looking murderous. The old me would have sat by her side, loyal to the end without even thinking about it.

I wanted to say "You OK?" in that fake passive-aggressive only-girls-can-hear-it voice. But I couldn't. Because I have known Stella forever and there is a part of me that knows only I see her as she really is, and that maybe somehow she knows that. So I ran back to the room and got the antihistamine my mum had given me, did impressions of Kourtney Kardashian giving birth and read *Ariel* to her in the voice of Donkey from *Shrek*.

I was wearing a bikini I had bought in a shop the day before. A proper, neon, look-at-me H&M bitch-face bikini. To be honest, it was the bikini of a girl who had lost her virginity long ago, but I wore it anyway.

10

SAM

We'd only been in the car twenty minutes before Ben passed out. Completely out. Chris slapped him in the face and he didn't even twitch. Although, since he started chain-smoking spliffs as soon as Robin put the key in the ignition, I suppose twenty minutes of consciousness was actually pretty good. Chris put Robin's novelty Rasta hat next to him in case he woke up and vomited.

Robin's driving, which is erratic at the best of times, was bordering on suicidal as we hit the highway and headed west toward Woodland Festival. I began to worry that his mum's Corsa wouldn't make it back in one piece.

He was *way* excited about the festival. We hadn't been to a festival together—him, me and Chris—since Reading, when we were fifteen, but that doesn't really count since we were only there for about five hours because our parents wouldn't let us camp overnight.

When Robin is excited about something it's nearly impossible to get him to focus on anything else. That's one of the things I like best about him, I suppose. However, as we were bombing down the M4 at 90 mph and he was tapping his right foot (the one on the accelerator) along to the music, it became a bit tiresome.

Three hours later we pulled into the shoe-sucking mud of the Woodland campsite. Ben—newly refreshed after his long sleep and now enthusiastically back on spliff-smoking duties—asked me if I wanted to "toss a Frisbee about," but I told him I'd rather just get going on setting up our tents. The clouds were already starting to gather. A few little ones directly above our field were openly scowling at us.

I was starting to regret telling my mum—who'd urged me to bring a stout pair of rubber boots—that "wellies were for children and farmers." I only had my old, battered skateboarding shoes with me. If it rained, I was screwed.

By seven p.m. it was raining. Actually, "raining" sounds too tame. By seven p.m. it was raining *really fucking hard*. Instead of just falling out of the sky like normal, these drops felt like they were being deliberately and angrily hurled at us. As if the clouds were irate neighbors trying to get us all to turn the music down.

But the music carried on despite the monsoon. So we decided to carry on, too. I prepared to leave the tent by strapping two Sainsbury's carrier bags around my already-sodden trainers. Ben had his dad's knee-length raincoat as well as a waterproof fisherman's hat to protect his spliffs, so he was fine. Robin had three cotton hoodies on, under the illogical assumption that because there were three of them, he somehow wouldn't get wet. Chris was wearing a trash bag like a dress. He had punched a hole in the top for his head to go through.

"I should wear this all the time," he said as he examined himself. "It's cheap and practical."

I noted to Robin as we were all leaving the tent that Chris still looked annoyingly good, even when wearing a trash bag.

Robin laughed. "If Chris gets *any* girls looking like that, I'll give you ten pounds."

I nodded and we shook hands. I've known Chris longer than Robin. Chris could get laid wearing Robin's Female Body Inspector T-shirt. And that's ten times more off-putting than a trash bag.

We headed straight out to the dance tent. Robin—who, as previously mentioned, had only five hours of festival experience under his belt—loudly proclaimed that the main stage was just for "idiots who've never been to a festival before."

Within thirty seconds of leaving our tents we were all soaked through. Getting to the dance tent was a nice break from the rain. We leapt about to the music like idiots just to get dry. Even Robin broke off from just nodding his head near the DJ booth. It was honest, stupid fun—the kind we hadn't had together for ages. Since way before exams, anyway.

That was until Robin spied a group of cute girls doing the same thing about fifteen yards away from us. He danced closer and closer and they danced closer and closer until eventually we were all dancing together.

This probably sounds weird, but I always get a bit annoyed when it comes to that part of the evening when we start trying to get with girls. The introduction of attractive females into a fun night makes everything immediately less enjoyable, because you're suddenly not allowed to act like a complete dick. You have to adopt this cool, unflustered persona. You've got to pretend to be someone you're not.

I suppose girls like Hannah are the exception to that— girls who you can just relax and be stupid with. And not worry about acting like a dick and talking about hot grape juice, because they're up for doing the same thing. The more I thought about it, the more I realized that ten minutes with her in the bathroom was a pretty unique experience.

These girls were *definitely* not like Hannah. Ben and Robin instantly went from laughing and joking and attempting purposely terrible break-dancing moves to smiling smugly, raising their eyebrows and shuffling about like they were in a fucking Justin Timberlake video.

Chris was still messing around and being totally goofy, doing shitty windmills on the floor, but he's such a handsome bastard he can get away with things like that and not scare girls off. I went for somewhere between the two— smiling smugly and raising my eyebrows while attempting purposely terrible break-dancing moves—and probably ended up looking like even more of a weirdo as a result.

As usual, the hottest girls in the group started talking to Chris and Robin. Ben saw his opportunity and offered the third girl a drag on his spliff. Which left me with no choice but to spark up conversation with the fourth girl in their group.

She was wearing little yellow hot pants and large hoop

earrings and had masses of strawberry blond hair yanked up into a topknot. She was pretty cute but quite clearly aware of this fact. She told me her name was Miranda, but she called herself Panda because it rhymed with Miranda and she really liked pandas. She liked pandas so much that she had a cartoon one stitched onto her backpack. She took off her sweater to reveal a Pixies T-shirt.

"I love the Pixies," I shouted over the thudding music. "What's your favorite song of theirs?"

She looked confused. "Oh, it's a band, too? I thought it was a clothing line by Pixie Lott. She's so awesome. Do you think she's here? I'd love to see her in real life."

I turned around to tell Robin, Chris and Ben that we needed to leave immediately, but every single one of them was making out with their respective girl. The good news was that—since Chris was still wearing his trash-bag gown—Robin owed me a tenner. The bad news was that we were clearly going nowhere. I turned back around to Panda.

"So we should probably kiss, right?" she said vaguely. "If that's what they're all doing?"

"Erm . . . yeah," I offered.

So that's what we did.

HANNAH

My dad had been a bit hesitant about the whole idea of us going to a festival. Not because he thought I would take drugs or get naked on TV, but more due to the camping aspect. He didn't seem to have a lot of faith in my Bear Grylls–style survival skills, which he obviously thought would be put to the test.

My mum had rushed out and bought a little pink tent with strawberries on it and said, "Make sure you bring it all back so it can be used again."

It took us three hours to put it up, and by the end every inch was covered in mud, and so were we.

"There's no way I'm taking it down," Stella said as she chucked her sleeping bag into it.

A guy in the tent next to ours asked me which bands I was here to see. I didn't know what to say. I'm not one of those girls who are *into* music. It's one of the questions I dread boys asking. It's like a litmus test for how cool you are. I usually respond with "I like all different types of music" and try to change the subject as quickly as possible. I miss the times when it was acceptable to like the music on the charts.

I didn't even look at the lineup online. Going to a festival was never about watching live music for any of us. It was just about wearing denim cutoffs with wellies and a hippie headband and being really tanned. I was still as white as anything. Kavos had made no impact whatsoever on the color of my skin.

Despite the driving rain, Stella was in high gear. She flirted with random dudes to get them to help us with the tent and stomped around the field in her limited-edition Hunter rain boots, jumping in puddles. Things were OK between us. We were friends just like always, but there was this detachment. We spoke every day but I didn't tell her about the massive argument I had with Mum about college housing or how I was getting nervous about leaving home.

Toilet Boy hadn't been mentioned, either. He was not

even a random I had kissed. Not even someone to add to our middle-grade crush book. He was just some guy at a party. Just another name on the Lobster Door. He was no one. At least that's what Grace, Tilly and Stella thought. To me he was still a secret daydream.

Kavos and everything that had happened there would supply us with all the sleepover stories and gossip we'd need until something else massive happened. If we were still having sleepovers. Which we weren't, really.

By the time we got to the main stage, it was dark, pissing down with rain and *freezing*. I was wearing my emergency hoodie and my dad's camping socks pulled right up to my shorts. So much for glamping. I'd already found an earwig in my hair and had to pee standing up behind a screen.

The main stage was packed. I was squashed next to Grace, being shoved forward into a man whose face I never saw but who was wearing a cow costume.

Grace tapped Cow Costume on the shoulder and asked him to lift her up onto his shoulders. He did. Up there, above the crowd, she was screaming in that faux "I'm a cute girl" way and waving her arms in case the big screen caught her. I could hear Stella and Tilly behind me, but it was too tight to even turn around to speak to them.

Suddenly, I thought Grace was hurt because she started screaming. At first I couldn't hear what was actually coming out of her mouth—it was just a kind of guttural wail. And then she started making words.

"Toilet Boy! Toooooilet Booooooooooy!"

He was *here*. Somewhere among all these frantic, dancing bodies he was here. Grace was waving wildly. I saw her look down. Her eyes were searching for me. I was frozen with panic. Stella grabbed my arm and screamed up at Grace.

"What? Are you sure?"

"Yes, yes! It's definitely him! He's over by the speakers!" Stella jabbed Cow Costume on the chest.

"Cow Man! Put her down! We need to get to Toilet Boy!" He looked confused. "You what?"

Grace dug her heels into his ribs.

"Just put me down!" She was using her Head Girl voice. Cow Man kneeled down, and Grace scrambled off his shoulders and plunged into the crowd. "Follow me!" she yelled at us. "He's this way!"

Stella grabbed my hand and Tilly's, and we surged after her. I felt seasick. Like I wasn't moving myself but being carried along with the current against my wishes.

"Toilet Boy!" Grace was screaming, as if that was his actual real name and he might respond to it. "TOILET BOY!"

Finally, the crowd parted and he was right there in front of us. Only he wasn't alone.

"Toilet Bo—" Grace's face dropped. "Oh . . ."

There was Sam, covered in mud but looking cuter than ever, making out with a redheaded girl in bright yellow hot pants.

Grace turned to me, her eyes bulging. "I'm sorry, Han—he wasn't—doing that a minute ago."

Before I could say anything, Stella rolled her eyes and stepped forward. "Grace, you idiot—that's not Toilet Boy. That's just Sam. Hey, Sam." She said it loudly, in a slightly bored-by-it-all-now voice

Hearing his name, Sam removed his tongue from Miss

Yellow Hot Pants's mouth and turned around. His eyes flicked from me to Stella and back to me again. Grace pinched Stella's waist and whispered, "Stella, seriously, that's Toilet Boy."

"Wait! Hang on," said Tilly. "That's the boy who was smoking weed in your cupboard?"

Grace and Stella stared at her.

There was no way out. It was going to happen. No lie I could tell would cover it up. I looked for an escape route but there were people squeezing me in on all sides.

Stella turned to me. "What the fuck is going on, Han?" she demanded.

I could feel myself shaking. Everybody was staring right at me now: Stella, Grace, Tilly, Yellow Hot Pants. And Sam.

SAM

I should have known it would happen at some point—me bumping into Hannah again, that is. I guess I should have hoped that if it did, I wouldn't be drunk, stoned and being groped by a girl called Panda, and she wouldn't be surrounded by a load of girls who were all referring to me as "Toilet Boy."

Why "Toilet Boy" anyway? That makes me sound awful. Surely "Bathroom Boy" works better? It has alliteration going for it and everything.

I knew it was a mistake to go to the main stage. But once Panda and her friends suggested it, Robin, Ben and Chris were hardly going to say no.

Thankfully, that horrible moment where we just stood staring at each other in front of everybody was interrupted almost immediately by a conga line that was making its way through the crowd. Chris, Robin and Ben, who weren't yet aware of the monumentally awkward situation unfolding next to them, latched on to the back, and we—me, Hannah, Hannah's friends and Panda's lot—all got dragged along, too. As more people joined, the line became increasingly chaotic. Within a minute I had lost sight of everyone I knew.

When I was finally spat out of the overflowing crowd, I saw Hannah, on her own, brushing herself down after having been spat out nearby, too. There was a split second where she hadn't seen me and I knew I could have walked away, but I really wanted to talk to her again. I didn't care if it was awkward.

"Hey," I said, approaching her. "That was nuts, wasn't it?"

She flashed me a nervous smile. "Yeah. Sorry, we didn't mean to, erm, interrupt you. Stella just saw you and we thought we'd say hi."

"Oh, no, it's cool," I said. "I was just . . ."

I was just making out with a girl named Miranda, who calls herself Panda because she loves pandas so much. A girl who isn't you.

"I was just . . . not doing very much, really." I couldn't think of anything better than that. She'd clearly seen me with my tongue down Panda's throat.

"Cool," she said, kicking vacantly at a bit of loose turf on the ground.

"Who else are you here with?" I asked, feeling my heartbeat quicken just a touch as a follow-up question formed in my head and made its way down to my tongue. "Is your, erm, boyfriend here, too?"

She jabbed harder at the loose turf, and it broke apart under her boots. "Erm . . . no. He couldn't make it. He's got stuff on."

"Oh. Cool." *What sort of stuff?* I wondered. Probably shopping for more vests.

A little silence fell between us as we both took turns prodding a new piece of loose turf with our feet. She unfurled a few strands of hair from her ponytail and started chewing on them. I felt a sudden urge from out of nowhere to grab her and kiss her. I channeled my frustration at having to repress this desire into kicking aimlessly at the damp soil.

Finally, she said, "Look, I should try to find Stella and the rest of them now."

"Oh yeah," I murmured. "I need to get back to my lot, too. But I guess I'll see you around?"

We had bumped into each other twice already, so there was no way we wouldn't bump into each other again. Or, at least, that's what I told myself.

"Yeah, definitely. See you, then."

She smiled and walked away. I noticed the sun had brought her freckles out even more.

As I watched her push her way back into the crowd, I stood there cursing her boyfriend, whoever he was, and realizing once again just how much I liked her.

HANNAH

I didn't even bother trying to find them again—I just headed straight back and got into my sleeping bag. The tent was hot and airless. Somewhere, in one of the fields, I knew they were all talking about me. I felt like a freak. A fraud.

Stella and me hadn't had it out yet. This whole summer. Maybe now it was coming. I knew they would have to come back eventually. After a while I sort of wanted them to come but they didn't. They were all out having fun without me. Maybe Stella was hooking up with Robin by now. They were probably talking about what an insane compulsive liar I was.

Lying in a tent listening to everyone around you having fun is probably one of the loneliest things you can do.

After what seemed like days, I heard the three of them outside, their voices getting louder as they got closer. It took Stella forever to figure out how to unzip the tent. I picked up *Vogue* and pretended to read. The silence between us felt real. Neither of us had anything to say. Maybe this is it. Maybe friendships actually end when neither of you has anything to say anymore.

"I'm really sorry, Han. This is so awkward. I kind of get why everything has been so weird between us now. It all makes sense. I wish you had told me."

It was real. I think. Real in that she thought everything was because of her kissing Sam. Real because she was sorry things had turned to shit between us. Real because she doesn't think about anything on any deeper level. All she sees is the headline news. Real because she never actually says anything real and this felt like it was.

"I feel like such a dick," I said. "I should have told you at the cinema."

"You're not a dick. Promise. Anyway, now we've kissed three of the same people, so it's all good."

"I haven't kissed Sam."

She smiled at me as she got her makeup bag out of her backpack.

"Haven't kissed Sam *yet*. . . ."

The tent conversation wasn't really the whole truth. So much more had happened to cause the rift between us. But I let it be so we could feel like us again. Actually, that's not true. I let it be because I'm weak. Stella had all the explanation she needed to put the whole thing behind us. To her, it was just something that had happened. But to me, the whole summer felt like way more than that.

As Stella wriggled down into her sleeping bag beside me, I thought about Sam and how cute he looked. Even wearing plastic bags on his feet, he looked hot.

"How will I ever kiss him, Stell?" I whispered as we were dropping off to sleep, thinking about the yellow hot pants girl. "He's clearly with someone."

From the depths of her sleeping bag, I heard Stella murmur, "Not for long."

SAM

After nearly an hour of muddy trampling, I finally found Ben and Robin back in the dance arena. They weren't dancing, of course. They were standing next to the DJ booth, nodding their approval at each new tune. Chris was still AWOL. Maybe he'd congaed his way back to London.

"Where the fuck have you been?" yelled Robin, bear-hugging me.

I couldn't contain it any longer. My excitement at seeing Hannah and remembering how much I liked her got the better of me. I told him everything—about meeting her in the bathroom at Stella's party, the double date, the fact that I was Toilet Boy.

"Fuck. Ing. Hell," Robin yelled over the ear-splitting techno. "So that whole time at the Westfield, that Welch's bloke Stella was talking about was *you*?"

I nodded, managing to feel simultaneously proud and embarrassed.

"No wonder Hannah was so weird. You just sat there in silence while Stella told us how much she loved you!"

Hearing Robin say it made it suddenly seem real, and I felt a surge of excitement pulse through me.

"What else could I do?" I shouted. "I couldn't have owned up while we were all sitting at that table—it would have been even more embarrassing for Hannah if you and Stella had known the truth. And I was supposed to be on a date with *Stella* anyway."

Robin shook his head. "You are never allowed to complain about girls not liking you again."

We suddenly spotted Chris bounding toward us through the swaying crowd. He was wild-eyed, shirtless and sporting freshly inked tribal-style henna tattoos on his arm.

"What the fuck happened to you?"

"I'm not sure," he said, grinning madly. "I stayed with the conga line. We went to some weird places. I think I got married to a mannequin at one point."

"I love this tune!" yelled Ben as the DJ dropped an abrasive techno song that sounded exactly the same as every other abrasive techno song he'd already played. We danced until we were too tired to stand up. Then we stomped back to the tents, muddy, drunk and happy.

The next day, we awoke to throbbing hangovers and unbearable heat. The walls of the tent felt like they were on fire. Robin kicked himself out of his sleeping bag, gasping and holding his head in his hands.

"Fresh air . . . ," he croaked. "Water . . ."

I unzipped the door and squinted out into the blinding daylight. The previous night's monsoon seemed to have washed the sky clean and the sun was blazing down intensely across the fields, baking the mud rock solid.

Ben and Chris went to get bacon sandwiches to remedy our hangovers. Robin stretched himself out on the damp grass, clutching our two-liter water bottle to his chest.

"So what's the plan today?" he said through a yawn. "You're going to see Hannah again, right?"

"I hope so. I think I really like her."

Robin raised an eyebrow. "You thought you really liked Jo. And she turned out to be a total misery."

It was true. But something about Hannah felt different. Liking Jo had always come with nagging, unsettling doubts. I couldn't think of one thing I disliked about Hannah. Except the fact she had a boyfriend, of course.

"There's one problem, though," I said. "She's got a boyfriend."

"Fuck him. He's probably an idiot." He took a swig from the water bottle and dried his lips on the sleeve of his T-shirt. "Hang on—if she's got a boyfriend, what was she doing on that double date?"

"I guess she just came along to be Stella's wingman."

"Wing*woman*," Robin corrected.

"Yeah, wingwoman. Or maybe she didn't even know it was a date thing."

Robin frowned. "I'm not sure about that. That sounds a little suspicious. If you had a boyfriend, I don't think you'd go out with your friend and two other guys, would you?"

"I don't know," I said. "Maybe her boyfriend's just cool with that sort of thing. Maybe he's a model or something, and he doesn't need to worry about her going out with other guys."

"Or *maybe*," said Robin, sitting up straight, his eyes twinkling, "she's not that into him. And *that's* why she got all hot and bothered about meeting a shithead like you in a bathroom at a party!"

I let this theory sink in for a moment. A huge grin spread across my face, and I felt my hangover dissolving. I wished I'd spoken to Robin about this whole Hannah thing earlier; it had gotten so twisted and confused being cooped up on its own inside my head. Apparently, a problem shared really was a problem halved.

"You *might* be right," I said, still grinning like a maniac. "But whatever the case, she's still with this guy. She told me so last night. Maybe it's just too big an obstacle."

"Nah," said Robin. "The bigger the obstacles, the more you're meant to be together, I reckon. Look at Ron and Hermione. Obstacles everywhere. But did Hermione give up on Ron when he was dating Lavender Brown? Did Ron give up on Hermione when she was hanging out with that Bulgarian quidditch bloke? Did they let the pressure of tracking down the final few Horcruxes tear them apart? No. All the drama they went through made it all the more poignant when they finally got together."

He noticed me grinning and checked himself.

"At least . . . I think that's what happened. That's what my sister said, anyway. I don't know."

I laughed and grabbed the water bottle from him. "It feels stupid thinking about girls and stuff when we've got bigger things to worry about."

"What do you mean?" he said. "Global warming? Because I figure that'll turn out all right. It's probably a big fuss over nothing."

"No, I mean scores. College. All that. I know I fucked up French."

Robin groaned. "You worry too much, Sam."

Ben and Chris returned with brick-sized bacon sandwiches, and the four of us ate, drank and played Frisbee as the afternoon sun beat down.

At about six p.m. we started getting ready to head out into the main field for the evening. My contact lenses were itching, so I went off to the bathrooms to take them out. I was slightly pissed off that if I bumped into Hannah again, I'd be wearing my glasses, which—as Robin likes to point out—make me look like "a crap hipster."

"I'll be back in a sec," I yelled.

11

HANNAH

I haven't seen a lot of penises. The list is:

1. My brother's (doesn't count).
2. Daniel Radcliffe's in *Equus* at the Gielgud Theatre (a long way away and not aimed at me specifically, so also doesn't count).
3. Freddie Clemence's at Alicia Miller's sixteenth birthday party. (I jerked him off. Well, sort of. I had no idea what I was doing so I just watched him do it himself, really, and occasionally touched it a little. It was embarrassing. Definitely counts but isn't exactly an impressive list for an eighteen-year-old who isn't a Christian or some sort of freak.)

Number four actual dick-sighting was at the festival. I saw a boy peeing into a plastic bottle.

Waiting in line for the bathrooms, I wished I could pee

like that, too. Waiting forty-five minutes to do something that you can do on demand at home is pretty depressing. By the time I got to the front I was crossing my legs and in moderate pain.

I saw Sam before he saw me. He was trying to wash his glasses under a tap. When they were clean he tried to dry them on his sweater, but it was muddy so he just smeared them again. I didn't know he wore glasses. He wasn't wearing them at Stella's house. Or at the Westfield. In the end he put them on wet. And then just as I looked down, he saw me.

It seemed to take him forever to decide what to do. And then he waved. The glands underneath my ears felt weird, like when you eat sour strips. My hair was so greasy. I couldn't bear for him to see it up close so I put my hood up. I actually put my hood up like some sort of gangster.

Walking through mud takes about ten times as long as normal walking. How many times can you awkwardly smile at someone as they make their way over?

"Hey," I said.

I thought he might lean in to kiss me, but he didn't, thank god.

"Hey" was all he said before a girl behind me tapped my shoulder.

"Are you waiting?" she asked. Which is a fucking stupid question when you've been standing in a line for longer than you do for Space Mountain.

I nodded. And then I said to Sam, "Just a second."

And walked to the porta-potty and opened the door.

JUST. A. SECOND.

I don't know how that came out of my mouth or what I meant by it. I basically ordered him to wait. Like we were friends. Like I had something to say to him. Like when I'm telling my mum something and am texting at the same time. I just sat on the weird metal toilet with blue liquid in it that stank and had no toilet paper, and I freaked out. I wanted to text Stella and say I had met Toilet Boy by the *actual* toilets and that she had to come NOW. But my phone had no signal.

The hood was ridiculous. Even criminals must put their hoods down to pee.

Sam was waiting by the sinks when I came out. Whenever I am with boys I just end up saying the most boring Mum-ish things.

"Are your glasses OK?"

"Yeah, I really hate being blind."

"My nan always says I shouldn't marry a man who wears brown suits, has facial hair or needs glasses."

He laughed. I'd basically told him he was a genetic failure. What I meant was "You are so cute and I think you might be The One."

I told him about how long I'd been waiting for the bathroom and about the boy peeing in the bottle.

"What are you guys doing now?" he asked.

I felt like I was on the spot. I didn't actually know. I didn't have a cool plan to meet up with cool people like he probably did. We'd seen the acts. I guess we were just going to wander around and maybe dance a bit somewhere and then go back to the tent. We are sort of lame, really.

My nan always says fortune favors the brave. But I didn't

do the next thing out of courage. I did it so I didn't have to share him with anyone else. "I've kind of lost the others."

"Oh shit, that sucks."

"Can you get any cell signal?"

"No."

"Me neither."

I felt like a lost child or something. I wondered if he felt compelled to stay with me. He probably wanted to get back to Yellow Hot Pants, who had impossibly perfect hair she didn't need to cover with a hood, and somehow wasn't splattered from head to toe with mud.

I wanted to tell him it was OK for him to leave. I knew exactly where the girls were. Grace had told me ten times before I left that they would be by the Innocent smoothie stand.

"Do you want to get some food?" he said.

I nodded and we wandered off. For a little bit I triple-checked everything I said in my head first, but then we just talked. Not like talking to a friend, but still talking. Still saying things you actually think. For a while we walked in silence and it wasn't that weird.

A man dressed all in yellow gave Sam a yellow poker chip with the word "happiness" printed on it in big letters.

"Hey man, get happy! Here's a Happiness Token for you and your girl," he said.

My stomach flipped because he had presumed we were together.

Sam didn't say, "She's not my girl. My girl is currently taking cool Instagram pictures of her yellow hot pants because she is incredibly hot." He just said, "I guess so; cheers," and gave me the token.

We walked to a field I had never been into and passed a tent with a sign outside that read SILENT DISCO.

So we went in and took some headphones and danced around. Not weird and pilled-up and crazy like the other people in there, but sort of like kids at a wedding. We just bopped about. Sam didn't seem that bothered about being cool. At one point this crazy old hippie started waltzing with him and he just went along with it.

Sam was awkward and gangly and sometimes he looked sort of anxious, but he seemed really kind, too. When we left, there was a shoe on the ground and he picked it up and put it on a bench so the person who lost it might find it.

We walked farther as the sun started to go down. We bought some cider and talked about what might happen if you went to the end of the universe and what you would fall into if you fell off the edge. And then we talked about what comforter covers we had when we were little and how mums always buy cheap cookies so they last longer.

We passed this doorway where a pagan priestess was conducting non–legally binding marriage ceremonies and watched some crazy drunk people, mostly drunk best friends, pretend to get married and dance around runes.

I could hear the soundtrack to *Bugsy Malone* playing. I love *Bugsy*. I've got the limited-edition DVD.

"I love Bugsy Malone."

It came out of my mouth before I could stop it. I made a mental note to say something effortlessly cool later to make up for it.

We walked toward the tent—which had a sign saying MAD HATTER'S TEA PARTY hanging above the entrance—and

Sam grabbed my hand and pulled me in. Inside there was a band playing, and a woman in a slinky dress and feather boa was singing Nina Simone songs.

There were little round tables and people drinking out of teacups. And a massive trunk that people were pulling clothes out of and dressing up in. When I looked over at the dance floor, everyone was in fancy old clothes. I pulled a red satin floor-length ball gown out, took off my hoodie and pulled it on over my tank top and shorts. My wellies stuck out of the bottom. I knew my bra was showing but it felt stupid to put my hoodie back on.

A girl trying on a tiara next to me said, "You look *amazing* in that dress."

Sam nodded and smiled at me. "Yeah, you do. Although, you've somehow managed to get mud on your *neck*. That's pretty impressive."

I had mud everywhere. Sam had put on a bowler hat and a black suit that was far too big for him.

A man dressed as a white rabbit took our drinks order. We both asked for gin and tonics and he served them to us from a teapot.

We danced around some more and a woman in seamed tights with 1940s-style victory rolls in her hair took a Polaroid picture of us.

We sat on velvet cushions and talked to the people around us while we drank our gin. Then we got up and tried to do the tango.

Finally, it got so late that the tent closed, so we changed back into our clothes and walked out into the night. People were starting to make their way back to their camps.

"Will Stella and the others be worried about you?"

"Nah, we're cool about stuff like that."

Grace had probably called the police and my mum, and the BBC for good measure.

Because of the mud and everyone trampling I hadn't sat down outside since we got here. But outside the costume tent the grass was still intact.

Sitting down and looking around at how empty the field was made me realize how late it had gotten.

"I feel like a cup of tea."

"Or some hot spiced grape juice."

It was the first time either of us had brought up that night. The night he had made out with Stella. I wanted to deflect from the memory of me wanting him.

"Will your friends be worried?" I asked him.

"Nah, they'll be fine."

"Oh, cool."

He stared down at his feet.

"How come your boyfriend couldn't make it?"

"Erm . . . he had to work."

"That sucks. Where does he work?"

"At Food Lion."

Even my fictional boyfriends are crap. Why didn't I say he was on a gap year? Or that he worked in a club?

We looked at the stars for a bit. If it was a film, he would have kissed me then. But if it was a film I would look like Yellow Hot Pants. And not invent fictitious shelf-stacking boyfriends.

SAM

I should probably have kissed her when we were lying under the stars. I kept thinking, *Now! Do it now!* But it just seemed like such a cliché. Maybe girls are into clichés, though. Crap romantic comedies are full of them.

Of course the main reason I didn't go in for the kiss was her boyfriend. I couldn't figure it out. If she was really with him, what was she doing lying in a field with me? Maybe Robin had been right.

I didn't feel like I needed to impress her. With Panda and Erin and Jo and pretty much everyone else I've ever had a crush on, I was always conscious of sounding like a dick. I couldn't allow a single sentence to leave my mouth without first running a mental X-ray scan on it, in case there was something stupid or uncool concealed inside.

It felt weird to think that me and Hannah had only really known each other for about seven hours. As we lay there I felt as comfortable with her as I do with Robin or Chris. More comfortable, actually.

Neither of us knew anything about astronomy, so we took turns making up constellation names. She pointed out "Kim Kardashian's Bum." I pointed out "Simon Cowell's Hair."

My phone had run out of batteries, so I couldn't tell how long we stayed there, but by the time we finally stood up, the sun was rising.

We walked back toward our tents through the main field. It was pretty much deserted compared to the previous night—just a few barely conscious bodies on the ground, most of them still clutching cider bottles or long-expired spliffs.

We passed through a little encampment of unbearably twee stalls where dreadlocked students were shilling tarot cards and hand-crafted wind chimes.

"Oh man, I can't stand stuff like this," I said, pointing at a large display of crystal skulls and yin-yang-symbol T-shirts.

"Yeah, me neither." She nodded. "I actually stopped lusting after Robert Pattinson when I found out that he owned a dream catcher."

"Very wise." I smiled. "At least he wasn't into astrology. That stuff bugs me the most."

Hannah gasped in mock horror. "My nan would never forgive you if she heard you say that. She's *obsessed* with star signs. She once told me the reason I messed up my physics exam was because Capricorns have short attention spans."

I laughed. "I just think the idea that the month you were born in has any bearing on what kind of person you are is ridiculous."

"When's your birthday?" she asked.

"Eighteenth of August."

"Typical Leo." She grinned. "Stubborn and hotheaded."

We both cracked up. I couldn't get over how fun, easy and just plain *good* it felt to talk to her.

"So where are you going to college?" she asked as we passed a little wooden booth covered with a thick velvet curtain bearing the words FORTUNE-TELLER.

I don't really like telling people I've got a place at

Cambridge. It makes me sound like I've got my head up my own ass.

"I've . . . sort of got a place at Cambridge, but I'm not sure if I'll get the grades."

Everyone says they're not sure if they'll get the grades.

"Wow. That's really impressive. To do what?"

"English."

"Hey, me too."

I was just about to ask which school she was going to when suddenly, from out of the dance tent, I saw Panda and her friends making their way merrily toward us. They must have been in there all night. They hadn't seen us yet, but it was only a matter of seconds before they did.

Without thinking, I flung back the curtain on the fortune teller's booth and yanked Hannah inside with me.

"Ah! Welcome, travelers!" murmured a heavily made-up middle-aged lady with a thick Eastern European accent. She was wearing a long silk robe and a makeshift "turban" that was quite clearly a tie-dyed bath towel. "You wish to know your fortune, I presume?"

The inside of the booth was only slightly less cramped than Stella's Harry Potter cupboard, and the sickly sweet smell of incense was overpowering.

"Sam, what are we doing?" whispered Hannah, understandably a little confused by the proceedings.

Through a gap in the curtain, I saw Panda and her friends oohing and aahing over a hemp yoga mat at the stall opposite. We weren't going back outside any time soon.

"Erm, yes," I said to the lady, "we wish to know our fortune." Then, turning to Hannah, I shrugged. "I just thought it might be funny."

She wrinkled her forehead at me. She clearly wasn't convinced. I didn't blame her.

"Excellent, travelers," muttered the lady. "But first, you must cross my palm with silver."

"How *much* silver?" I asked. I didn't want to bump into Panda, but I also wasn't hugely eager to hand over the rest of my festival money to a woman with a towel on her head.

"Five pieces of silver each, so it's ten for the both of you."

"And how much is ten pieces of silver?"

"Ten pounds."

"Ten pounds?" I protested. "But pounds aren't even silver!"

"It's a figure of speech."

I glanced through the crack in the curtain again. Panda was still right outside, trying on a bright green headscarf.

"What do we get for ten pounds, then?" I asked.

"You get a glimpse of your future, my dear," whispered the lady dramatically.

"Yeah, but are you going to tell me good stuff or bad stuff? I don't want to give you a tenner and then find out I'm going to get mugged or run over or eaten by a shark or something."

"Eaten by a shark?" said Hannah, raising her eyebrow.

"It could happen," I said, raising an eyebrow back.

"It could indeed," purred the lady. "All you have to do is cross my palm with silver and all will be revealed."

"You mean all I have to do is give you ten pounds and you'll make some stuff up."

The lady's enigmatic smile dissolved into an irritated frown. "Look, love, if you're not going to pay up, can you piss off? I've got other customers waiting." Her exotic Eastern European drawl had given way to a broad northern accent.

Before I could protest, Hannah thanked her politely for her time, swept back the curtain and pulled me out into the sunlight.

Panda and her cohort were just leaving the stall, armed with their ludicrous purchases. Thankfully, they didn't see us, but Hannah saw them.

"Erm, Sam, isn't that the girl you were with yesterday?" she asked, watching Panda and her friends as they wandered off.

"Who?" I said, pretending not to understand the question.

"The girl? From yesterday? When we first saw you in the crowd . . ."

I squinted in the direction of Panda's back. "Erm, yeah, it might have been her. I can't really be sure from this distance."

Hannah glanced at the fortune-teller's booth and then smiled at me.

"Sam, you could have spoken to her if you wanted. I wouldn't have minded."

I don't know what it was—maybe the fact I was still half drunk, or weary from lack of sleep, or maybe just because Hannah looked so cute at that moment, smiling up at me so brightly under the morning sun—but I just decided to tell the truth.

"I didn't want to speak to her. I only hooked up with her yesterday because all our friends were making out with each other. I didn't even particularly want to. She's called Miranda but she calls herself Panda because it rhymes with Miranda and she loves pandas."

Hannah giggled. "That's ridiculous."

"I knew you would find it funny! Literally no one else found it funny except me. Even Robin said it was a cool way to show support for an endangered species. I guess I . . ." I paused, trying to summon the bravery I needed from somewhere inside me. "I guess I would rather have been with you. I haven't really been able to stop thinking about you since Stella's party. I'm sorry, that's a shit thing to say when I know you've got a boyfriend, but I can't help it."

Her smile widened, and she blushed a little.

"I thought you liked Stella," she said quietly. "Why else did you go on that date?"

"Because my friend Robin would have killed me if I hadn't! Stella just came up and started kissing me at the party—I didn't really know what was going on. I tried to find you, but I guess you'd already left with your boyfriend, maybe."

The "maybe" hung in the air, like an echo in an underpass. Hannah laughed and shook her head.

"Yeah, the thing is, Sam . . . some of the things I said about my boyfriend weren't strictly true."

"Which things?"

"Well . . ." She looked me straight in the eyes. "All of them."

I felt confusion and elation jostling for position inside me.

"What do you mean? So you're not with anybody?"

She shook her head again. And then, not under an impossibly beautiful starry sky but in the midst of dream catchers, incense sticks and fortune-telling rip-off merchants, I kissed her. And she kissed me back.

When me and Robin and Chris talk about kissing girls, we always talk about the mechanics of it, the cold facts: their technique, how much they use their tongue, how wide they open their mouths. But kissing Hannah, I realized that none of that actually mattered. What mattered was how you felt about the person. That was what made this the best kiss I'd ever had. It was just . . . right. There was no other word for it.

"What shall we do now?" I said, once we'd finally come up for air.

"I'd better go back and find the girls."

We wandered back to the field Hannah was staying in, but it turned out she couldn't remember where her tent was.

"What does it look like?" I asked.

"I don't know—it's a tent."

"That's not going to narrow it down in a field full of tents. What does it *actually* look like?"

"Erm . . ." She pointed to a tent. "It looks a little like that one."

"In what way?"

"In that it's a tent."

"Oh good. With deduction skills like those, we'll find it in no time."

She pinched me on the forearm and grinned.

Eventually, she spotted a mud-spattered little tent with a flowery design that was just visible beneath the dirt.

"I think that's it!"

She ran over, unzipped the entrance and crawled inside. I followed her in.

The floor was littered with apple cores and rolling papers and empty beer bottles.

"You absolutely certain this one is yours?" I asked.

"Erm . . . no, actually," said Hannah. "We're in someone else's tent."

We both cracked up. She looks so hot when she smiles. I pulled her toward me and we dropped down onto a (slightly dingy) sleeping bag and started kissing. It was muggy in the tent—that kind of aggressive, claustrophobic heat that can only come from zipping yourself into a tiny polyester igloo under the blazing morning sun—but that did nothing to kill our passion. With our lips still stuck together, we wriggled sweatily onto the blow-up mattress, reaching under each other's T-shirts and she moaned gently—a good kind of moan (I hoped).

I was beginning to regret having used the Febreze in the backseat of Robin's car as deodorant. But since I'd left my roll-on at home, I didn't really have much choice. Anyway, the various unorthodox odors already inside the tent were doing their best to mask my Alaskan Springtime scent.

We writhed about, ignoring the yawns and groans and shuffles of people waking up in the tents around us. Totally oblivious to everything except each other.

We were moving fast. She started to unbutton my jeans and sat up while I pulled her T-shirt over her head. We lay back down, breathlessly, and kept kissing.

"Sam," she whispered, as I kissed her earlobe to try to divert attention away from my fumbling inability to undo her bra. "Sam . . ."

"Yeah?" I said, giving up on the apparently unconquerable bra clasp for the moment and hoping she hadn't noticed.

"It's just that . . . I should tell you . . ." She breathed heavily as I decided to try my luck on her jeans button instead.

"What?" I gasped.

"I'm . . . This is my first time. I'm a virgin."

I sat bolt upright, nearly exposing my very obvious boner. This was her first time! She *hadn't* got "jiggy" with dipshit Freddie! She hadn't got "jiggy" with anyone! She was—she was just like me! I cupped her face in my hands and kissed her.

It briefly entered my mind to try to play it cool, like I had with Erin. To tell her that I'd been with two or three girls, and she shouldn't worry because I knew exactly what I was doing. But I couldn't contain myself. It was like a weight had been lifted. I came up for air from the kiss and smiled at her. "It's my first time, too."

A brilliant grin broke across her face, and she pulled me back toward her. We were moving even faster now, hardly thinking about what we were doing. I went for round two with the bra clasp as she unzipped my jeans and edged them down until they rested around my ankles. This was it. This was actually it—and it didn't feel scary or weird or stupid. It felt amazing.

Then, from nowhere, there was rustling and coughing and laughing right outside the tent. Hannah and I froze and stared at the entrance. The rustling got louder, and suddenly the zipper started moving upward. Someone was coming in.

I slid off the sleeping bag—fully exposing my very obvious boner this time—and yanked the zipper back down to the ground. Hannah let out a howl of laughter and quickly slapped a hand over her mouth to silence herself. The zipper was wriggling in my hands. The tent's owners were still trying to get in.

"Oi!" we heard a girl shout outside. "Is someone in there?"

Hannah couldn't stop. The nerves and general ridiculousness of the situation had gotten to her. She was paralytic with giggles. Still holding the zipper in place, I chucked a sleeping bag over her to muffle the sound. It didn't do much good. People in the next field would still have heard her hissing and snuffling.

"Let us in our fucking tent!" screamed the girl outside. "We're really hungover!"

I couldn't see any way out except to try to cut a hole in the lining and crawl out the back, so I accepted defeat.

"OK, OK," I said. "We're coming out. Sorry."

"You've got ten seconds!" said the girl.

There was a pause.

"Or what?" I asked.

Another pause.

"Yeah . . . I don't know. That seemed like an appropriate thing to say. Just be as quick as you can, please."

I pulled my jeans back up and Hannah put her shirt on and (eventually) managed to stop laughing/hyperventilating. As I was about to unzip the entrance she suddenly said, "Stop! We should leave the place in a decent state, don't you think?"

I laughed. "Yeah. OK."

We smoothed out the sleeping bags on the airbed and collected up the apple cores into a discarded plastic bag— even though they weren't ours. And then, once we were happy with the condition of the tent, we unzipped the door and crawled out.

The commotion had drawn a crowd. About thirty hungover-looking people were standing around the entrance. As I poked my head out, they all started laughing, cheering and applauding. Hannah emerged behind me, and the cheering and clapping got louder.

"Let's hear it for the romantic couple!" shouted someone in the crowd. "Let's hear it for the tent fuckers!"

Hannah and I looked at each other, shrugged and then smiled and raised our arms, taking in the praise. No tent fucking had *actually* happened, obviously, but the fact we were finally together felt like an achievement in itself.

"Thank you, thank you," we said, shaking the dozens of hands that were being enthusiastically thrust at us.

Even when we'd walked to the next field we were still laughing about it. It hadn't sunk in that I'd just missed my best chance ever to lose my virginity. It just seemed hilarious. And anyway, it didn't feel like the chance was gone. I felt sure Hannah and I would be in a similar situation soon. Just not in someone else's apple-core-strewn tent.

"I'd really better find Stella and the girls now," said Hannah, smoothing down her tousled hair. "They'll be worried."

"Yeah. I guess we've been gone nearly twelve hours now."

I pulled her toward me and hugged her.

"Let's meet back at the Mad Hatter's Tea Party tonight," she said. "I'll bring Stella and Grace and Tilly. You bring Robin and everyone."

"OK. See you there at, like, nine?"

She nodded and smiled.

As we kissed goodbye, I could still hear the cheering and applause in my head.

12

HANNAH

I finally found the tent and crept in. I lay next to Stella, waiting for her to wake up. I couldn't bear it. I kept coughing to speed up the process. Stella is the only person I have ever met who wears a satin eye mask to bed. In a muddy, earwig-infested tent it seemed even more ridiculous.

"Are you awake?" I knew she wasn't. I stopped trying to be subtle and gave her ponytail a yank. "I kissed Sam."

She pulled her eye mask up and found my face right opposite hers.

"Fuck off!"

And then she screamed. We heard someone in a nearby tent shout, "Shut up!"

I love how Stella gets involved like it's her own life.

"Oh my god. Tell me *everything*! Like a movie. From the beginning. I knew you'd found him. I told Grace you had. She was all, like, 'Oooohhhh, she's been stabbed in a mosh pit.' But I knew. It was my bestie sixth sense. It was speaking to me. It was saying, 'Hannah's getting laiiiiid!'"

And then she got onto her knees, still in her sleeping bag, and fell on me.

"Hannah's getting laiiiid!"

"Don't make me laugh! I need to pee and I can't face the line."

She picked herself up and fell on me again.

"Stop! You're hurting me."

"You'll be hurting more later when you're getting lai—"

We were both hysterical.

"Don't laugh, Stell. I've found The One. Sam is my lobster. Fact."

The tent was so hot we wiggled outside, still in our sleeping bags, and lay on the grass, eating chips and talking about Sam. About how he had changed his hair and was a bit tanned and looked even cuter than before. About what Stella would wear as a bridesmaid. About how big his wiener might be and whether I should take Advil before doing it like Grace had.

Stell was surprised when I told her he was a virgin.

"But he's so *tall*."

"And?"

"I don't know. . . ."

Grace and Tilly emerged from their tent and then we were all discussing it. We said our names out loud.

"Hannah and Sam, Sam and Hannah."

"Sannah!" said Grace.

Stella snorted. "Sannah's shit. It should be Ham."

All I'd felt with Freddie was nerves. But not good nerves. More fear. Or embarrassment. I wanted him because I wanted what he could give me. A checked-off box, maybe. A sort of cast-iron proof I was OK. Because I kissed people who were cool and who got with hot girls. Hooking up with him had never physically felt like anything, really. Just like someone putting their tongue in my mouth. Or touching my boobs. Or whatever.

I actually *wanted* Sam. Not because he was hot, even though he was. Just because I really wanted him. I could actually imagine being his girlfriend. Not in a shit, meet-at-Westfield-and-get-off-with-each-other fourteen-year-old way. Hooking up with him in the tent didn't feel like any other time I've been with a boy. I wanted to touch him. I wasn't having an out-of-body experience and pushing myself to be brave and do stuff. I wanted him to touch me. I wanted him to be close to me. It was weird that I'd only just experienced that. Maybe everyone always felt like this when they made out with someone. But I never had. Until now.

If those people hadn't come back to their tent, I would have let him, I think. I would still have been shit-scared, but I wanted him to. Before he kissed me, he pushed my hair behind my ears and kissed my cheek. Like he really liked me.

Tonight is our night.

Grace lent me her black bra. I didn't have any nice underwear, though. In the end I had to wear my *Adventure Time* ones because they were the newest and my other ones said

KISS MY ASS on the back and I would die of embarrassment if he thought it was instructional.

We got to the Mad Hatter's Tea Party earlier than the previous night, so people weren't really acting crazy and dressing up yet. We sat on the big cushions and drank gin and tonic out of teacups. I was wearing denim cutoffs and a silk camisole and a flower-garland headband. Grace had drawn flowers and butterflies in glitter all over our bellies and shoulders and around our eyes. Thank god it wasn't raining.

"You're glowing," Tilly announced.

"I'm not pregnant."

"Yeah, but you're in love."

I didn't even deny it. I knew I wasn't actually in *love*. Because we hadn't known each other long enough, but it did feel special.

I couldn't look at him at first, and when he came over and kissed me on the cheek we both acted cool, like we were friends who had just happened to bump into each other. And we made stupid small talk, and then his friend Robin came over and kissed me on both cheeks and ruffled Sam's hair and said, "This guy . . . what a guy. He is . . . What can I say? You couldn't wish for a nicer fellow."

Sam laughed. "Shut up, Robin."

Their hot friend, Chris, cut in next. "This guy. I tell you, if I was going to get it on with any guy in this room . . . it would be Samuel Eugene Moran."

"Your middle name's Eugene?" I giggled.

Sam slapped Chris on the back. "Thanks for that, man. Appreciate it."

"No worries, Eugene, old son," said Chris, thumping him on the shoulder.

"Let's hug," said Robin. "GROUP HUG!"

He dragged me in with him, Chris and Sam, and we all laughed.

We danced together and everyone dressed up and took photos. On the wall, there was a gallery of Polaroids from the night before. I found the one of me and Sam. We looked really happy. When no one was looking, I pulled it off the wall and put it in my pocket.

I noticed Robin talking to a girl and Stella saw it, too. We danced and danced and the boys danced, too. Sam was next to me.

"Right," he said, "let's dance like . . . an old couple on a cruise."

And he put his hand around my waist and took my other one and we waltzed around.

"Oh, Beryl," he said in an old-time American accent. "You do look a dream this evening, darling."

Even when he called me Beryl my cheeks burned.

"Now hippies at Woodstock."

And we swayed, made peace signs and twirled around.

"Hip-hop gangstas."

Nothing could have been more ridiculous, but I did it anyway.

And then right in the middle of me doing some aggressive hand gesturing, he came up from behind me and put his arms around my waist and I felt sick. Because even though we had kissed loads and almost had sex, I still felt nervous in that moment.

My ears were so hot I wondered if he had noticed. And my mouth went dry. He turned me around by my waist. And I put my arms around his neck and then he kissed me. He felt damp and smelled like sweat and mud. And then after he kissed me he smiled at me. No one has ever smiled at me after kissing me.

I felt another arm around my waist.

"Toilet Boy," Stella said to Sam. "You can't hog Hannah. We're going to play Never Have I Ever." We went over to where the others were sitting in a huddle.

Stella explained the rules, even though I'm pretty sure everyone there had played it before. "We go around in a circle and take turns saying something we've never done. So, for example, I might say that I've never been to America. And if you *have* been to America, you have to drink."

"Robin would be drinking on that one," said Chris, nudging Robin in the ribs. "He's just got back from America, haven't you, mate? Which theme park did you go to again?"

Robin looked down at his drink. "Nowhere. Doesn't matter. Let's just play the fucking drinking game."

We all sat on the floor cushions. Sam sat next to me, close enough to touch my hand every so often and smile at me some more. Robin started with, "Never have I ever kissed anyone in this circle."

And Sam and me drank. And then I looked up and saw Stella was drinking, too.

Stella said, "Never have I ever had sex."

And everyone drank except for me, Sam and Tilly. Everyone made cooing noises, even the boys, although theirs were of the sarcastic variety. Their friend Ben, who seemed to be

203

permanently stoned, said, "Well, you know what they say, there's no time like the present."

"You should be drinking, you big sex zombie!" Stella yelled at Tilly.

"What's a sex zombie?" said Robin.

Tilly's face turned red and she downed her drink. Grace went next.

"Never have I ever cheated on an exam."

Grace is so sweet. Everyone drank except Sam, me and Grace. Stella was in her element, and Robin was getting more and more into her. I noticed them catching each other's eye every few minutes. It was obvious they were going to hook up.

Scanning the tent, I suddenly saw the outline of someone I recognized. Tall and muscular and tanned. I knew who it was before he turned around. Pax. My stomach lurched. He was wearing a ratty black T-shirt, mud-specked rain boots and camouflage shorts. I couldn't help thinking how cute he looked, and about how just thinking that he was cute made me feel guilty. I turned around to see if Stella had noticed him. She hadn't, but Grace definitely had. Her eyes were wild as she grabbed my shoulder and whispered through clenched teeth.

"James is over there!"

I had been so consumed by the sight of Pax that I hadn't even spotted James, Harry and Jordan standing next to him near the speakers.

"I'm freaking out," hissed Grace. "I thought I'd never see him again!"

She turned her head and let her hair fall over her face as a disguise.

"I feel so awful about hooking up with him, and Ollie wrote me this letter last week about how he wants us to stay together through school and be together forever. I really love him, Han."

Her eyes were glistening. Grace is the overreaction queen. I had to get her outside before she either cried or hyperventilated. I tapped Sam on the shoulder.

"Me and Grace are just going to the bathroom. We'll be back in a second."

Sam kissed me on the cheek, then cupped my face in his hands and kissed me again, this time on the lips.

"I'm so glad this finally happened," he said.

"Me too." I smiled as Grace led me toward the exit.

SAM

I wasn't trying to act like her boyfriend. It just sort of . . . came naturally. I didn't even think about putting my arm around her or kissing her—I just did it because it felt good.

As soon as we met up in that Mad Hatter's Tea Party tent, our friends started giving Hannah and me shit about how couple-y we were being. Neither of us cared, though. We couldn't stop smiling. Or squeezing each other.

At one point, Robin even took me aside like a proud dad and said, "She's all right, you know. You two are really sweet together."

"Thanks, man," I said, not quite able to look him in the eye. "I really like her. I don't think I've ever liked anyone like this."

"It's good," he said, eyes on the ground but smiling. "It's really good, man."

There was a pause, and then he blushed and grunted and punched me in the kidneys before running off to flirt with Stella. He was flirting with Stella *a lot*. I was secretly really grateful, since it took a lot of the focus off me and Hannah.

While we just occasionally pecked each other's cheeks or held hands, Robin and Stella were running about, punching, scratching and mercilessly mocking each other in an entirely unsuccessful attempt to mask the obvious sexual tension between them.

I was about six gin and tonics deep when Hannah went outside to the bathroom with Grace. It was just me, Stella, Tilly, Robin and Chris left sitting there. Ben had gone outside in search of Cheetos and not come back. He was almost certainly standing near a DJ booth somewhere, nodding furiously.

We were just starting another round of Never Have I Ever when Stella suddenly jumped up off the grass and started waving her arms, trying to get the attention of a stupidly good-looking guy who was navigating his way through the jammed, swaying crowd. He looked like the sort of guy you see in ads for Armani Exchange. Or at the parties they always show in fancy beer ads. The sort of guy who would give Chris confidence problems. He didn't really look real.

"Oh my god, Pax!" screamed Stella, desperately flailing her arms around as he finally saw her. "This is so random! What the fuck are you guys doing here?"

Me, Robin and Chris all mouthed "Pax?" at each other.

"Just when I thought Panda had the Stupidest Fucking Name at the Festival Award all sewn up," I whispered.

"Panda's got nothing on Pax," Chris laughed.

"Yeah," said Robin, eyeing Pax warily. "If your parents christen you Pax, then clearly you've got no other choice in life other than to become an absolute dickhole."

After muscling his way through a sea of drunk and dancing bodies, Pax was suddenly upon us. Stella leapt into his (admittedly sizable) arms and squeezed him tightly. He didn't look totally comfortable with this; he bent his head back to avoid the most of her cheek-kisses and forced a smile that was only an inch away from a grimace.

"Who the fuck is this ass hat?" whispered Robin, who had now upgraded from wary to really pissed off.

Chris and I shrugged. Robin is used to being the center of attention in social situations. He wasn't enjoying playing second fiddle to a *Rich Kids of Beverly Hills* extra. I hadn't seen him this angry since he was twelve and Alex Harvey told him the Sorting Hat would have put him in Hufflepuff.

Stella didn't make the introductions. After twenty seconds of heavy flirting, she sent Pax back off to the bar, not taking her eyes off him the entire way. When he was out of sight, she sat back down next to us and sighed heavily.

"Sorry about that," she laughed. "That's Pax. A really good friend."

"Pax?" snorted Robin, not hiding his contempt particularly well. "Is that short for Tampax?"

"No, actually," sniffed Stella. "It's Latin for 'peace.' What's 'Robin' Latin for?"

"It's Latin for 'What kind of pretentious douche bag has a Latin name?'" said Robin, and he shot me a wink as if to suggest this was a devilishly clever comeback.

I winced at him to let him know I wasn't entirely convinced.

"Where do you know this Pax from, then?" asked Robin, making air quote marks around Pax's name.

"We met in Kavos. And you don't have to do that," said Stella, mimicking his finger punctuation. "It is actually his real name."

"I should fucking well hope so," said Robin. "Being given that name is one thing. Giving it to yourself is quite another."

"Shut up, Robin," Stella snapped.

Me and Chris raised our eyebrows at each other. They'd gone from newlyweds to bitter divorcees in a matter of seconds.

At this point, Pax strolled back from the bar with some equally ridiculously good-looking friends in tow, his hands and pockets clinking with bottles of pear cider. Just as Robin, Chris and I were getting ready to snub him, he handed us a bottle each.

"There you go, guys," said Pax. "I thought I'd get a round in. Any friends of Stella's are friends of mine."

Chris and I instantly decided we couldn't go through with the snub after a gesture like that, so we leapt up and shook all their hands. Robin, however, was not to be won over that easily. He grabbed the cider from Pax but stayed sitting down, which looked a bit odd as all eight of us were now standing up in a circle around him.

"You all right down there, man?" said one of Pax's friends.

"Hmm?" said Robin, pretending not to hear. "Yeah, man, I'm cool. Just not really in a standing mood."

"Too wasted to get up?" laughed another of Pax's friends. "Like it."

"I can get up if I want," snapped Robin. "I'm just more into sitting down right now. I feel like standing up's been 'done.' "

Chris bent down to Robin's level. "Robin, stop being a tit and stand up," he hissed. "He just bought you a cider."

"So just because he bought me a cider, that means he's all right, does it?" Robin fired back. "I'm sure Hitler bought his fair share of ciders, Chris. I suppose that makes him a decent guy in your book, does it?"

"Yeah, good point well made," said Chris, tousling Robin's hair. "You stay down there."

Stella hadn't even noticed Robin wasn't up at her eye level. She had her sights firmly set on Pax.

"So, oh my god, Pax," she said, beaming. "It's been literally ages. How *are* you?" She playfully punched his massive tanned arm. Down on the damp grass, I saw Robin wince and down half his cider.

Pax seemed distracted. "Yeah, good, thanks. How are you?" Before Stella could answer, he added, "Where's Hannah?"

I swallowed my cider too quickly. I don't know why, but it felt weird just knowing that Hannah *knew* someone that good-looking. If guys like him were asking after her, what was she doing with me? But then, *I* know Stella, and I guess most people would say Stella is more attractive than Hannah. Not me, though.

Stella had the same look on her face that Robin had when Pax first strolled into view. Clearly she wasn't used to being second on a boy's agenda.

"Oh, she's around here somewhere," she said slowly. Then

she flashed me a smile—a weird, cold smile—and turned to talk to one of Pax's mates.

HANNAH

"Fuck. What are the chances?" said Grace. "I can't believe they're here. I thought they lived in Devon?"

We were huddled outside the tent, trying to decide what to do.

"You do know we're in Devon *now*, Grace," I said. "They've got every right to be here." I wasn't thrilled to see them but it wasn't Armageddon like Grace was making out.

She wasn't listening. "Yeah, but what are they doing here? Why are they here? I don't want to see James again. Oh, god."

"Grace, it's fine. Nothing's changed. Ollie isn't here. He doesn't know anything about it. Why would he ever know anything about it? There's nothing to freak out about. We'll just say hi and then leave it."

"What if Stella wants to get with Pax again?"

"Well, so what? It doesn't mean you have to hook up with James, does it?"

Grace shook her head, but she didn't look entirely convinced. I kind of understood her wanting to keep James frozen in her memory.

In my mind, Pax only existed in Kavos—tanned and grinning under the Greek sun. Seeing him out of that context had freaked me out a bit, too. I was keeping it together in front of Grace, but I was starting to feel uneasy about how I would react when I was face to face with him again.

We kept walking toward the bathroom and I chatted about other stuff to take Grace's mind off James.

I put my hand in my back pocket and felt the bag of Haribo I'd been saving to share with Sam later. We linked arms.

"Do you feel like you and Sam are meant to be?" Grace said.

"Yeah, I do. Because we met again. He wasn't invited to Stella's party, but he showed up. And after that I thought I'd never see him again, but now I have. I think it's fate."

"He's so perfect for you, Han. He's a cool geek."

"And he's really kind. And he smiles after he kisses me." She snorted.

"See," I said, "the dream team did find Toilet Boy. We said we would and we did."

"Fate brought him to us . . . Ham is my new favorite couple."

"I still prefer Sannah," I laughed.

"OK, Sannah. Sannah is the new power couple. I'll have to accept that Grollie has lost the top spot."

Being out in the cold air made me feel drunker somehow. I put my sweater on as we walked back toward the Tea Party tent. I imagined Stella was probably already making out with Pax in there. I didn't care, either. They really *were* right for each other. The same way Sam was right for me.

13

SAM

As I swallowed the dregs of my cider, I realized I hadn't been this drunk in a while. If I closed my eyes, it felt like I was on a boat. I took a few deep breaths. I needed a glass of water.

Chris had gone outside for a piss and still hadn't returned. He and Ben were lost in the festival ether. Both their phones were going straight to voice mail. Stella, Tilly and Pax's gang were all loudly reminiscing about some night out they'd had in Kavos. Robin was still sitting on the floor, moodily scrolling through his text messages. I bent down to speak to him.

"I'm going to get some water. Do you want anything?"

He didn't look up from his phone. "Oh, no. I'm sure Pax the Latin Lover will sort me out with whatever I need. He's such a great guy."

"OK, fine." I stood up again. "Let me know when your little sulk is over and we can start having fun again, OK?"

As I trotted off toward the bar, Robin shoved his phone back into his pocket, jumped up and followed me.

"Don't just leave me with them. I don't want to sit there by myself, hearing about how 'crazy' Kavos was."

We muscled our way through the crowd and joined the back of the line at the bar. It was much busier here; bodies crushed up against us from all sides. I closed my eyes again and felt the tent spinning. I really needed that water.

As we waited in silence, pushed this way and that as the scrum edged closer to the bar, I spotted Hannah and Grace making their way back in.

Hannah looked so pretty, even from right across the tent. I loved the way she didn't barge through the crowd like everyone else; I could see her politely asking every person if she and Grace could just squeeze through.

As she approached Stella, Tilly and the rest of them, I caught sight of Pax pushing through the crowd toward her. He wrapped his arms around her waist, picked her up and twirled her around and around. He was shouting something. The tent felt hotter all of a sudden.

Hannah was laughing and shaking her head. She seemed a little overwhelmed. She made a playful effort to escape Pax's grip, but Pax held tight and kept spinning her.

Stella's mouth was hanging open. She was standing, arms folded, watching the whole thing. She had said Pax was a "really good friend." Clearly, he was also a "really good friend" to Hannah. Maybe that's all I was to her, too. How many "really good friends" did she have?

Robin whacked me on the arm. He was finally at the front of the line.

"Hey! I'm getting you another gin and tonic, yeah?"

I couldn't take my eyes off Hannah and Pax. I could just about see them if I peered over the crowd on my tiptoes.

"I just want water," I muttered. I didn't hear his response.

Pax put Hannah down and started talking frantically at her. He still had both his hands on her waist. She moved them away gently, but he put them straight back, and she laughed. I wished I could hear what he was saying.

Robin turned around and forced a gin and tonic into my hand. "There you go."

"I said I wanted a water! I'm too drunk as it is."

"You can't be too drunk at a festival, Sam. That's mathematically impossible. Do you think anyone at Woodstock ever said, 'Oh dear, I'd better slow down a little. I don't want to have a headache in the morning'?" He took a sip of his own drink and finally saw the scene I'd been staring at for the last few minutes. He lowered his glass and took it in.

"What the *fuck* is this?"

Pax was now dancing with Hannah. Or, at least, he was *trying* to make Hannah dance with him. Hannah, still grinning broadly, was shaking her head in embarrassment, while he moved her waist in time to the tinny reggae blaring from the speakers. She kept looking around, but she didn't stop him.

"Who the *fuck* does this guy think he is?" snapped Robin. "First he's all over Stella and now he's making a move on Hannah. For a dude whose name means 'peace,' he seems pretty keen on causing conflict."

I took a hefty swig of my gin and tonic. Anything to soothe my sandpaper-dry mouth.

"They're probably just friends," I murmured. It sounded even more stupid out loud. Pax pulled Hannah close and whispered something in her ear. She wriggled free. For the first time since she'd seen him, her smile faded slightly. She looked around her again. I wondered if she was looking for me, hidden behind the blur of bodies at the bar. She said something to Pax and then turned and started speaking to Stella.

"Are you going to let him do that?" Robin asked.

I didn't know what I was going to do. Did I even have any right do *anything*? Any girl in her right mind would have chosen Pax over me. I couldn't really blame Hannah for that. I considered just slinking out and going back to my tent. It felt like the school homeroom all over again, watching Jo fiddling with Toby McCourt's tie or messing with his hair and wanting so badly to go over and just whisk her away. But all I ever did was duck out into the hallway and stand there, feeling hot and confused and furious at myself for doing nothing.

Before I could make a decision, Hannah was squeezing through the crowd toward us.

"Hey!" She shot a grin at me and then Robin. "I was wondering where you guys went to."

"I just needed some water," I said.

She wrinkled her brow, grabbed my gin and tonic from me and sniffed it.

"You do know this isn't water, right?"

I took it back from her and downed nearly half the glass. "Yeah."

Robin broke the ensuing awkward silence by clearing his throat loudly.

"Well . . . if you'll excuse me, I'm going to find Ben and Chris." He pulled his phone out and tapped it. "Sam, give me a shout when you leave."

He gave me a grim smile, pushed his way into the crowd and disappeared.

I finished my drink and dropped the plastic cup on the ground. My mouth felt drier than ever.

"Is everything all right, Sam?" Hannah asked.

"Yeah, fine."

It came out too quickly, too defensively. I couldn't look her in the eye, so I just focused on the mud beneath her feet. I wished my head would stop spinning so I could think a little more clearly.

"OK, well . . . good." She laughed nervously.

I wanted to step toward her and touch her. To feel close to her, to feel the same way I did when we were dancing together last night. But all I could think about was the way Pax had held her by the waist. He'd done it in front of everyone, too. I felt the shame of it swelling inside me. The silence built until it was unbearable.

"Look," said Hannah, "if you want to go and hang out with Robin and that lot, I don't mind."

"Would you rather I did that?" I directed my question at the mud, rather than at her.

"Of course not! I want you to stay here!" She sighed. "Sam, what's going on? This feels weird."

I looked up at her.

"Yeah, sorry. Listen . . ." The words were off my tongue before I could yank them back. "Are you with that Pax guy or something?" I tried to make it sound casual. I'm pretty sure I failed.

Hannah exhaled a loud laugh. "Oh my god, no! Sam, literally . . . no. The only reason I know him is because he had a thing with Stella in Kavos." She touched my arm. "He's just friendly. He was just pleased to see me, that's all."

"Yeah, *really* pleased." It sounded more cutting than I had intended. "Sorry, it just looked like there might be something between you."

She coughed up another high-pitched, almost hysterical laugh. I hadn't realized it, but she was clearly just as drunk as I was.

"Sam . . . he's with Stella. Or, at least, he *was* with Stella."

Now it was her turn to stare down at the mud. I waited for her to say more, but nothing came.

"Is there something between you and him?"

"Sam. My . . . best . . . friend . . . likes . . . him."

"Yeah, you keep saying that, but that isn't what I'm asking you." My cheeks were burning and I could hear my heartbeat in my head.

She still wouldn't meet my eye. "There's nothing between us, OK?"

"Do you like him like that?"

"What?"

"Do you find him attractive?"

The music seemed louder suddenly. I was shouting without even meaning to.

"That's totally irrelevant."

"It's not totally irrelevant to me."

She shook her head and sighed. "Well, he *is* attractive. So yes, I suppose I find him attractive. But I find lots of people attractive."

"Great." The throbbing in my temples was building steadily. "Has anything ever happened between you and him?"

Her silence answered the question, but I asked it again anyway.

"Has something happened between you and him?"

She nodded slowly, still looking down at the floor. No wonder she hadn't minded his hands all over her. She'd probably been waiting for this moment since she left Kavos.

"So wait . . . you like him, you've kissed him already and you've still got feelings for him?"

"Sam, you make it sound awful. That's not how it is at all."

"Well, the only reason I know it's like that is because you just told me."

"No, I didn't. Well, I kind of did, but I didn't mean it to come out like that."

"Well, I'm glad it did. I don't want to stay here and make a complete dickhead of myself if it's him you want and not me."

She grabbed my shoulder and looked me straight in the eye. "Sam, don't be ridiculous! Of course I want you!"

I shook her hand off. I needed to get out. "I'll see you later. I'm going to find Robin."

"Sam!"

I swayed toward the exit and the crowd swallowed me up.

HANNAH

I just stood still and let everyone move around me for a while. Listening to snippets of conversations shouted over the noise. A random girl and her boyfriend asked me if I was OK and then Grace and Tilly were suddenly in front of me.

"Are you all right?" Grace shouted. "We've been looking for you everywhere. Where's Sam?"

I shook my head. "I don't know. We had a fight. He thought Pax was hitting on me."

"What? *Was* Pax hitting on you?" Tilly's eyes met mine dead on.

"No. Of course not."

But I thought about his mouth brushing against my ear and whispering, "It's really, *really* good to see you. You look so good."

"He was just being super-friendly like he always is. And Sam just . . . took it the wrong way."

I knew it wasn't strictly the truth but I didn't really know what kind of mess the truth would lead to.

"What? That's ridiculous. What a doofus," Grace said.

Tilly nodded in agreement. "He can't get jealous when you talk to a guy your friend is getting with. That's crazy."

I felt bad letting them think Sam was some controlling, jealous psycho. But I didn't know what else to do.

"Yeah, but I feel like it might have looked a bit dodgy. I feel like I should try to find Sam and explain." I desperately wanted to see him. To be alone with him and make him understand how much I liked him.

"OK, let's find him, then." Grace went into practical mode. "He probably went to the dance tent because that's obviously where Robin and them are."

Even walking short distances in mud that deep required serious fitness. We had been trudging along for about a minute when I stumbled out of my left boot and fell into the mud. Grace pulled me up but my legs were soaked.

"Maybe we should give up and get a pancake." Tilly looked hopeful.

"No, Tills, we have to find Sam," Grace said firmly. We trudged on slowly, arm in arm, supporting each other through the quagmire, when suddenly Tilly dramatically jumped in front of me and put her face right up against mine. Her eyes were huge; she looked terrified.

"Han, shut your eyes right now."

"What?"

"Hannah, let's just go back to the Tea Party tent."

I leaned to the left so I could see past Tilly. On the other side of the field, right in the open air, with his hand down the back of her yellow hot pants, was Sam—making out with Panda.

For a second I couldn't process it and I just kept staring. I felt like I'd been punched in the stomach.

If we were on a reality TV show I would have launched over and grabbed Panda's hair and got in an epic bitch fight with her. Or if I was a power woman with a *Sex and the City* career I could have coolly sauntered over, made a cutting comment and walked away. All I could feel was everyone looking at me. Waiting for me to react. But I didn't know how. I felt Grace's hand land softly on my arm as she led me away.

"Let's just go."

"Where's Stella?" My voice came out like I was half asleep. "We should tell her . . . you know . . . that . . . we're . . ." I trailed off.

He was kissing her neck now. She was giggling.

Grace stepped in front of me this time. "Don't look. What's the point? It's just some spoiled bitch with a fucking stupid name."

When Grace swears it sounds ridiculous. I couldn't help looking. He was only thirty feet away. "Let's go back and get Stella."

So we turned around and walked back. Except for the occasional "Fuck, this is horrible," no one really spoke.

We found her very quickly. I knew from her rain boots. The rest of her was obscured by Pax, as they stood kissing in the corner of the tent. He didn't exactly waste much time. Tilly marched over and tapped her on the shoulder. I saw her untangle herself while Tilly explained what had happened. Pax looked almost upset, Stella looked militant. She left Pax and strode across the tent toward us.

"I'm going to fucking *kill* that Panda bitch."

The thing is, when Stella says it, you know it could happen.

"I want to leave, I want to leave now." Something in my voice stopped Stella in her tracks. She nodded and held my hand and we left.

Pax said he'd walk us back to our tent. Maybe he thought

Stella would commit a violent crime if she saw Panda. On the way I heard Stella telling him that she would just do whatever I wanted to and that she would be there for me no matter what. Stella will always have my back. Whatever happens between us, when something hits us from the outside she will fight until the death. I love that about her.

When we got back I expected the obligatory kiss on the cheek, but Pax gave me a huge hug and said, "Shit, Hannah, I hope you're OK." If he felt any awkwardness about what had happened earlier, it didn't show. I still couldn't figure out if he was Mr. Darcy or Mr. Wickham. Maybe it was possible to be both?

We all talked it through, over and over, and decided to sleep in one tent for solidarity. Lying in our sleeping bags, eating the Haribo, we just repeated the same conversation.

"I wish one of us had some battery so you could call your mum."

It was weird how Grace sensed I wanted to talk to Mum. Thinking about her and Dad was what made me start crying.

I wriggled farther into the sleeping bag. Listening to my friends hate Sam was sort of comforting because it helped to drown out the thoughts in my head.

"He's a complete prick."

"And a psychopath."

"Definitely. Or maybe a sociopath."

Stella cut in. "Or he's an evil, whore-fucking douche bag who gets off on trying to break people's hearts."

Hearing her say "trying" made me know he had. Or maybe it was *my* fault for saying that horrible hurtful stuff

about Pax. I kept replaying it in my mind but with me saying different things that made it better, not worse. Everything was completely fucked.

Everyone talked and talked until they dropped off to
sleep. I lay in the quiet, listening to the rain and people
walking back to their tents, and Grace talking in her sleep
like she's done ever since she was ten.

I just wanted to evaporate. To disappear. To just never
have been there in the first place. I felt in my pocket for the
Polaroid. I could smell the mud. It smelled like Sam.

SAM

It was a long trip back from the festival. I mean, obviously,
it was the same distance as the drive *to* the festival, but it
seemed a lot longer.

Ben was passed out next to me in the back of the car.
In fact, thinking about it, I have no memories of Ben being
conscious for longer than about an hour during the entire
weekend. Robin and Chris sat up front, arguing about which
route we should take to avoid traffic, while I stared out the
window at the houses and trees flicking past.

I would have told them to shut up but I was quite enjoying the distraction; their bickering gave me something to
concentrate on besides the big fucking mess that was my
life.

Everything had been going so well. I should have
known it couldn't last. That's the good thing about being a
pessimist—if things go well, that's great, and if things don't
go well, then at least you can say you predicted it.

I always manage to cock everything up in one way or

another. I definitely cocked up that French exam, which means I also cocked up my chances of getting into Cambridge. I *literally* cocked up my one actual opportunity to lose my virginity with Erin. If I didn't find a way to cock up my work experience next week, it would be a miracle.

Worst of all, though, I cocked everything up with Hannah.

It really *was* like Jo in homeroom all over again. I just walked out of the tent. I couldn't deal with it anymore. Of course she wanted Pax. Every girl in there wanted him. I kept thinking of him leaning into her with his big, stupid, bronzed hands on her waist. And her just standing there, smiling back at him.

I barged through the crowd, spilling about fifteen people's drinks en route. I'm surprised no one punched me.

I felt drunker than ever. I needed to find Robin and Chris. I also needed to find a glass of water. I didn't manage to find any of them.

My phone was still dead, so I couldn't call anyone. Once I was outside, I decided to head toward the dance tent. I was almost certain to find Robin or Ben, stoned and head-nodding in there. Chris could have been anywhere—and with anyone—by then.

I'd only made a few stumbling steps when I saw a pair of bright yellow hot pants lighting up the path in front of me.

In the middle of the field, shaking her iPhone madly at the sky, was Panda. She spotted me and grinned. She stuffed her phone back into her bag and smoothed down the wispy strawberry blond hairs that had wriggled free from her topknot.

"Hey, Sam! I was wondering when I'd run into you again. I'm having an absolute signal nightmare. I can't find my friends and my phone's not working."

I approached her, my feet feeling increasingly unsteady. "Me too. I've lost everyone and I'm totally out of battery."

She took her phone back out and starting waving it up at the stars again. "I'm trying to download this really cool app that's supposed to help you get reception at a festival." She stopped waving and checked her phone. "But I can't download it because I can't find any signal."

I nodded. "It's a catch-22."

She looked confused. "No, I think it's called the Festival Reception App."

"Right. Sure."

I was just about to wish Panda good luck with her un-downloadable download and carry on to the dance tent when I thought about Hannah and Pax and what they might be doing right now. That image of him leaning in to whisper in her ear stopped me in my tracks.

I was fed up with letting the Paxes and Toby McCourts of this world have all the fun. Why should I spend my life ducking out of homerooms and festival tents while they got exactly what they wanted? What about what *I* wanted?

Instinctively, I lurched forward and put my hands on Panda's hot-panted waist.

Panda stopped waving her phone about and looked at me. A smile spread slowly across her face.

"Hello, Mister!" she laughed. "You're a little bit forward tonight, aren't you?"

I took a deep breath and leaned into her, just like Pax had leaned into Hannah. She giggled.

"So you kiss me two days ago and then just *expect* to be able to kiss me again whenever you like, is that it?"

I nodded. Her smile widened. She put her hands on my waist. It felt good. Well, not *good*, but . . . better. This was what I'd been missing out on all my life. This was why the world was ruled by Paxes and Tobys; they saw what they wanted and they took it.

Then I kissed her. And she kissed me back. There was no emotion in it, just drunkenness and confusion. Closing my eyes brought the seasick feeling straight back, so I kept them open. I watched a group of guys all dressed as WWE wrestlers staggering past as Panda massaged my tongue with hers. She tasted like cigarettes and falafel. It felt so different from kissing Hannah that I couldn't even believe it was the same verb.

HANNAH

My nan picked a movie and then I picked a movie. She picked *An Officer and a Gentleman*, I picked *Finding Nemo*. She picked *Pretty Woman*, I picked *The Princess Bride*, and so on.

Nan always takes loungewear seriously. "You never know who's going to knock at your door," she says.

Today she was wearing matching lime-green pants and a top with a sequined kettle and cup of tea on it. I'd been back from the festival for three days, but I hadn't taken off my *Adventure Time* pajamas once. Joe was staying at his friend's and Mum and Dad were at work.

I knew watching the orgasm bit in *When Harry Met Sally* wouldn't be as awkward with Nan as Mum. I've heard my nan say "blow job" before. And she views a DVD as a back-drop for a chat more than an event in itself.

"How is that Stella anyway?" she asked.

"Yeah, really good."

"I bet she can be a piece of work, though."

"Sometimes, I guess."

"She's a pretty girl, but those kinds of looks fade. She's got a face like a mouse, if you ask me."

"She's my best friend."

"Still got a face like a mouse. She's not beautiful like you."

I couldn't hold it in.

"Stop it, Nan. Stop trying to make me feel better. I'm not an idiot. I can see myself. I *know* how I look. Trying to make me feel better about being ugly just makes it worse."

"What is going on? You're a beautiful girl. You've got lovely eyes."

Lovely eyes. That is the worst. I bit my lip.

"I'm going to read upstairs."

I tramped to my room and just sat on the bed, looking out the window and leaving Nan still watching *When Harry Met Sally*. Like she's witnessed a million people stomp out of a room, like she's Old Father Time.

I replayed the Sam/Panda moment in my head con-stantly, and systematically hated him, then her and then myself. After everything that had happened between us at the festival, after we almost lost our virginities to each other, he just went straight out and hooked up with her. It made me question everything about anything ever.

Maybe I just disgusted him. And he used the Pax thing as an excuse to wriggle out of things with me. Maybe I was just a warm-up act and Panda was the headliner.

I tried to console myself that I would have a different sort of life. That it didn't matter that I would never have a boyfriend and I'd always be a virgin. I just want to wake up one morning and be the type of person who is so good-looking that these types of things can never happen to them.

I heard Nan coming up the stairs. She knocked on the door as she walked in.

"Only me."

She handed me a mug of hot chocolate.

"Hannah, if something is wrong . . . if you're in trouble . . . you know . . ."

I had no idea what she meant.

"I'm not in trouble."

Did she think I'd joined a gang or something? That I'd run up gambling debts?

"Not trouble. It's not trouble nowadays. It's just . . . what it is."

What the fuck was she on about?

"Nan. What?"

"I want you to do everything. Because you can. Anything you want, you can have . . ."

I stopped staring at the dots on the mug in my hand and looked up at her. Her voice was softer. Her hands were smoothing the same section of her pants again and again.

"Nothing is irretrievable, you know. There's no mistake that you can't come back from."

"I'm not pregnant, Nan."

I laughed as I said it but it didn't feel funny. She sighed deeply.

"You don't seem right."

"I'm just nervous. About results."

She knew I was lying, but what could she say? I watched as she fiddled with her rings. She wears them stacked on all her fingers; each one marks an occasion—a birthday or an anniversary.

"Which is your engagement ring?" I asked.

"I didn't have one. We couldn't afford it. But this one is my wedding band. I had to get it widened because my fingers got all fat when I got old. Don't ever get old—it's awful."

She took three off her finger and handed me the wedding ring. It was a dull gold band. Her plainest ring. I rubbed it between my fingers.

"How did you meet Granddad?"

"At a wedding. I was a bridesmaid for my friend Pamela and he was the best man. He was so handsome. But I looked like a piece of work. She made me wear this lavender dress that her mum made. Except she was no good at sewing, and it was too short and too tight and made my bosoms look all lumpy."

"You must have looked all right if he went for you."

"I suppose so. A lot better than I do now, anyway."

"What was the first thing he said to you?"

"I can't remember anymore. He danced with this girl Sue all evening before he came over and talked to me."

"Why?"

"I don't know."

"Why didn't you ever ask him?"

"Maybe I did once; I can't remember."

"Where did he ask you to marry him?"

"Outside the Hammersmith Palais."

"Did you say yes?"

"Of course I did! How else would I be here with you now?"

We both giggled. I gave her the wedding band and she put the rings back on in the same order. Then she took my empty mug and stood up.

"I didn't mean to upset you earlier."

"I'm sorry I got mad. Life just feels so hard."

"Sometimes it is."

She bent down and kissed me on the head.

After she left I lay there looking at my wall. At the models from *Vogue* shoots and the photos of us all on nights out. If only Nan knew how ridiculous it was for her to ever think anyone would want to sleep with me. That I'll never know what sleeping with someone feels like. What sleeping with Sam feels like.

There is no one I can talk to about it because they will just say the standard things. That I'll meet someone. That Sam is a dick. That I'm only eighteen. I almost wish someone would just say, "Just get over it. It's never going to happen." At least it's the truth.

14

SAM

A week after coming back from Woodland, I felt more like an actual adult than I ever had in my life. I was working in an office (sort of), I had a girlfriend (sort of) and I'd had my heart broken. (There was no "sort of" about that last one.)

My (sort of) office job was the week's work experience in my mum's friend's office. I'd been there three days and was still not entirely sure what it was they did. The staff was exclusively made up of spoiled, hot and permanently hungover girls in their late twenties, named either Vicky or Sarah or Sophie.

In between sending me out to bulk-buy candy for them, they attended meetings in glass rooms with Banksy stencils on the walls and beanbags on the floor, where they discussed "social media strategies" and wrote things like "Stats show most retweets happen at lunchtime" on a massive whiteboard. Below is some sample dialogue from an average day in the office:

Vicky [slamming down phone]: God, she sounds fat.

Sarah: Who was it?

Vicky: Becky at Judy Morgan's.

Sophie: God, do you think? I think she sounds stunning.

Vicky: I really think she sounds fat.

Sarah: Apparently, she's stunning.

Vicky: God, she's doesn't sound it. She sounds fat. Like she has fat arms.

I was supposed to be learning about life in the real, adult world. However, the only thing I'd learned so far is that girls fucking *love* peanut M&M's and it's possible to judge the size of someone's arms by the sound of their voice.

My (sort of) girlfriend was Panda. I didn't intend for her to be my sort-of girlfriend. It just sort of happened. She texted me the day after we got back from the festival. Rather than a casual "Hey, it was nice drunkenly making out with you a couple of times—do you wanna meet up again?" message, hers said, "So what shall we do on the weekend hun? xxxx"

She clearly assumed we were already a couple, so I just went with it. When I showed him the text, Robin shook my hand and congratulated me on the four Xs. It was, to use his phrase, "major progress."

I hadn't seen or heard from Hannah since that night. That's the beauty of not being on Facebook, I guess. Although, since Robin had eagerly befriended Stella about twenty minutes after our disastrous double date, there were still opportunities for some mild stalking. Once we spotted a few pictures of Hannah and Pax together in Kavos. In one, Pax was clearly sneaking a glance at her in her bikini. I felt a bit sick looking at it.

She hadn't even called or texted. And obviously I wasn't going to call or text her after what she'd said. The trouble was, I was struggling to remember exactly what she'd actually said. It had definitely seemed bad at the time, what with the gin and the ciders and watching Pax's big, tanned hands flapping around her, but I had an awful, sick sensation in the pit of my stomach that I might have overreacted. I asked Robin what he thought, but he just shrugged and said, "I dunno, man. It definitely *looked* bad from where I was standing." And that's what kept running through my head every time I got the urge to send her a late-night text: *It definitely looked bad.*

In a way, I was glad that exam results were looming, since it gave me something else to worry about.

Me and Chris were at Robin's house watching terrible homemade hip-hop videos on YouTube and talking about what would happen if we didn't get the scores we needed, when Chris spotted something on Robin's Facebook.

"Shit. Stella's having another house party."

We read the invite in silence. It was happening the night we were going to get our results.

"Fuck that," Robin said finally, sitting up in his chair. "We can find better parties to go to than hers."

"Like whose?" I asked.

Robin paused. "Yeah, all right, hers will be the best. I was trying to make you feel better, you dipshit."

"Thanks, man."

"Unless . . . ," said Chris.

"Unless what?"

"You could go with Panda."

"Oooh, Panda! Yes, you could go with your girlfriend, Panda." Robin had started doing a thing where every time he said Panda's name he pitched his voice up three octaves and pouted his lips. I had considered asking him to stop but, annoyingly, it was pretty funny.

"I suppose I could go with Panda," I said. The idea didn't fill me with joy, to be honest.

"Do you know what, Sam?" said Chris as Robin was on the brink of upgrading his high-voiced pout into a little dance. "The problem with Panda—if you don't mind me saying?"

"No. Go on." I was genuinely interested. I knew there were several problems with Panda; I wanted to see which he thought was most pressing.

Chris nodded and continued. "All right, so the problem with Panda is that she's one of those girls who *thinks* she's funnier than she actually is."

"Yeah!" Robin nodded excitedly and slammed his fist on the table. "Definitely, man. Girls who *think* they're funnier than they actually are, are worse than girls who aren't funny at all."

"Wait," I said. "So just to confirm—is she funny or not?"

"She's a *little* funny," said Robin diplomatically. "And you can talk to her. She's not one of those girls you literally cannot speak to. One of those girls who are like a different species or something."

"Sophia Demico," said Chris.

"Exactly," said Robin.

Sophia Demico is the hottest girl in our school. However, she's also possibly the dullest human being alive.

Robin continued. "Talking to girls like Sophia Demico is

a bit like talking to a cat. You say things at them and they sort of blink and move their head to acknowledge that they heard you, but you can see in their eyes that they haven't actually understood a word. Then eventually they just skulk off to rip up a chair or shit in the garden or something."

"Are you still talking about Sophia?"

"No, that last bit was just cats. As far as I know. But anyway, you get what I'm saying. Panda's not like one of those girls—you *can* actually talk to her."

Chris leapt in. "Yeah, but because you *can* talk to her, she thinks you *like* talking to her."

"Exactly," said Robin. "Just because she's not mortally offended by sex and swearwords, she thinks she's one of the boys."

I considered this. It seemed pretty spot-on.

"Sam can confirm whether or not she's one of the boys, can't you, man?" said Chris, nudging me in the ribs.

"Well, he *can't*, actually." Robin grinned. "Since he hasn't actually seen or felt her genitals. Have you done *anything* with her yet?"

"Like what?"

" 'Like what' means no."

"No, it means fuck off."

Robin snorted. "Honestly, Sam, if you haven't slept with her, or *anyone*, by the time you go to school, you might have to start telling people you're religious or something. That's the only feasible explanation for still being a virgin at this age."

I chucked a pillow at his head. Chris laughed and switched off the computer.

HANNAH

On the way back from the movies, the train broke down at Ravenscourt Park and everyone had to get off. Stella and I walked to the end of the platform, where we had stood every day after school since we were eleven. We sat on our bench.

"We'll probably never be at this station again."

Stella rolled her eyes. "That is such a *you* thing to say."

"Well, why would we? The only thing that's here is school."

"Georgina Foster lives over there."

"You fucking hate Georgina Foster. You spread a rumor that she got off with Mr. Donaldson."

"She probably did—she frickin' *loved* science. Do you remember when she did that display where she fried the Play-Doh and talked about Zac Efron's hair?"

"That was Esther."

"Ergh, I hate Esther, too."

"You hate everyone."

"Except you."

"And Pax."

"He doesn't count. He's a boy."

I kind of liked hearing Stella say that. She'll never be one of those girls who is obsessed with someone. Well, she does get obsessed, I suppose. But not outwardly. She'd never admit it.

"You do like him, though."

"Well, he's really hot and really cool. What's not to like?"

She was right. What had happened between me and Pax at the festival flashed into my mind. I was still struggling to figure out if what he had done was wrong. Whatever the case, Stella was selling him short. Boys who are that hot usually act like massive dicks, but he didn't.

"You and him are perfect."

I wasn't being disingenuous. I meant it. There was nothing of any real substance between me and Pax. There's a photo of him and Stella in Kavos on Facebook. They mirror each other's perfection, and make a sort of glowing sun of limbs and symmetry and gloss.

"Are you excited about seeing him?" I asked her.

"Yeah, of course."

Pax and Casper were coming up to London at the end of the week. Stella and Pax had been speaking for hours every day since Woodland and they were basically an item.

I was really looking forward to seeing Casper again.

Stella looked at me. "Sam is a cunt," she said.

Even Stella never says that word.

"I know," I said, then felt guilty for saying it. Stella had been Sam-bashing enthusiastically ever since we got back from Woodland. I just let her get on with it. It was better that she thought Sam was just a c-word who had randomly broken my heart than for her to know there had ever been anything between me and Pax. Especially as there *definitely* wasn't anything between us now.

"He really is, Han. And he's a fucking psycho. You deserve better. He is not your lobster."

"You don't believe in the lobster."

"Whatever. I believe *you* believe in the lobster. It's like fairies. It comes to those who believe."

For Stella, this was a pretty profound thing to say.

"Well, why don't you start believing in the lobster?"

"Because what's the point of finding The One now? Say we found The One tomorrow. . . . It would just ruin everything. We'd have to go to college with the shackle of the lobster. Basically wearing Sebastian from *The Little Mermaid* around our necks."

"Stella, Sebastian is clearly a crab."

"He's a lobster, you moron! We'll Google it when we get back. Anyway, Freddie loves you—why don't you just go out with him?"

I wanted to say "Because I want Sam to want me," but Sam clearly didn't want me. If he ever had, he definitely didn't anymore.

We'd seen on Stella's Facebook that Panda had written on Robin's wall: "Can u put me and Sam down for Ben's next night plz hun??"

Stella had just snorted and said, "Ugh, she's such a *twat*. He deserves her."

We let a train pass.

"It feels strange that school is over. That everything is ending. That next month we're not coming back."

Stella just shrugged. Sometimes I think she only exists for tomorrow. Even the second that's just passed is meaningless to her.

"What if we change? What if everything changes?" I wasn't being rhetorical. I really wanted an answer. "I hate it."

"Why? We'll visit each other and go and stay with Tilly and Grace. It's not that big a deal."

"I hate endings."

"You're so emotional."

That's true. I cried at the baby squirrels on *Naturewatch* yesterday.

"Are you scared about scores next week?" I asked.

"I just hope that if I've fucked it up they'll still let me in."

"You're so practical. I feel sick when I think about it."

"Hannah, you'll get three As. You will."

I hate it when people say that to me. They think I'm being typically negative when I say how badly History went. But it really did.

"You'll get three A's and then we'll find you a new improved Toilet Boy at my party. Maybe you can upgrade to Shed Boy or even Bedroom Boy."

We talked for hours on the bench. I must have stood on this platform thousands of times but I could only remember a handful. When I kissed Freddie for the first time after *Dreams of Anne Frank* rehearsals. When I cried waiting for the train when my granddad died. When Stella and I saw Mr. Cross getting off with Miss Nailor.

We were talking so much we missed the last train in the end and walked back to Stella's.

I texted my Mum to say I was staying out and she texted back:

Happy you're happy again. So is Dad.

I was feeling better, I suppose, but I still flinched when I thought about Sam and Panda.

Lying head-to-tail on the bed with Stella, I said, "Do you wish you'd waited until you'd met Pax? To have sex, I mean?"

"No, because at least now I know what I'm doing, so I won't seem totally clueless. I just hope he doesn't want me to give him a blow job because it grosses me out. They literally piss out of there."

I groaned. "I think I'll be a virgin forever."

"I think you will be too if you don't grow some balls and realize that Toilet Boy is, and clearly always was, a toilet."

SAM

Before I could think about Stella's party, I had another social engagement to attend to: an after-work "drinks."

It was the penultimate day of my week at the office, and I'd just returned from the shop with nearly a metric ton of peanut M&M's, which I dumped on the desk between Vicky, Sophie and Sarah (I was still not totally sure which was which). Rather than doing what they usually did and grunting "Thanks, hun" without taking their eyes off their computer screens, one of them looked up at me and smiled.

"You know, Sam," said Vicky or Sophie or Sarah. "You've been a real sweetie this week. You should come to these drinks tomorrow."

"What drinks?" I asked, slumping back into my seat.

"We're having drinks in the office for a few clients," said Sophie or Sarah or Vicky. "Everyone in the building's coming. It's your last day—you have to come."

"I sort of have plans with my girlfriend, but I can probably get out of them."

Instantly, all six of their eyes lit up. They were looking at me like I was a new species of creature they'd just discovered.

"Oh my absolute *god*!" said Vicky or Sophie or Sarah. "You've got a *girlfriend*?"

"Ah, how sweet!" added Sophie or Sarah or Vicky.

"Oh my god!" Sarah or Vicky or Sophie gushed. "You absolutely *have* to bring her to the drinks on Friday."

The others squealed their approval at this suggestion.

"What's her name?"

Her name. No matter how many times I have to explain it, it doesn't get any easier.

"Her name's Miranda," I mumbled into my computer keyboard, "but she calls herself Panda because it rhymes with Miranda and also because she likes pandas."

There was a pause while Vicky/Sophie/Sarah, Sophie/Sarah/Vicky and Sarah/Vicky/Sophie took this in. I waited for the mocking peals of laughter but they never came.

"That is actually awesome," said Vicky or Sophie or Sarah finally. "I wish my name rhymed with an animal."

"Yeah," said Sophie or Sarah or Vicky. "It would be so awesome to be called, like, Miraffe or Mirelephant."

"Oh my god, yeah," agreed Sarah or Vicky or Sophie. "I am totes naming my daughter Miraffe."

"What if you have a boy, though?"

Sarah or Vicky or Sophie chewed her pen while she considered this. "Maybe I'll go for a more masculine animal, like Mirhino or Mirocodile."

"Yeah, Mirocodile's gorgeous, actually."

"Well, I've already got dibs, so you'll have to take Mirhino."

The conversation continued in this vein until all the peanut M&M's were finished and it was time for us to go home.

. . .

I met Panda outside the office at six-thirty on Friday. To be fair, she did look really good. She'd clearly made an effort. She was initially quite annoyed that it clashed with Ben's club night, but when I told her it was an office party, she changed her tune completely.

She said, "Oh my god, I'm hoping to get a job in an office someday."

I guess she assumed that every office in England was interconnected, and that if she made a good impression in this one she'd be set for life.

The "drinks" consisted exclusively of really expensive gin and tonics. Even the smell reminded me of that night with Hannah. I left mine on the table and went to get some water. By the time I got back, Panda had already polished off two glasses.

The Vickys, Sophies and Sarahs seemed to be enjoying themselves purely because all the people they usually spoke to on the phone were now actually here in the flesh. And thus they could finally assess how much flesh they had on them. Below is some sample dialogue from when I walked past them, huddled around the photocopier, on my way for a piss:

Vicky: God, have you seen the state of her?

Sophie: God, who?

Vicky: Becky from Judy Morgan's.

Sarah: Oh my absolute god. Is she here?

Vicky: Yeah.

Sophie: Oh my god, which one is she?

Vicky: Um . . . which do you think? Look for the fattest arms in the room. She's the one attached to them.

Sarah: Oh my god, Vicks! You totes called it.

Vicky: Yeah. Her voice was a dead giveaway.

Since they were all too concerned with arm girth to pay any attention to Panda and me, we spent the first hour or so standing idly around the nibbles table, sipping water (me), guzzling gin (Panda) and not talking much.

At the festival I never really got the chance to see just *how* ill-matched we really were. We were always drunk and distracted by friends, loud noises and the fact that I'd just had my heart bent out of shape. I'd seen her a couple of times since, but we'd usually just met outside a cinema, kissed, gone into the cinema, sat in silence for two hours, come out, kissed and gone home.

Now that I was stone-cold sober and stuck with just her, it made me realize how little we had to say to each other. I thought about standing with Hannah in Stella's bathroom and walking around the festival with her at dawn. We hadn't stopped talking once.

"I *love* street art," said Panda, filling a huge conversational hole and nodding toward one of the millions of Banksy stencils on the office wall. "It's so quirky."

I couldn't think of a response to this that didn't involve banging my face on the table, so I said nothing.

Panda drained her fourth gin and tonic and looked around irritably.

"This is boring," she said. "Let's go somewhere and . . ." She gave me a sideways glance. "You know . . ."

"We can't go somewhere and . . . you know," I said. "We might get caught."

Panda laughed. "Getting caught is the whole fun of it, stupid!"

"I'm not sure about that," I said. "I think a burglar would probably take issue with that motto."

"Shut up, Sam."

She slammed her glass down, grabbed my hand and strutted across the room. I checked to see if the Vickys, Sophies and Sarahs had noticed but they were still too busy mentally weighing people in the corner. Panda wandered out into the hallway and I followed her.

"There!" she squealed, pointing to the door of the supply closet.

"No," I said, shaking my head. "That's the supply closet. We can't go in there. It's for stationery."

"Isn't it kind of . . . naughty to go in the supply closet?" she said, squeezing my ass.

"I can't think of anything less naughty than stationery," I said, removing her hand from my butt. "When was the last time you saw a hole puncher in a porno?"

"I don't watch porn," said Panda, screwing up her face in disgust.

"No, I don't, either," I said, quite convincingly, I thought. "But I don't imagine they feature much stationery."

"Stop being a baby and live a little," she whispered, and she opened the door and pulled me inside.

The supply closet was literally the least sexy place in the world. Unless you find the smell of printer toner arousing.

Yet Panda was talking about it like it was fucking Paris at sunset.

"Yeah," she whispered, gazing around in awe. "This is perfect."

We started kissing. I could taste the gin and tonic on her tongue. She loosened my belt and started to undo my jeans. With a flick of her finger and thumb, they collapsed and fell in a little denim pool around my ankles.

I felt my stomach churning. I wasn't sure how far I wanted this to go. I'd got it into my head that my first time would be with Hannah. Which was stupid, since, obviously, the same thought had never crossed her mind. She was probably holding out for Pax. Regardless, was I really prepared to lose my virginity in a windowless room full of staplers?

Panda put her hand inside my boxers and pulled out my dick. I prayed that the problem I had with Erin wouldn't come back to haunt me now.

"Panda! Wait!"

"Let's do it here," she whispered. "Let's fuck right here."

"Erm . . ." I thought about Hannah and Pax. If I *was* going to wait for the "right" person, clearly I'd be waiting forever. There was no time like the present. Even if the present smelled like printer toner.

Before I had time to make a real decision, we heard muffled voices outside. We both froze. The door handle rattled. Someone was coming in.

Quick as a flash, Panda ducked behind a rack of Post-it notes and highlighters. I sprang after her but tripped on my jeans and came crashing down on the floor, bringing several boxes of pens and a few pads of legal-size paper with me. As I struggled to haul myself up, the door opened.

It was Vicky or Sarah or Sophie. With a guy. They'd clearly had the same idea as Panda.

Their mouths—which had previously been pressed against each other—now hung open as they stared down at me, sprawled on a pile of stationery, pants around my ankles, desperately—and unsuccessfully—attempting to cover my semierect penis. I tried to speak, to call for Panda to show herself, but nothing came out.

The man blinked and ushered Vicky or Sarah or Sophie back out the door. "We'll, erm . . . we'll let you finish, man," he muttered.

"No, I'm finished! I mean . . . not *finished*, I haven't started! I wasn't doing anything!"

It was too late. They had gone. I heard their howls of laughter receding down the hall. Panda moved out from behind the rack and dusted herself off as if nothing had happened.

"Phew," she said. "That was kind of close, wasn't it?"

"Kind of close?" I yelled, stumbling to my feet and dragging my jeans back up. "I just got caught with my cock out in a supply closet!"

She grabbed me by the collar and kissed me. "I told you getting caught was the whole fun of it!"

I wriggled free of her grasp. "Getting caught was literally the *least* fun part of this experience! What could possibly be fun about making people think you've left an office party early to go and have a wank on some legal pads?"

Panda exhaled loudly. "God, Sam, you're so boring sometimes. When I met you, I really thought you were a free spirit. Like Bob Marley or Nick Grimshaw."

"Well, I'm not!" I was getting angry now. "I'm not a free spirit who likes humping in cupboards and quirky street art and 'living a little.' I like sitting inside, drinking hot grape juice."

I don't know why I said it. It just came out.

Panda wrinkled her nose, confused. "Is there such a thing as *hot* grape juice?"

I sighed and opened the door.

"Come on. Let's just go."

We left in silence down the fire escape—I couldn't face going back into the office. Outside, by the bus stop, I told her that I didn't think things would work out between us. She nodded glumly. I don't think she thought it was true love, either.

We hugged and I walked off. As I passed the office I saw Vicky, Sophie and Sarah huddled by the photocopier, laughing. At least I know that if I ever want a reference, I can call them up.

"Sam has a good typing speed, a helpful attitude and a penchant for masturbating in supply closets."

Brilliant.

HANNAH

We met Pax and Casper at Paddington station. Stella wore hot pants. It was like she was going to war with the faceless—well, not so faceless, due to Facebook stalking—girls of Pax's world. Girls from his travel-year photos draped all over him at foam parties in Thailand. Girls from school in his senior pictures. The girls who wrote try-hard comments that seemed effortless but that any girl would know took two hours to compose.

We met them by the Paddington Bear Shop and talked about our various feelings on marmalade. The kind of chat that fills up time until you feel comfortable.

I'd been pretty nervous about seeing Pax again, but it was clear straight from the get-go that he was here purely to see Stella. There was no mention of what he'd said to me at the festival. He was so wasted at the time he'd probably forgotten all about it. After giving me a big, friendly hug, he didn't take his eyes off Stella once.

On the tube to Stella's I sat next to Casper. We both knew to give Pax and Stella time alone. Casper seemed more relaxed than he had in Greece. He looked more comfortable in his clothes. He was wearing baggy jeans with thin blue and white stripes, a plain white T-shirt and yellow Converse.

"I like your shoes."

"I picked yellow because I thought it would be like having sunshine on my feet, even in the rain."

It didn't sound cheesy the way he said it.

"Will you be OK with those two?" I asked. Four days must have seemed a long time stuck with Stella and Pax. Stax. Stella would probably prefer Pella.

I looked over at the two of them. They weren't making out with each other but you could tell it was only because we were on the train in the middle of the day.

"Yeah. There's loads of stuff I want to see. I've made a list."

He unzipped the front pocket of his backpack and pulled

out a notebook. As he riffled through it I could see a few sketches of people and lots of ones of birds' beaks. He found the page.

"OK. So, in no particular order . . . Punch Drunk theater company. Spaghetti ice cream. Thames midnight walk. Buy new pants."

He paused.

" 'Buy new pants' is an incidental addition to the list. Because I need new pants."

Before I could ask about what all the other things meant we had to get off the tube and walk to Stella's. My mum and dad would not be OK with two random boys that I met on vacation coming to stay. They probably wouldn't be that all right with the concept of random boys we met on vacation in general. It's weird to think that Stella didn't have to check with anyone.

We got to Stella's house and almost straight away Stella and Pax went upstairs. The bedroom door slammed after them. I made Casper and me a cup of tea.

"Do you just want to come back to my house for dinner? I feel bad leaving you here alone. And what if Stella's cleaning person comes back and you're just randomly in the house?"

"That would be a bit weird, I suppose. Is that OK?"

I texted my Mum:

Bringing my friend Casper around for dinner. Don't be weird.

We ate loads of the fancy cookies at Stella's house and then left them a note saying where we were going.

From the moment I saw my nan's silhouette coming to open the door I knew it was a mistake. Even through stained glass I could tell she had blow-dried her hair. She looked like a magician's assistant. She was wearing a powder-blue chiffon blouse with matching wide-legged blue pants, a massive gold belt and gold wedge sandals. She belonged on a Nile cruise, or with Tom Jones.

"Come in, come in," she said, welcoming me into *my* house, which she didn't even properly live in.

She fussed over Casper, taking his coat and leading him into the kitchen. Mum and Dad looked exactly the same as they always do. Dad was eating chips and dip from little bowls on the table.

"A few nibbles before dinner?"

My mum bristled as my nan said it. We are never allowed to snack before meals.

Casper sat down at the table. He asked my dad about his day, he talked to my mum about Devon and how he was staying there with Pax's family because his parents were going through a tough time. He is the most honest person I have witnessed in conversation. He just said things without being embarrassed.

It didn't even feel like he was over-sharing. It seemed brave and special. My family never talks about things like that but all of a sudden my dad was talking about his parents' divorce and how hard it had been. It was like being in a strange alternate universe where my family was made up of completely different people and I had come to a dinner party with them.

In Kavos, Casper had seemed so awkward, someone

to be pitied. But here he seemed totally at peace with his surroundings.

"Does that piano still work?" he asked.

My granddad's piano is in our kitchen, even though none of us can play. My nan didn't want to get rid of it, but it seemed pointless shipping it to Spain.

"Yes," said Nan.

"Can I play a little? My parents had to get rid of theirs. I haven't played in forever."

When Casper said it, I think Nan was at the point of getting down on one knee and proposing. He played "I Want to Hold Your Hand" and Nan and Mum danced. And for two minutes they actually got along.

Sitting back at the table after the song had finished, Nan said, "Where are you staying, Casper?"

"At Stella's house with Pax."

"Oh dear. What a gooseberry. Stay here with us."

I looked to Mum to gauge her reaction.

"Of course; we can make up a bed in Hannah's room."

It was a little weird that they hadn't asked me if it was all right.

"Um, yeah, that would be great, if it's really OK?"

I think he was asking me more than them.

"Course it is," I said. "We don't have Milanos cookies like at Stella's, though."

I could tell Nan was offended. "Well, I've never liked that Stella. She's hard as nails."

"Maybe she has to be." Casper just said it, matter-of-factly. And left it at that.

Lying in bed, I wondered what Pax and Stella were doing.

If they were wildly and passionately having sex under her princess canopy, next to her lilac fairy lights, *Breakfast at Tiffany's* poster and the collection of Beanie Babies she kept hidden under her bed. Probably.

We spoke to each other through the darkness and eventually the conversation came around to Stella and Pax.

"Are you jealous?" Casper asked.

I closed my eyes and thought about the first moment I'd seen Pax by the boat.

"Maybe. Yeah, I guess I am, but not because of Pax. Just because they seem to fit together."

"You think?" He sounded doubtful.

"And I want to fit together with someone like that."

Nothing needed saying about Sam. I was sure Pax had filled Casper in on what had happened at the festival. Even though the light was off I glanced at *The BFG* on my bookshelf, with the Polaroid of me and Sam hidden inside.

"I'm sorry he didn't turn out to be what you thought he was."

I groaned and rolled over. "Where is my lobster?" It was a rhetorical question, directed at the universe more than Casper.

"Your what?"

"My lobster," I mock-wailed, drawing the word out and pounding my fists on the mattress like a spoiled child.

He laughed. "What the hell is your lobster?"

"Lobsters mate for life. I want to meet my lobster."

Casper shook his head. "Well, first off, they don't, and second—"

I sat up in bed and looked down at him. "What?"

"What?" he shot back innocently.

"What do you mean they don't mate for life? Yes they do. It's a thing. It's one hundred percent a thing."

"Well, I'm going to college to study marine biology and I'm telling you it's one hundred percent *not* a thing."

I flopped back down onto the bed and stared up at the ceiling blankly. "How can my whole life since I was eleven be based on a lie? That is just *typical*."

"Hang on," said Casper. "You've been basing your whole life since you were eleven on the incorrect assumption that lobsters mate for life?"

"Yes."

"Well, the next time you base your whole life on something I suggest you Google it first."

He got out his phone and seconds later was reading out a list.

"Bald eagles mate for life, apparently. Oh, hang on . . . what about *Schistosoma mansoni* worms? That's got a romantic ring to it. They also cause the snail fever disease, so that's two for the price of one, there."

I rolled over grumpily. "Well, I want to find my bald eagle, then."

"What, just before you go to college you want to meet the love of your life and then be torn apart as soon as you've found each other?"

He had a point. "Yeah, I suppose . . . ," I said.

Casper smiled and switched his phone off. "Night, Hannah," he said.

"'Night."

A few seconds went by in silence, then I said, "Casper?"

"Yeah?"

"You know Sebastian from *The Little Mermaid*?"

He laughed. "Yeah?"

"Is he a lobster or a crab?"

"Crab. Definitely a crab. Good night."

"'Night."

I grabbed my phone off the bedside table and texted Stella:

Sebastian is a crab. Lobsters don't mate for life.
Have you done it yet?

15

SAM

It's weird that your entire life can be decided at eight a.m.
Surely, if you're potentially about to discover you'll spend
the next fifty years working in McDonald's, you could sleep
in a little to prepare.

Still, it was eight a.m. and we were outside the school
gates, waiting to be let in. Results day. It seemed like it
would never arrive, but here it was.

Me and Chris were totally silent as we waited. Robin
talked—to himself more than anyone else. He'd been saying all summer that he didn't care about getting into Loughborough, but as he stood there glancing at his watch and
hopping up and down on one leg like he needed a pee, it was
obvious that whatever was in that envelope would mean
something to him.

"This is bullshit," he muttered, digging his hands even
deeper into his pockets. "Getting up at the crack of dawn

to trek all the way here just to open an envelope. You know Ben's school lets them check their results online? I'm going to lodge a formal complaint. I could be in bed with my laptop right now."

It was raining—was that a bad omen? Or maybe a good omen? Sometimes the rain can indicate happiness and good things—like at the end of *Four Weddings and a Funeral*, for example. I can't think of any other examples, though, so that could just be a one-off.

I had been fully prepped on the morning by my mum. She'd given me a waterproof folder with all my college and personal details and pretty much every phone number in the whole of Cambridge University—plus thirty pounds fresh credit on my phone—in case I didn't get the grades I needed. *God*, I thought, *I hope it doesn't come to that.*

Mr. Harris from Geography gave us a grim smile as he unlocked the gates and we trooped past him to the main hall to pick up our envelopes. Robin made jokes to try to ease the tension. It didn't work.

Once we'd picked up our envelopes, the three of us stood outside the hall, in the drizzle, holding them, not saying anything.

"Who's going first, then?" asked Chris finally.

None of us reacted. I let out a nervous laugh. I really didn't want to go first.

"Fuck this," said Robin, ripping open his envelope. Apparently, he was going first. He pulled his piece of paper out and studied it for a second or two. Chris and I kept quiet in case it was bad news.

A huge smile split his face in two.

"Two Bs and a C!" he beamed, holding the paper up to show us.

We both gave him a big bear hug. He needed three Cs at least to get into Loughborough after his ridiculous American summer camp adventures.

"Thank fuck that's over," he said, stuffing the paper and torn envelope into his backpack and sitting down on the steps, despite the rain.

"It's not over yet," said Chris irritably as he ripped his envelope open. "We're all in this together."

Slowly, Chris took in the contents of the letter. He needed at least three B's for Warwick.

He exhaled loudly and craned his head skyward. "A and two Bs! I got in!"

Me and Robin jumped on him, screaming, "Yes!"

There was only me left now. I looked at the two of them. Robin was drumming his fingers on his backpack and chewing his lower lip. He seemed more excited about my results than his.

"I shouldn't have gone last," I said. "There's more pressure."

Chris groaned. "Just open it, dickhead."

I stared at the envelope. If it contained anything less than three As, my life was basically over. For some reason, Hannah popped into my head. I wondered if she had opened hers yet.

I offered the envelope to Chris. "I can't do it. You open it for me."

"Stop being such a fucking girl!" Robin leapt up to punch me on the arm. I flinched to avoid him and, in the process, dropped the envelope into a large—and extremely deep—puddle by my feet.

"Fuck!"

Robin and Chris burst out laughing. I yanked the envelope out of the murky water, but it was too late—it was soaked through. I tried to open it, but it but just tore apart. My entire future was waterlogged.

"You massive fucking idiot!" I slapped Robin around the head as hard as I could. He was still cackling so hard he could hardly breathe.

"It's all right," he managed to say, gasping between laughs. "We'll just go and speak to the secretary—she'll have all the results on her computer."

The three of us sprinted across to the secretary's office. Thankfully, by the time we arrived, Robin and Chris had regained their composure. Robin put a hand on my shoulder and looked me straight in the eye.

"You'll be all right, Sam. Whatever happens."

I smiled at them both. "Wait for me outside, yeah?"

"Yeah."

I walked into the school secretary's office. The school secretary is a large, bubbly lady who is usually speaking loudly on the phone or eating a muffin. At this moment, she was doing both.

She mouthed "Come in" as I popped my head around the door.

"I'll have to call you back, Kathy," she said into the receiver. "I've got a wet, rather upset-looking boy at the door." She put the phone down and gave her full attention to the muffin.

"What can I do you for, dear?"

"Hi, I'm Sam. I, erm, dropped my envelope in a puddle. Can you tell me my results, please?"

She looked at me over her glasses. "In a puddle, you say, dear?"

"Yes."

"Well, that's careless, isn't it?"

"It wasn't entirely my fault."

"I mean, puddles are quite obvious things. You can spot them a mile away."

"As I say, it wasn't my fault. Could you please just tell me my results?"

"Yes, all right, dear. No need to snap. I'll just go to the website."

She clicked her mouse. Her eyes widened as she stared at the computer screen. She slapped a hand to her forehead in dismay.

"Oh no," she said, shaking her head. "Oh dear, dear, dear. That is *awful*."

I slumped into the nearest chair with my head in my hands.

"Oh shit," I groaned. "What is it? It's a D in French, isn't it? I *knew* I screwed up French."

She glanced up at as if she'd forgotten I was there.

"Hmm? Oh, no, sorry, dear. It's just Facebook. My friend's posted pictures of her new baby. Awfully ugly little thing. Looks like that bald one in *The Lord of the Rings*."

"Right, fine. Can you *please* tell me my results?"

"Your results? Oh, yes. That's what we were doing, wasn't it? Right."

She clicked her mouse a couple more times.

"Right, here we go," she said, squinting at the screen. "C?"

My heart stopped.

"C?" I yelled, panicked. "C in what? French?"

"No, dear, I mean your surname—it starts with C, doesn't it?"

My heart started again.

"No, M! Moran. Sam Moran."

"Oh, sorry. I know there's a Sam Cassidy in your year. I thought it might be you."

"Well, it's not—it's Moran! Sam Moran!"

She clicked her mouse a few more times.

"OK, Moran, Moran, Moran . . ." She squinted as she scrolled down the screen. My grip tightened on the arms of the chair.

"Can I just come around and see for myself?"

"No, dear, you stay over there. Ah, here we are. Sam Moran."

Sweat prickled on my forehead. She cleared her throat.

"English—A."

My shoulders relaxed a little.

"Geography—A."

My shoulders relaxed a little more. Please, please, *please* let me not have screwed up French.

"And the last one . . . French—B."

My hands gave up their grip on the chair and dropped limply to my side. French. I *knew* I'd screwed up French.

Outside I could hear the faint screams and cheers of

people opening envelopes that contained the results they wanted. I wished so much that I was one of them.

The secretary tipped her head to the side and gave me a sad, comforting smile.

"I'm so sorry, Sam."

I thanked her, stood up and walked out; I was on autopilot. But there was still hope. I scrambled around in my waterproof folder and found the number I needed for Cambridge University. I phoned it. I told the lady my name, my ID number and my results. She listened patiently and said she'd call me back in fifteen minutes to let me know if I still had a place next year.

I walked outside. It had stopped raining. Robin and Chris ran over to me. I told them what had happened. We all sat quietly on the steps outside the secretary's office until, fifteen minutes later, my phone rang.

The lady at Pembroke told me that unfortunately they wouldn't be able to accept me as a student next year. Robin and Chris wrapped their arms around me.

"Fuck man, I'm sorry," Robin said.

"Yeah, that's so shit," Chris said.

I didn't say a thing. My whole future was dissolving in front of me.

All I could think was, "Fuck. I'm going to York."

HANNAH

I woke up at five a.m. and checked the College Board website for the millionth time, even though I knew it wouldn't say anything. I padded around the house and then just sat on the floor, leaning against the fridge. I kept thinking my mum or my nan would come downstairs, sensing I was awake. That they'd make me tea and I'd be unresponsive. But they didn't.

I sat and got angry that the only person who gave a shit about my exam results in the house was me. On my mum's family organizer on the fridge it said *"Han Results"* in blue pen next to today's date, and then in another color *"call tree man"* and then underneath *"Linda?"* Like it's just part of the list, not the fucking rest of my life at stake.

But then when I crept out of the house at seven a.m. and opened the gate, I heard a tap and turned around. They were all at the upstairs window. Mum, Dad, Nan and Joe. They all held their hands up and crossed their fingers. They are so random, but so sweet. And probably scared of saying the wrong thing and making me even more insane.

I walked to Stella's house and called her. She opened the door fully made-up, hair straightened, and off we went. We got off the tube at Ravenscourt Park.

"OK, so *this* is the last time," she said. "Thank fucking god."

I couldn't speak. I felt like I wasn't even in my own body.

"Ergh, there's Carmen." Even now, Stella's priority wasn't the fate of the rest of our lives. "She dyed her hair red. Typical."

By the time we were at the gates we were just part of the crowd. Waiting for the doors to be opened felt like an eon. I could hear Stella prattling on about Kavos and her shoes. Then Grace and Tilly arrived. I could see Grace felt the same way I did. Neither of us spoke.

"Why won't they just fucking let us in?" said Grace between clenched teeth.

And then, as if they had heard her command, the doors opened. I felt Stella's hand find mine and squeeze it. And we walked in together. The hall smelled the same. The teachers looked the same. I found my envelope on the table and picked it up.

I went to the corner, faced the wall and opened the letter. I couldn't even make it out at first. The rows of letters and numbers and modules and boards. I could feel myself welling up.

I walked onto the playground. Stella was there with Tilly and Grace. I didn't want to speak in case they were upset. But they were all smiling.

I smiled, too, still in shock, and then I found my voice. . . .

"Fuck! I'm going to York!"

I could smell pancakes before I even opened the front door. In the kitchen the table was laid and the family was all there. There were balloons that said CONGRATULATIONS and flowers from the garden in a vase on the table.

My mum hugged me first.

"Well done, well done, well done," she chanted in my ear, and kissed my cheeks.

Dad put his arms around Mum and then around me, too.

"Three As. And all summer you've been beside yourself about that history exam."

Nan winked at me and opened a cupboard and pulled out a Tiffany's bag.

I have never been given anything expensive in my life. My family just doesn't have money for stuff like that.

"I wanted you to have a bit of sparkle."

I think Mum was a bit shocked. "Oh, Mum," was all she said.

"Audrey, that's very kind," Dad chipped in.

I opened the turquoise bag and saw two boxes.

"Open the new one first," Nan said.

It was a chain with a solid silver heart pendant. It was gorgeous. I put it on straight away and hugged Nan.

The other box was cardboard and battered and old. I opened it and saw my mum's face change. Nobody spoke. I took the ring out of the box. Joe broke the silence.

"What is it?"

"It's my wedding ring, love. I wanted you to have it."

"Are you sure, Nan? You wear it every day," I said.

She laughed it off, but after breakfast, when we were cleaning up, she said, "I wish you could see yourself the way I see you."

"You're my nan. You have to think I'm great."

"Yeah, and you're my granddaughter and I say you're pretty special."

I knew I couldn't laugh that away.

"Thanks, Nan."

"Every time you look at the ring remember that I think you're perfect. Even when I'm gone."

"Nan, you're only seventy."

"I mean when I'm back in Spain, you cheeky twit."

I laughed so much I started choking. We talked about

York and what clothes I wanted to buy for school and what dorm I'd get.

"That ring's been lucky for me. I reckon it'll be lucky for you, too."

It felt like the longest day in the world. By noon I needed a nap. The rain made the house feel cozy, so I got into bed and watched it hit my skylight. My mum went to meet Linda and my dad went to work. Nan was having a coffee date with a retired plumber named Keith, and I could hear Joe playing computer games downstairs.

It's weird to think of my room being empty when I go. Of things getting dusty. Everyone says you shouldn't go home in the first semester because it makes you homesick. When I come back at Christmas and climb into my bed I will be different. I will have changed. It should be exciting, but it makes me scared. Like I want stasis. Everything to freeze. I don't want to forget how I feel now.

I don't know when I fell asleep, but when the door creaked I thought it must be Joe.

It wasn't Joe. But it was fucking surreal.

"Hey, Hannah."

Pax was standing right there in my room.

Underneath the comforter I was wearing my bra and panties and nothing else. Which I *never* do. Only American girls in movies wear their underwear to bed, but today I'd gotten into bed in my clothes and then just wriggled them off.

I felt massively pissed off with Joe for letting him in the house and just waving him on upstairs without warning me.

I stayed lying flat with the comforter up to my neck. I had to admit, he did look amazing. His hair had grown longer over the summer and he was a wearing a pale green T-shirt that matched his eyes.

"Hey," I said. "This is so weird."

"Yeah, sorry. I should have called."

"I don't mean bad weird. It's just weird you being in my house. I don't associate you with it. It feels freaky."

"Sorry. I know what you mean. Like when you see teachers outside school. I'm on my way home, and I haven't really seen you so I thought I'd come and say goodbye."

"Oh, that's so sweet." As flattered as I felt, I suddenly wondered where Stella was and what exactly was going on. "I was actually just going to watch a movie, but—"

"That sounds great," he said, cutting me off before I could finish. "My train's not till five."

"Oh, right," I said. "Cool."

Why had he left Stella's three hours early?

"I'm really sorry but I'm not actually dressed," I said. "I just need to put something on."

He laughed and put his hands over his eyes. "And I thought *my parents* were hippies. Is this a nudist house, then?"

"No way. We are so *not* naked people."

"So you're the rebel?"

"Stand in the hall for a second."

He obliged. From outside the door he said, "I have seen girls' bodies before, you know."

I wanted to say, *Yeah, Stella's. Or a load of thin, super-rich, model-type models called India and Effie and Miranda. Or Panda.* Her popping into my head made me think of Sam.

But the thought of Pax seeing the stretch marks on my hips and my not-shaved-for-three-days legs distracted me.

"Oh yeah, what a player you are," was what came out instead. I meant it to sound funny, but it came out sounding old-ladyish.

"I didn't mean it like that . . . ," he said.

I wondered how many girls Pax had slept with. And whether he had already slept with Stella.

"OK, you can come in."

I didn't want to care about what I was wearing and if he thought I looked nice, but I did. It felt like a situation we definitely shouldn't be in. I wanted him to leave, or at least tell me what was going on. I did think he was cute. It was impossible not to. But it was just being in proximity to that hotness, nothing else.

I got out my laptop and we picked *Stardust*. I felt guilty because I knew Joe was downstairs and it's the one film we actually both like. Being on my bed so close to Pax felt odd. Every time I moved I was aware of my body. I couldn't relax. It was like my life was in HD. I tried to sit in an attractive way and not breathe really heavily or sniff loudly. I wanted it to feel like friends hanging out, but it didn't. Bringing Stella up made me feel better, so I did it a lot.

"Are you gonna miss Stella when you go home?"

"Yeah. I guess."

"Do you think you'll go and visit her in Birmingham?"

"Yeah, maybe."

I couldn't think of anything else to say. Why was he being so cold about her? He leaned back and put his head against his arm.

"I do like Stella—"

I could sense more was coming but I cut in.

"She's beautiful. Totally stunning."

He didn't say anything. He picked up the York reading list.

"Oh shit, I forgot to say congratulations! Stella told me you got in."

"Yeah," I said. "Good news about Casper, too. He texted me this morning. Three As."

"Yeah, it's awesome. I can't wait to see him later to celebrate."

"How come you're not staying up for the party tonight, then?" I asked.

"I just . . ." He looked down at the floor. "I just can't. Got to get back." There was a pause, and then he tapped the University of York logo on the reading list with his finger and grinned at me. "Hey, so we'll both be there next month. I'm really glad you're going, too."

"Yeah, we can go to classes together."

Why do I always say the geeky thing?

"Yeah."

There was this weird silence. I wanted desperately to make it normal. To make it like a scene from *The Big Bang Theory*. For us to be jokey and cool.

But he stayed silent. Like he was daring me to stay silent, too.

Suddenly, he stood up and started pacing the room frantically.

"I wish I'd never fucking hooked up with Stella in Kavos.

Everything is fucked! If I sleep with her and then dump her I'm the bastard that took her virginity."

Why had she told him she was a virgin? *Was* she a virgin? But that wasn't the issue. Well, it sort of was.

"*Dump* her? I thought you loved her?"

I didn't mean to say "love," really. I meant that she loved him, I suppose.

"Love her? Love her? You don't love people until you're, like, twenty-three or something. She's just too . . . intense. She's acting like we're married or something. She's even put that we're in a relationship on Facebook. She's talking about coming to visit me in York during Freshers' Week. It's not that I don't like her, it's just . . . too much right now."

"Why did you come to London, then?"

"I don't know. Because Casper was coming anyway and he told me he was going to hang out with you. . . . And, well . . ." He stopped pacing for a moment and looked at me. "And the thought of him getting to hang out with you . . . I don't know . . . I suppose I was a little jealous. I mean, I do like you. I tried to tell you that at the festival." For the first time ever, he looked shy. "There is something between us. Well, there is for me. And it makes me even more of a dick because now I've got myself into this situation with Stella and you're her best friend."

I didn't know how to react. It was all too much to take in. For a split second I wanted to kiss him. Like I had that night in Kavos when he wanted me. He sat back down next to me on the bed, then leaned over and put his forehead against mine. We just sat like that. His mouth was so close.

"I would never betray Stella."

He was so close to me that I barely had to whisper it.

He kissed my cheek and I let him. And then he kissed it again but closer to my mouth.

I pulled away and looked at him.

"She's my best friend."

And that was it. He stood up and ran a hand through his hair. "OK, shit . . . I'm sorry. I'll . . . Maybe I should go, then."

I nodded. "Yeah."

He picked up his backpack and said, "Hannah, please don't tell Stella about this. It would only upset her."

"What are you going do, then?" I asked. "You can't just leave it like this with her."

"Yeah, I know. I'll call her tomorrow. I don't want to ruin her party."

I nodded again.

"See you at Freshers' Week, then," he said. And he was gone.

My instinct was to call Grace or Tilly straight away. But I knew, in some way, that would also be betraying Stella. I felt like this was something that needed to stay between me and Pax. I turned over and buried my face in the pillow. Why was everything so fucked?

I heard the front door bang; Nan was back from her date. She came upstairs and craned her neck around the door.

"If you don't want *him*, babes, then I don't know what it is you want."

And then she winked at me.

Feeling so many things at once is exhausting. So I just shut it all out and went back to sleep.

Nan has kept clothes that have memories attached to them. My favorite is a black minidress. It's got really long sleeves but is tiny. She wore it to her engagement party. There's a black-and-white photograph of her wearing it in an album. She's wearing boots that cover her knees and false eyelashes. She looks like a movie star. I have tried it on many times in my parents' bedroom but never seriously thought about wearing it out. I'm not brave enough to wear vintage stuff. I'm not cool or kooky. I have nothing. I don't have Sam, and now that I know how liking someone the way I liked him feels, I don't want to settle for something less. Even if the something less is as good-looking as Pax.

The person I wanted didn't want me, and I was leaving to go to college at the other end of the country. Tonight was just one night. I could just go to Stella's party, have fun and not care about anything.

So I went upstairs and put the dress on. When I came back down, Nan and Mum were in the kitchen. They stopped arguing when I walked into the room and Mum said, "When did you get so beautiful?"

And Nan said, "It's like looking at myself."

Mum snorted. "Modest as ever."

"What should I wear it with? I don't have boots like you had."

"Eyeliner. And lots of it," said Nan.

So I went upstairs and traced around my eyes three times. Then I just put my Converse on and left like that.

SAM

I got the text in the middle of a discussion with my mum. I say discussion—it was more a long, uninterrupted and highly emotional monologue from her about my lack of dedication to French homework.

"Oh, Sam . . . it's such a shame. If only you'd concentrated more on the pluperfect tense. You always said that was your weak point."

I don't understand why parents do this. I've already let myself down—do I really need the burden of knowing I've let someone else down, too?

The beep of the text message arriving made my mum stop mid-flow and say, "Oh, Sam, is that . . . *them?*"

She thought Cambridge was texting me to say they'd made a mistake and I'd actually got in:

Gr8 newz Sam—u in Cmbrij nxt yr! Lol ;-)

"No, Mum, obviously it's not them."

She sighed and went back to fiddling with her coffee cup. I picked up my phone and left the kitchen. It was a good excuse to get out of there for a while.

The text was from Robin. It read:

This is why you need to be on Facebook you dick! Stella's just updated her status to say: Stella Carmichael is in a relationship with Pax Sinclair!!!

My heart leapt. There couldn't be anything between him and Hannah now. If there ever *had* been anything, that is.

Over the past few days, my unsettling feeling about having overreacted at the festival had hardened into a grim certainty. Maybe she had thought Pax was cute, and maybe she'd even kissed him, but that was before that day we spent together. That day had meant something to me, and I was pretty sure it meant something to her, too. I'd let suspicion and stupidity and my permanently low-flying self-confidence mess things up with Jo; I couldn't let it happen with Hannah as well. Hannah was different. I *really* wanted her; I didn't just want to want her.

It was strange to miss someone you'd spent so little actual time with. But I *did* miss her.

I called Robin right away. He picked up after just one ring.

"You get my text?"

"Yeah."

"So it looks like that Pax prick is out of the picture. Well, out of the picture for *you*, at least. He's still muscling in on my patch, apparently."

"I'm not quite sure how Stella qualifies as 'your patch,' since you've only met her twice, but still."

"Come on, man—you must be pleased! There *can't* be anything going on with Pax and Hannah now. If Facebook says it, it must be true."

"That's excellent logic."

"Cheers. So . . ." He paused.

"So, what?" I asked.

"So, are we going to Stella's party tonight, now?"

Stella's party. I didn't know how I felt about that.

"I don't know, man," I said. "What are our other options?"

"Erm . . . we could go to Sophia Demico's party."

I groaned. "You said yourself those girls are so boring."

Robin corrected me. "Boring and *hot*."

"I could always stay in," I offered.

Robin actually tutted. He sounded like my mum. "You're not *staying in*, Sam, for fuck's sake. It's results day."

"Yeah, and my scores were crap."

"They were better than mine," he said. "Technically."

"Yeah, but you got what you needed! And anyway, I can't just phone Cambridge and say, 'In case you didn't realize, my results were *technically* better than my friend Robin's, so that should now make me eligible for your university.' I'm fucked, man. I don't know what I'm going do."

"Even more reason for you to go out and get absolutely drunk off your face."

I considered this.

"I do want to see Hannah again," I said.

I thought Robin would either laugh or sigh at that statement. He didn't. He just said quietly, "Yeah, man. I know. That's why we should go."

There were a few seconds where neither of us said anything. I could hear the clink and splash of Mum cleaning up in the kitchen.

"I don't know," I said finally. "It seems like too much to fuck up Cambridge and get publicly rejected by Hannah in the same day."

Robin snorted. "Sam, firstly, that won't happen. Probably. And secondly, fucking up Cambridge could be the greatest thing that ever happens to you! It means you can come with me to the American summer camp hump-a-thon, for a start."

A few days ago this statement would have seemed totally laughable. Now it suddenly seemed like a genuine option.

"So?" said Robin. "What do you think? You can stay inside, weeping about your B in French, or you can grab life by the nuts!"

I laughed. I genuinely didn't know what to do. I wanted Robin to make the decision for me. All I could think about was how much I wanted to see Hannah's smile again. I knew it would be awkward after the way I'd just walked off at the festival, but I didn't care. I had to see her again. To apologize. To tell her how I felt. To try to turn that amazing day at the festival into something more substantial.

"OK," I said. "Fuck it. Let's go. We can always leave if it's shit or if there's any drama."

Robin sighed. "Let's face it—with Stella and Hannah around, there definitely *will* be drama."

16

HANNAH

Stella's place was packed when I arrived, and it was still early. People clearly thought this would be the most bonkers of all the results parties. They were right.

Tilly and I danced like crazy people to cheesy '80s music and we took photos pretending to present Oscars to actors we have crushes on. Stella took tons of pictures of me in my dress doing Twiggy poses.

I sang to Bob Dylan—"when you got nothing, you got nothing to lose"—and danced all by myself. When I finally flopped down next to Tilly on the living room floor she pointed not very subtly into the kitchen.

"I can't believe *he* came," she said.

Charlie was standing, looking shifty, by the fridge with one of his disgusting friends.

"It doesn't surprise me," I said. "I don't think he actually cares about Stella, do you?"

Tilly shook her head. "I know. It's just weird because now

she has a boyfriend. You would think he'd feel a bit awkward."

We watched Charlie open the fridge and take out a yogurt before tearing off its lid and digging into it with his finger.

"I don't think Charlie is exactly a sensitive guy."

Tilly laughed. "Her and Pax seem really serious, though."

On Facebook they had been "in a relationship" for the last ten hours. If Charlie cared, eating fruit-on-the-bottom yogurt and drinking beer with his friend, you couldn't tell.

Nine hours ago, Pax had been sitting on my bed. But now he was gone and with no one at the party able to confirm that it had happened, I was beginning to wonder if it actually had.

I could see Grace getting stressed about the number of people streaming into Stella's house, and Ollie trying to calm her down, as usual.

"It's not even your house and Stella clearly doesn't care," he laughed as he put his arms around her.

Stella clearly didn't. She was right in the thick of it, like always, laughing, talking and dancing at a hundred miles an hour.

It was getting so hectic and crazy that I went upstairs into Stella's room and sat on the bed. It felt like a museum. Some sort of exhibition about a time that had passed. History. Collages of photos from all the years between when we were eleven to now, tickets to gigs we'd been to and films we loved, napkins from restaurants on which we had written lists of the people we had kissed. For so much of my life I had felt her room was our room. Her lilac wallpaper with tiny pansies that had gradually been eroded by posters and photos. You couldn't even see it anymore. But I knew it was there. The dramatic part of me thought of leaving her a note, telling her that Pax wasn't as into her as she thought. But that felt cowardly and melodramatic. And I wanted to tell her. I felt as though I should. If I kept the secret for him it was as though I was on his team, when of course I was on hers.

A pair of boxer shorts was lying just under the bed. It made me think of them in bed together, of Stella choosing him as her lobster, knowing Charlie didn't really want her. Not enough. And now Pax didn't, either. Not enough.

And then, as if thinking about her had made her appear, there she was.

"Hey . . . I saw you dancing like a crazy bitch," she said. "Are you wasted? It's only, like, eleven o'clock, you know?"

"No, I'm just . . . emotional, I guess."

"About what? School being over? Going there today and seeing Miss Collins just made me frickin' elated that I never have to go back."

"I don't know. This whole summer has been really weird."

She came over and sat on the bed and crossed her legs.

"You really liked Sam, didn't you?"

I nodded slowly. "Yeah, I really did."

She put her head against my shoulder. "Life sucks sometimes."

I nodded again. "Have you slept with Pax yet?" I wanted to see what she would say.

She answered in an excited whisper. "No, we were going

to do it tonight, but he had to go home. I guess we'll have to wait till I visit him in York. It's going to be so awesome being able to see him and you in the same place."

Going to York was my thing. It wouldn't be the same if Stella was there during Freshers' Week; if I tried to be even a little bit different, she would know.

I stared at a picture of us on her wall in a three-legged race, age twelve, and took a deep breath. "Do you think Pax is your lobster?"

"He's my lobster for now," she said.

"I just . . . I don't know. . . . Do you really want to start college with a boyfriend? Especially one who's on the other side of the country?" I tried to make it sound offhand but failed miserably. Her voice came out distant and cold as she moved away from me slightly.

"What do you mean?"

"I dunno. I didn't think you wanted a boyfriend. . . ." It sounded so lame.

"It's not a big deal. . . . Why are you being weird?"

"I'm not, I just . . . I really like Pax and you together. . . . I just . . ."

"Just what?"

"I dunno . . . Pax . . ."

"Just because Sam is a bastard doesn't mean Pax is."

"Sam didn't want me," I snapped. "That doesn't make him a bastard."

"OK, so Sam can make out with another girl in front of your face and he's a nice guy, and Pax treats me amazingly but you've got a problem with it?"

In her world—where Sam was just an evil, emotionless sociopath and Pax and her were the perfect couple—she had a point.

"I'm not saying Pax is a bad person," I said.

"So what are you saying?" She got up and stood in front of her dressing table, picking up tubes of lipstick and checking what color they were.

"Just that . . . maybe he isn't right for you."

She laughed a bit and shook her head. She still had her back to me but I could see her trembling slightly as she fiddled with a tiny pot of hand cream. "Oh right, I see. And who were you thinking he was right *for*, exactly?"

"What do you mean?"

"Someone who thinks they're cleverer than everyone else and deeper than everyone just because they read fucking books about women killing themselves? Someone who whines all the time about how ugly she is just so people like Tilly and Grace can kiss her ass? You knew you'd get three A's but you made us all talk about it all summer. You make yourself out to be the victim all the time, but you're not. You're just boring, Hannah. Really boring. And that's why Sam got off with Panda. That's what Pax says."

My whole body was trembling.

"What do you mean, 'That's what Pax says'?"

Stella turned around to face me and clamped her hands to her hips. "Well, we were talking about why Sam would just have randomly gone off and made out with someone else, and Pax was like, 'Hannah's kind of boring. Maybe he just thought he'd have more fun with that Panda girl.'"

I gripped the comforter tightly so my hands would stop shaking. Stella wasn't finished.

"Don't fucking make out like I'm the bitch. You always do that. Go home and cry to your nan about how mean I am."

"I wasn't going to," I said coldly.

Neither of us moved. Footsteps coming up the stairs made us both flinch and then Charlie walked in.

"Hey, ladies. Stell, I was wondering where you'd got to." He smiled broadly. Neither of us responded, so he smiled again, but this time more tentatively. "Everything all right?"

Stella sighed as if she was bored. "Hannah's just being a little . . . weird."

I picked up the overnight bag I'd left in her room and started putting the makeup I'd taken out earlier back in.

"Yeah, that's right, Charlie. I'm just being a little weird. Weird like making your friend wander around Kavos in her pajamas so you could get with some guy. Weird like thinking you are the only person who has the right to buy a dress. Weird like lying about your fucking virginity for no reason whatsoever except that you're a controlling, psychotic bitch."

I'd never lost it like that before. She just stood there. Charlie whistled under his breath as if he'd just witnessed something slightly perplexing.

"Not everyone in the world wants you, Stella. And even if they do, they wouldn't if they knew what you were really like. Pax doesn't even want you. He came to my house today and told me."

I saw her break. She looked almost like a child. I had destroyed her. I regretted it right away.

"You're a fucking liar."

"I thought you two were, like, best friends," Charlie said, shifting his weight from foot to foot and looking at the door.

"So did I," I said.

"You're jealous of me and you always will be." Stella didn't look at me as she said it, but her voice was shaking.

"Why don't we go downstairs and get a drink? It's a bit intense up here."

Charlie reached his hand out and Stella took it and then they were gone.

Being in there felt wrong after that, but I didn't want to leave.

I can't function like other people. I can't *do* life. Everyone else seems to just be able to live. Have friends, look OK, have boys actually want to go out with them.

I walked into her bathroom and let the door slam shut behind me. I pressed my face up against the cold of the tiles and looked at myself in the mirror. *When you got nothing, you got nothing to lose.* I had nothing.

SAM

We got there late. Around eleven o'clock. We could hear the party from three streets away. I don't know how Stella's neighbors let her get away with it. If I so much as strum a single chord on my acoustic guitar, Mrs. Hodson from number 6 is banging on our front door within seconds.

Me, Chris, Ben and Robin had been drinking Robin's dad's Coronas for three hours beforehand, so all of us were well on the way to being fucked. I needed to be. I couldn't take being sober and seeing Hannah. I had no idea what was going to happen.

Weirdly, the whole not-going-to-Cambridge thing had made me feel braver, too. If I had no future, why should I worry about the present? Regardless, I kept glancing into the car windows I passed to make sure I looked OK.

Chris rang the bell. A wall of noise hit us as the door opened and a guy none of us had seen before stood in the doorway. He was brandishing a half-empty whisky bottle and was wearing the lid of a flip-top trash can on his head, like a (literally) rubbish Dalek.

"Yes!" he yelled at us. "More party people! Get the fuck inside!"

He hugged all four of us in turn as we shuffled through the door. The party was absolutely massive. Bodies blocked the stairs, the halls and the doors to the front room. Everywhere you turned, someone was asking, "How did you do?" "What did you get?" or "So, what college are you going to?" I just prayed no one asked me.

We squeezed our way through toward the kitchen, passing that little cupboard under the stairs where I'd first told Robin and Ben about Hannah a few weeks back. It seemed like years ago.

We poked our heads into the kitchen, but there was no sign of Hannah or Stella. Or Pax or Grace or Tilly, or anyone else we knew.

"Stella *must* be here somewhere," mused Chris.

"Yeah." Robin nodded. "Unless she's *so* cool that she doesn't even go to her *own* parties. Is that a thing? Do you think some people are so cool that they organize parties and don't even turn up?"

We all ignored Robin's questions and shuffled our way out into the yard. It was mayhem; even busier than the first party. Four girls were lying flat on the trampoline while two drunk boys bounced them up and down energetically. They shrieked with glee. There were clusters of people covering every single blade of grass. All you could hear was laughter and screaming and clinking bottles.

I spotted Hannah's friends Tilly and Grace sitting with a group of boys by the fence. They didn't see us. I didn't want them to, either. I wanted to see Hannah before I saw anyone else.

We ducked back into the kitchen. There was still no sign of Hannah or Stella in there. Robin edged toward the fridge and pulled the door open. He yanked out four cans of Red Stripe.

"We'll just have a quick break for light refreshment."

He cracked his open and handed one each to me, Chris and Ben.

"Ah!" he said, smacking his lips and wiping the froth off his chin. "That's better."

Two short, pretty girls with thick black eyeliner and punky, peroxided hair sidled over and barged in front of us. They were both scowling at Robin.

"Hey!" said one of them. "Those are our beers, man!"

"I'm terribly sorry, ladies," said Robin in his fanciest accent. "But my friends and I have opened them now, so it's probably best if we finish them, too."

"You what, mate?" snarled the other one.

At this point, Chris cleared his throat behind them. They both turned around to look at him, beaming his brightest, toothiest, I-should-have-been-a-male-model-iest grin down at them. Instantly, their frowns dissolved into coquettish grins. They both began twirling clumps of their bleached hair around their fingers.

"Oh, no, sorry," giggled the first one, still melting in the heat of Chris's smile. "I guess you guys can have them. Share and share alike, right?"

"Thanks so much," said Chris. "That's so kind of you guys."

"Yeah," added Robin. "Nice one. So, are you having a good night so far?"

Notwithstanding the fact that the numbers didn't add up (two of them, four of us), I wasn't particularly keen on the idea of chatting up angry punk girls in Stella's kitchen. My mind was only on one thing.

"I'm going to find Hannah," I said. I'm not sure any of them heard me. Chris was nodding politely as the first girl outlined how upset she was at getting a D in Sociology, while Robin and Ben began an in-depth dubstep discussion with the other one.

I left them all to it and muscled my way through the kitchen and out into the hall. I even checked the Harry Potter's bedroom cupboard that we'd hotboxed last time. There was nothing in there but a mop and some boxes. I thought I could still smell a faint odor of weed. I tiptoed my way up the staircase, dodging several drunk couples kissing. I crept up to the bathroom—that same bathroom where we'd first met—and tried the door. It swung open, and there, in tears, sitting under that intense, Welch's-colored shower, was Hannah.

She flinched as the door creaked back to reveal me standing in the door. Her eyes were swollen and damp, and her freckled cheeks were traffic-light red. My first instinct was to rush over and throw my arms around her, but the look on her face stopped me.

"Sorry," I said. "I didn't . . . I wouldn't have come in if I thought you were in here."

She blinked slowly, releasing two fresh streams of tears down her cheeks. "You shouldn't have come at all, Sam. What are you even doing here?"

Her voice was hard and angry.

"I'm sorry—I just had to see you again," I said. "I was . . . I acted like a dumbass at the festival. I was drunk and stupid, and I got things twisted up in my head. I didn't mean to say all that stuff. I don't care if something happened between you and Pax."

She let out a loud, despairing cry and hauled herself up to her feet.

"Me and Pax!" she yelled, her body quivering with rage. "Who gives a fuck about me and Pax? There never even *was* a 'me and Pax'!"

I stepped toward her, trying to interrupt her.

"I know, I know, I'm sorry, Han—"

"No!" She cut me off. "You can't just come here and say sorry and expect everything to just magically be all right."

"I don't know what else to say," I shouted. "I told you I was drunk, I was a jackass! I feel horrible for the things I said."

"The things you said?" She laughed bitterly. "What about the things you *did*, Sam?"

I opened my mouth to speak, to tell her I didn't know what she meant, when an image of Panda drunkenly waving her phone at the sky outside the Mad Hatter's tent flashed into my head.

"I saw you, Sam," she said softly. "You went straight outside and kissed her. Like that whole day never happened."

I felt like I'd been punched in the stomach. The thought of her standing there watching as I kissed Panda was unbearable. The words scrambled across my tongue as I tried desperately to explain.

"Hannah, I'm so sorry," I garbled breathlessly. "I don't know what I was thinking. I got it into my head that there was something between you and Pax. I'm such an idiot. All I wanted was you, and I fucked everything up."

"You really hurt me, Sam," she said. Her anger was gone; it was like she'd yelled herself empty. She just looked tired, standing there limply with her arms dangling down by her sides.

I couldn't take it any longer. I reached forward and pulled her toward me.

"I'm sorry," I whispered. "I really am."

For a second, I held her hot, trembling body against mine. And then she broke away. The tears were working their way steadily down her cheeks and onto her chin.

"It's not that easy," she said.

I wasn't listening. All I could think about was holding her. I pulled her back into my arms and kissed her, feeling the wet warmth of her cheeks against mine. She pulled away again and stared right into my eyes, breathing heavily. Then she grabbed me by the shoulders and kissed me back. We stood there, under the shower nozzle, clinging to each other, gasping for air between kisses.

That was until Hannah's friend Grace came bursting through the bathroom door, red in the face and panting.

Every time I'm getting somewhere with Hannah in this bathroom that girl *has* to come in and fuck it up.

"Hannah!" she yelled, barely even registering me. "There you are! You've got to come downstairs *now*!"

17

HANNAH

"What is it?" I said.

"Just come. Right now."

"What's happened, Grace?"

But she grabbed my arm and was dragging me. Her grip was painfully tight. I didn't even have time to process what had just happened with Sam.

"Grace. What the fuck?"

"I don't know. I don't know."

That was all she said. The music had been turned off and people were starting to leave. There was a circle of girls all focused on something. Grace pushed through, and Sam and I followed her.

Stella looked impossibly small. Lying there she could have been a seven-year-old. Her head was banging against the floor violently. It was knocking so hard against the wood that the noise vibrated around the room. There was a trickle of vomit coming out of her mouth but her movements were spraying it onto her top and around her face. Something came out of her nose and was running toward her eyes. She wasn't there. Her whole body was writhing and moving but she wasn't conscious. Her eyes were all white.

"She's having an epileptic fit."

Sam was beside me.

"We need to call an ambulance."

Grace looked at me. "Charlie was here. He . . . they . . . I think he gave her . . . something."

"Fuck. Oh god." I knelt next to her. I was too scared to even touch her. "Where's Charlie?" I demanded.

"Gone," Grace said.

"Well, someone call him and ask him what the fuck he's done to her!"

Sam stepped forward and knelt beside me. I felt his hand on my shoulder.

"Hannah, go and get a pillow from the sofa. Grace, call an ambulance now. Tell them she's taken drugs but you don't know what sort."

"It was coke. She told me." Tilly said it quietly. She was starting to cry.

Sam spoke to the emergency services and followed the instructions, answering all their questions calmly. He told everyone to leave but they were going anyway. People don't want their parents associating them with drugs, out-of-control house parties and ambulances.

It was only when the paramedics came in and Sam stepped aside that I saw his hands were shaking.

"Two people can come with us," said one of the paramedics.

"We'll go," Sam said, looking at me.

In the ambulance they asked us questions. Her date of birth, her blood type, her allergies, and whether she had any preexisting medical conditions. I knew everything about her. As much as I knew about myself.

The whole way to the hospital she kept on convulsing. In the end they strapped her to the bed. It was barbaric. I couldn't believe it was happening. I couldn't look at it.

"You all right, dear?" the paramedic asked me. I just nodded.

The emergency room wasn't like it is in American movies. A crowd of people didn't rush her into a room with this massive sense of urgency. They took her away and wheeled her behind a curtain. I caught glimpses of people behind other curtains. An old woman in a pink nightie looking confused. A little boy sitting up in bed playing on an iPad with his mum next to him.

We told the woman at the front desk everything we had already told the paramedic. They didn't tell us what to do. So we went and stood looking at Stella. She was stiller now. Her tiny body in the middle of the bed. Every so often she would jerk and her eyes would half open but she still wasn't there.

Eventually, a nurse told us that the doctor was going to examine her and that we could go and sit in a room down the hall.

"I'll come and get you when the doctor's finished," she said.

We sat down next to each other, staring out at the posters about bowel cancer and how to spot meningitis. And then it hit me.

"We have to call her parents."

I knew I had phoned their house in Italy before, when Stella had been there one summer, but I couldn't find the number on my phone.

"Will your parents have it?" Sam said it gently. As if he knew my parents hadn't entered my head.

I nodded. How much I wanted them suddenly hit me.

"What time is it?"

"Twelve-thirty."

They would almost definitely be asleep. It rang twice before Mum answered.

"Hannah. Are you OK?"

I wanted to say something but I didn't know what words to say in which order.

"Stella . . . Stella . . ."

I wasn't crying. I just couldn't make my mouth move.

Sam touched my shoulder and took the phone out of my hand.

"Hi, is that Hannah's mum? This is Hannah's friend Sam. Hannah is fine but Stella is in the hospital. She's had a seizure."

Had a seizure? Is that the parent-friendly expression for taking a drug overdose?

He gave my mum information. She said they'd be there in twenty minutes.

I put my head against Sam's shoulder. And then the nurse walked in. We shot to our feet.

"We need to do some blood tests and we're going to admit her to a ward to monitor her, but she is stable and she's going to be OK. You can see her in ten minutes or so."

It didn't feel like a weight had lifted. It was like I could feel myself and how tired I was and that I was real. Like my senses came back.

SAM

I honestly thought she was going to die. I've never seen anyone die before but she looked the way people look when they're about to die on TV. Spluttering and gargling and blinking in and out of consciousness. Fucking terrifying. I don't think I'll ever be able to watch *House* again.

I don't know what came over me at the party. I'm not usually the sort of guy to start telling everyone what to do and organizing everything. But no one else seemed to be taking charge. Even Robin looked too freaked out by it all to step in. And I *really* thought she was going to die.

At the time, I was in autopilot mode, not stopping to think about what I was doing, but afterward I felt quite proud of myself. Mainly for not fainting when Stella did that eyes-rolling-back-in-the-head thing that made her look like the girl from *The Exorcist*. That's something else I can't ever watch again.

After the nurse told us Stella would be fine, me and Hannah collapsed back onto the ridiculously uncomfortable seats in the ER waiting room, exhausted but relieved. I texted Robin and Chris to let them know everything was all right. Then I spoke to Hannah's parents and asked them to come to the hospital.

We sat in silence beneath a flickering fluorescent light. After the last hour of shouting and sweating and worrying, it felt strange to be so still and quiet. The waiting room was empty except for us. That intense moment in Stella's bathroom suddenly seemed like a long time ago. Hannah was just staring straight ahead at the wall. I wished I had even the slightest idea what she was thinking. Why the hell are girls so impossible to read? I can tell exactly what's going on in Robin's head just by the way he hunches his shoulders.

"So that Charlie guy sounds like a total shithead," I said, just to punch a hole in the silence.

"Yeah." She nodded. "He's a dick. At least Stella knows it now, I guess."

"I don't think I could ever take cocaine," I said. "I hate stuff going up my nose. I can't even use those Vicks inhalers when I get a cold."

"Were you one of those kids who had to use the chest rub instead?"

"Yeah," I said. "So when they invent a form of cocaine that you can rub into your chest, I'll be all over it."

She laughed quietly and then shook her head. "God, I'm so glad Stella is going to be OK."

We slumped back into silence again, listening to the low hum of the lights and the faint clip-clop of feet echoing through the corridors around us. I gritted my teeth and decided to try another apology.

"Hannah, I really am sorry about what happened that night at the festival. I'm such an idiot."

She unfurled a few strands of hair from behind her left ear and chewed them. God, I had missed seeing her do that. She stared blankly at the wall as she chewed, apparently absorbing what I'd just said. Finally, a very faint smile spread across her face.

"I don't know," she said. "I'm not sure 'idiot' is quite strong enough, to be honest."

I laughed out of sheer relief. "No, no, it's not! It's way off. What about 'asshole'? I'm an asshole?"

She cocked her head to one side in consideration, her smile widening gradually. "Asshole is better," she said. "Still not quite there."

"Fucking asshole?" I offered immediately. "Massive fucking asshole? Massive fucking idiot asshole dickhead."

Her smile was now at full stretch. "I think that just about covers it, yeah."

"I could go on. I'd be happy to try a few more variations until we've got it right."

"I don't think that'll be necessary, but thank you."

I was on a roll. I decided to go further.

"Look, I know this sounds stupid and cheesy, but I really like you, Hannah. I've spent all summer liking you."

She blushed. I was blushing too, but I didn't care.

"So it just seems stupid that we don't keep . . . seeing each other. What do you reckon?"

"Yeah." She nodded. "I'd really like that."

I edged closer to Hannah and put my arm on the back of her chair.

"What are you doing?" she asked, grinning.

"I was trying to put my arm around you in a charming, sexy, subtle way."

"Yeah, there's nothing sexier or more charming than a hospital waiting room."

I withdrew my arm. Hannah laughed. Then she clasped my hand tightly.

"Shit, Sam, I forgot to ask about exams! Did you get into Cambridge?"

With everything that had happened in the last hour, I'd completely forgotten about Cambridge.

I shook my head. "No. I fucked up French. I didn't get in."

Her face dropped and her grip on my hand tightened. "Oh no. I'm so sorry. Are you all right?"

I thought about it. Weirdly, I did feel all right. I had time to figure out exactly what I wanted to do. It didn't feel daunting; it felt exciting.

"Yeah," I said. "I am all right. I'm really all right."

"Well, that's good."

"So what happened with you?" I asked, my cheeks still faintly smoldering from the ill-prepared "I really like you" speech. "Were your results OK?"

She nodded. "Yeah. I got in, so that's good."

"Got in where?" I couldn't believe that after all this time I didn't even know where she'd applied.

"York."

"York?" My stomach did a perfectly executed backflip. York was my second choice. The place there was probably still mine if I wanted it.

I looked across at Hannah, who was still chewing a strand of her straw-colored hair and smiling that wide, bright, incredible smile. I wanted her, I was sure of that, but maybe we could make it work between us even if she was in York and I was in London, America, or *anywhere*. If we wanted it badly enough, it would happen. And I *did* want it badly enough.

"That's amazing," I said. "Well done."

I wrapped my arm around her and she put her head on my chest. For the first time I could remember, I had absolutely no idea what life had in store for me. It felt brilliant.

HANNAH

I opened the door to my bedroom tentatively, but Stella was awake. I went and sat at the end of the bed. She had slept on and off for forty-eight hours.

"I brought you some hot chocolate."

She sat up and took the mug out of my hand. She was wearing my hedgehog pajamas, even though they swamped her. With no makeup and her curly hair unstraightened and braided she looked like the version of her I had made best friends with in grade school.

"Your grandparents are on their way."

She nodded. "Cool." It was flat and emotionless.

I knew what she wanted to hear—that her parents were coming—and not being able to say it made it hard for me to look at her. I stared at the pattern on the comforter.

I handed her a yellow envelope with scrawly boy's writing on it.

"This arrived this morning."

She opened it. It was a cheery, colorful Get Well Soon card. She read it silently and handed it back to me.

Hey Stella,
  I hope you're feeling better. I've been really worried about you. Eat lots of spinach so you get well soon

and can come to York and make some epic memories with me.

Lots of love,
Pax

Underneath he'd drawn a little stick man holding a can of spinach. I put the card down on the bed and looked at her. She smiled, and some of the weight and the sadness seemed to lift from her face. All I could feel were good things about Pax, because he was responsible for easing something inside her, even for a moment, that I didn't fully understand. She was scraping her nail polish off with her fingers. Little shards of it fell over the comforter.

"I think he did like you . . . in Kavos," she said quietly.

"Stella, Pax wants you. He has always wanted you. Remember on the boat how it was *you* he sat talking to for ages? How it was *you* that he kissed on the first night?"

Stella took this in. "But I'll never understand why you didn't just say to me in the Westfield café, 'Stella, this is Toilet Boy. He is my lobster. The end.'"

"Because I thought he wanted *you*. Because you had already kissed him. And I felt like an idiot for making it seem like we had this Romeo and Juliet connection in the bathroom, when he made out with you five minutes later."

"So what? You knew I was only doing it to make Charlie jealous. And I didn't give Sam much choice in the matter."

"Yeah, but that wasn't what it was about. It didn't matter whether or not you wanted him. It was the fact he didn't want me."

"Yeah, but he did."

"All right, Little Miss I-Know-Everything. It's all good to say that *now*. It sounds simple *now*." We were both smiling.

"So that stuff with Pax . . ." She was trying to sound casual. "What you said at the party about him not wanting me . . ."

It was the moment. I would only get *that* moment but I didn't even hesitate.

"I just said it. I don't know why. Of course Pax didn't say that. You know what a nice guy he is. He's totally into you."

Whether he was or not didn't feel like the important thing. Her feeling loved and getting better right now was what mattered.

She nodded. "I forgive you. All for one and one for all."

I had forgiven her, too. For less tangible and labeled things. For the things I couldn't describe out loud or put my finger on but I knew were there.

I put my legs under the comforter and wriggled down, and we were head-to-tail in my bed for probably the thousandth time. Stella turned onto her side, into the position she always fell asleep in. She yawned.

"You're blatantly going to do the deed with Sam soon, aren't you? Which means I am going to be the only virgin left."

Her confession hung in the air. On some level I think I had always suspected that she was lying about Charlie. Maybe on some level she had known she deserved better. I really hoped that Pax was going to be just that. This was her clearing the decks.

"No, you won't be," I said. "Tilly's still in limbo."

18

HANNAH

You can only lose your virginity once. It's the only big life event that comes between being born and getting married.

I didn't feel shy or embarrassed with him. I was ready. I wanted to do it. My body just didn't seem to want me to. My family had gone up to my aunt's in Whitby, so we had the house to ourselves. He asked me so many times if I was sure. If I was *sure* I was sure. And that's the thing—I was.

But when he put the condom on and started to push it inside me it just wouldn't happen. It wasn't even that it hurt. Although it *did* hurt. It's just there wasn't anywhere for it to go. Maybe my vag is deformed or something because I know for a fact that his penis will not fit in it. It only just snugly fits a tampon. Maybe we can never have sex. Maybe we will break up because I have a thimble cooch.

I had to tell him. "Look, it won't fit. It's too big. I'm sorry."

SAM

"It won't fit. It's too big. I'm sorry."

I don't know why she said sorry. It's pretty much the best thing anyone's ever said to me. "It's too big." I kept repeating it to myself as I walked home. This must be how porn stars feel every day. I told Robin and he spat his Coke out, laughing.

"*Too big?* Yours? She must be messing with you, man. Has she never seen one before?"

He offered to show her his, to help her "properly understand the scale of them."

I thanked him but declined. It would have been nice if we'd managed to do it that night, but I didn't even mind that much that we didn't. It was weird how un-weird it felt with Hannah. To be lying there, naked, laughing about how stupid it was that we couldn't have sex. It felt like we were in it together. Nothing could embarrass us because it was . . . well, *us*. She's coming over tomorrow. Maybe we'll have more luck then.

HANNAH

I can hear the little boy who lives next door to Sam practicing his violin. Lying here naked while Sam puts the condom on, looking at the broken skateboards nailed to his bedroom wall and the yogurt cup that has been by the door for a week, I feel a bit pointless. Like I should offer to do something, but what? I can't actually do anything except lie here. He has to do the rest. He's the only one who can make it happen.

SAM

I probably should have cleaned up my room a bit. Made more of an effort. That fucking Alistair kid next door with his violin . . . he couldn't have picked a worse moment. I hope I'm in this room in ten years' time when he's losing his virginity next door, so I can ruin his big day by loudly misplaying "Chopsticks" through the wall.

I am so shit at putting on condoms. I wonder if Hannah's noticed. You're supposed to glide it on smoothly, but that never works for me. It takes me three tries to get it on right because I keep trapping my pubes, painfully. Finally, it's on.

HANNAH

It feels awkward. He doesn't know where the hole is. I don't even know if I know where the hole is. I can feel him pushing up against a place that definitely isn't that place. I don't know if he'll be offended if I sort of guide it. But I don't want him to feel embarrassed. I hold it in my hand and poke it into the entrance bit. All he has to do is push.

SAM

I have literally no idea what I am doing. She keeps kissing me. Doesn't she realize that I need to concentrate? I can't do two things at once.

HANNAH

I know he isn't pushing hard enough. It's like something is blocking it.

"It's OK, I'm fine. Just do it," I say.

And he pushes a bit more and it just goes in. All of a sudden it is in all the way. I feel like I should be staring into his eyes but I am actually staring at Mila Kunis's perfect butt because her poster is right by his bed.

SAM

I think it's in. I'm pretty sure it's in. She kind of grunts and squirms and lets out a little sigh. Does that mean it's in? There should be a light that comes on somewhere to let you know it's definitely in, like when you plug your charger into your laptop. I wish she'd stop looking at that Mila Kunis poster.

HANNAH

Now that it's in I'm not worried. Because I know what's going to happen now. It is sore. It feels like something alien is in me. Like my body knows it shouldn't be in there. It doesn't hurt, it just feels sore. Every time he pulls it out a bit and pushes it back in I wince. I don't know whether I should make noises. I mean, if I make noises like I'm enjoying it, it'll be absurd. But then lying silent is also weird. . . .

SAM

This. Is. Fucking. Brilliant. It's not so painful and tight after a while and it just feels amazing. Hannah's making some slightly strange noises but I don't think she *totally* hates it. At least, I hope she doesn't. It's hard to tell, to be honest.

HANNAH

Afterward, we lay there side by side in his single bed and I rested my head on his chest. I don't know if he's my lobster, but he definitely feels more right for me than anyone else ever has.

The muffled squeals and screeches of violin practice were still coming through the wall.

"I think he's actually getting worse," I said. "If that's even possible."

Sam laughed. "If only he knew that he's been serenading a momentous moment."

He lifted my head gently and got out of bed.

"I'll just be a second," he said. "I remembered something."

He pulled his pajama bottoms on and traipsed down the stairs. I could hear him banging about in the kitchen. I slid out of bed, got dressed in my T-shirt and panties and went over to the mirror.

I looked the same. This weird part of me had thought I might look different, more adult, more complete than half an hour ago. I remember watching *Shakespeare in Love* when I was twelve and being totally freaked out about how Judi Dench could tell that Gwyneth Paltrow had lost her virginity just by looking at her. Like being old and wise meant that you could just see someone and *know*. I imagined walking into the kitchen at home later, and Nan giving me a knowing, Judi Dench–type look and announcing to my mum that I'd been "plucked." Maybe if we shoved Tilly in front of her, too, it would solve the whole hymen limbo thing once and for all.

I bunched up my hair and tucked it under itself, making a bob. I pictured myself in York, wearing chic autumnal clothes, wandering through the cobbled streets with Sam. I didn't feel any more complete than I had this morning. But maybe I never will. Maybe I'm just not that sort of person.

I heard Sam's footsteps as he clumped back up the stairs and appeared in the doorway, grinning. He was holding two mugs, wisps of steam rising from the top of them.

"That's what you remembered?" I said. "That you had to make a cup of tea?"

He shook his head and put the mugs on his bedside table.

"Hot spiced grape juice," he said. "Seemed appropriate, seeing as this is, y'know, an important occasion."

I laughed. "Well, you know what we do on important occasions. . . ."

Our hands smacked together in a perfect high ten.

Acknowledgments

Firstly, and most importantly, to Polly, Rosaline, Juliette, Rain, Sarah J, Sarah M, Megan, Flavia, Shanice, Kate, Hannah, Alex/Laura and all the other Green School Dream Teams. Your stories are the best stories.

And a massive thank-you also to Anna McCleery, Celia Rees, Nick Sayers, Astrid Holm, the real Robin and all our other Latymer mates; Barry, Rachel L, Rachel H, Tina, Elinor and all at Chicken House; Trevor and all at Runcible Spoon; Jo Wyton, Ersi Sotiropoulos, Ben Illis, Vicky Clarfelt, Eleanor Malcolmson, Gemma Cooper and John Bardsley.

Plus, huge thanks to our US editor Kate Sullivan and US agent Allison Hellegers for their incredible work on taking Sam and Hannah across the Atlantic!

About the Authors

Tom Ellen and Lucy Ivison met at the end of high school and quickly became sweethearts. Though they broke up in college, they remain best friends. Lucy runs the online teen magazine *Whatever After* and teaches in girls' schools across London, specializing in building confidence and creativity. Tom is a journalist and has written for *Time Out*, *Vice*, *ESPN*, *Glamour*, and many other publications. They cowrote *A Totally Awkward Love Story*, which was partially inspired by their own high school relationship, with Tom writing Sam's chapters and Lucy writing Hannah's. This is their first novel.